Fire In the Wind

Judy Bruce

MERRIAM PRESS

HOOSICK FALLS, NEW YORK
2017

First published in 2017 by the Merriam Press

First Edition

Copyright © 2017 by Judy Bruce
Cover design by Joseph Gentzler
Book design by Ray Merriam

ISBN 9781576386224
Library of Congress Control Number: 2017937973
Merriam Press #F6-P

This work was designed, produced, and published in
the United States of America by the

Merriam Press
489 South Street
Hoosick Falls NY 12090

E-mail: ray@merriam-press.com
Web site: merriam-press.com

FIRE IN THE WIND

For Jenny and Tom

Other books by Judy Bruce

Death Steppe: A World War II Novel
Voices in the Wind
Alone in the Wind
Cries in the Wind

Chapter I

I died once, but only for a minute or so. Still, it should rank with distinction in the category of unusual circumstances. I've also killed four men in the last four years, which must be a record for Nebraska attorneys under the age of thirty. But I planned to stay out of trouble—I failed in the past and it cost me dearly.

Yet calamity came even faster than I expected. Starting at dawn on Sunday, a disturbance tormented me—the sense of foreboding in my guts persisted throughout the day and into the evening. After a delicious supper I barely tasted, portent began to pulse through my arteries. So I set out for my "backyard," as I called it. Five miles of rugged land north of my house stretched before me, pocked with peculiar land forms. I passed over a grassy mound named Rufus located half a football field from the house then weaved through the five small buttes dubbed the Seven Dwarfs, located southwest of a bluff called Big Leo. The second year of the drought kept the soil beneath the gray-green buffalo grass crusty hard.

What was bothering me?

A prairie dog popped his head out of his hole, barked at me, and then disappeared. I turned to face the early August wind, waiting for answers, but none came. I didn't even hear Beverly Wilson, my neighbor whom I had loved like a mother in the absence of my own. Why didn't I hear her soothing voice? I jogged over to Big Leo and climbed the east slope. Once atop the bluff, I stood by the Fort, the small hut of wood framing and glass windows that my Uncle Bill and others built for me last December.

Then it struck me—the door was unlocked. The inside was void of much besides benches for me and my guests to use in the winter to keep out of the sting of the gusting north wind. I examined the lock, which did show scratches around the keyhole; it was probably an easy lock to pick. This unsecured door could be meaningless, but my roiling guts argued back.

So I spent a half hour searching for answers. Using the binoculars I stored under one of the seats, I first scanned the Beast, a larger bluff to the north; Pooper's Canyon, a dry ditch near the Wilson property to the west; Raccoon Creek, a shallow stream marked by cottonwoods that cut through dry earth to the west; and finally Miss Gulch, a deep, dry gully to the northwest. I loved this scraggily wasteland, replete with cherished memories of my childhood with Derek and Vonny Wilson. Yet it was also a place that haunted me from my earliest days here as a toddler, with eerie voices in the wind that tortured me with longing. It worried me that a new, disturbing event might scar my land.

Back home, my mother, Elizabeth, known as Beth to most, but Mom only to me, asked, "Trouble?"

I nodded. Uncle Bill dropped his head into his chest and my Lakota housekeeper, Patty, murmured and rubbed her temples.

"God above," said my mom.

I called State Patrol Officer Warren Merritt on his cell phone. We'd been though several "incidents" together. When I told him something was wrong, he knew to respond with alarm.

"What do you think it is?" Merritt asked.

"I don't know, but I think it's here at my house or probably out to the north."

"Lordy, Megan, you've been through enough. I'm off today, but I'll get a cruiser and take a drive around the area. Promise me you'll stay inside."

"Gotcha."

"And call your uncle."

"Oh, Bill is standing right here. He knows I'm agitated."

"Okay, I'll be in touch."

I set my phone on the kitchen counter as I felt the stares of my uncle, my mom, Patty, and my war vet boyfriend, Zane.

All I could say was, "Something…I don't know what…but something."

That failed to mollify them. Uncle Bill began scratching his late day whiskers with both hands. Patty, here on her day off, left and returned with four flashlights. Mom and Zane just stared at me, waiting. I turned from their gazes to call Bo Schnitzel, the Dexter deputy on duty. He promised to check the Cowpoke, the Dexter tavern, Custer's diner, and Spittle's, formerly the Pizza Shoppe, to find out who was in town and who might be looking for trouble. My next door neighbor James Wilson knew me even better than Merritt or Bo—he brought his shotgun. In time, we settled in the family room and turned on the Sunday night baseball game as twilight deepened into darkness.

Suddenly, Barnaby and Traddles, James and Bill's dogs, began barking. With the family room curtains open, we saw it as soon as it started.

I jumped up from the sofa. "What the hell?"

Mom called the police while Bill dialed his cowhands and friends. Zane and I rushed out to the patio.

"My God! I don't believe this!" he said.

I dashed back into the house and took James by the shoulders. "James, I need you to stay here, no matter what. Please. Guard my house. Barnaby will guard yours."

Benumbed, he just stared at me.

Then to Patty I said, "Tackle him if he leaves."

After retrieving my Glock from the study, I grabbed two flashlights. Out on the patio, I handed one to Zane. Under the rear porch light, Bill was hooking up the backyard hose. The horror of the scene atop Rufus caught my breath. God Almighty!

A burning cross.

"Zane, go to the right!" I yelled as I headed to the west side of the knoll.

America's most heinous symbol of hatred rose thirty feet into the night sky, its fiery malevolence befouling my house and land with its light. It made my stomach turn over.

I looked for Zane as I approached the side of the mound. I didn't see him at first then I spotted him, still back where I left him. Damn! This was a lousy time for his shell-shock to kick in. I sprinted around the side of Rufus then swept a beam of light to the west and north. Lights flashed and sirens blared on the highway. As I ran forward, I shone the light to the east. I worked my way through the Seven Dwarfs, never seeing a soul. As the sting of smoke hit my nostrils, I recognized the smell of hatred. Shit. I really wanted to shoot the bastards who did this; yet I was angry that I felt the need to carry the gun that I wanted to leave locked away in storage.

By the time I worked my way back to Rufus, a huge blast of water was dousing the fire and sending smoke into the night sky. Someone caught me in a flashlight beam and ran toward me from the house.

"Megan, it's Warren Merritt. If you've got your hand on your gun, please put it away."

"No, you're safe," I said.

"Have you seen anyone?"

"No, and I got out here right away. They cleared out damn fast and I never heard a truck or car."

"All right, then. Walk back with me. Maybe we can avoid getting water-hosed."

When we returned to my backyard, it was filled with State Patrol, firemen, reporters from Sidney and Kimball, and curious locals. I didn't stop to talk to anyone, but headed toward the house. I hated publicity and reporters in general. I never talked to them, no matter who I'd shot. When I met my mom on the patio, she handed Merritt my camera.

"You'll want this," she said. "I think I got some good shots before the fire department started soaking the damn thing."

"Good thinking, Mom. And you cussed. I think that's a first."

"Well, I'm mad. You might hear more."

Just then we heard creaking wood and the sounds of the beams crashing into a heap. A blast of smoke shot into the night, shrouding the stars as embers flew in all directions. Shots of water covered the grassy hill, making sure the fire didn't spread.

"How's James?" I asked.

"Speechless. He's with Patty and Kayla. I gave him a large brandy."

"Will you go get Zane? He's still frozen to that spot."

Mom nodded and walked out into the yard.

"PTSD?" asked Merritt.

"Yeah. His last tour was a rough one. Let's go over here."

I led him to the side of the house. I wanted to get out of Zane's way, for he wouldn't want to see me just yet. He'd gone numb and I had acted—men don't handle that well.

"Did you see anything this afternoon?" Merritt asked.

"Well, the door to the Fort on Big Leo was unlocked, though it could've been that way awhile…but I don't really think so. I bet they used it to scout the area or James. I wish now that I'd stayed out there."

"If they were set on doing it, they'd wait."

I nodded. Jack and Bud, Bill's cowhands, stood a few yards off to the side, as if they were waiting for instructions; Bill must have called them. I led Merritt over to them. The men had become acquainted after the Shootout in the Eldritch barn.

"Thanks, guys, for showing up," I said. "Now promise me you won't go out there. They might just be waiting to ambush somebody…though I'd appreciate it if you checked on the horses."

"Sure thing," said Jack. "This just makes me sick. Now everybody's gonna think that Nebraska has the KKK."

"Lordy," murmured Bud.

"We'll do a search in the morning," said Merritt. "Nobody but you, Megan, knows this land well enough to run around in the dark."

"Well, I have done that a few times, but not since I broke an ankle. Will you excuse me? Goodnight, guys."

As Bud and Jack left and Merritt walked over to another trooper, I headed over to a cowboy I didn't recognize.

"Did Foxworthy send you?" I asked.

"Yes, ma'am," said the tall, broad-shouldered silhouette of a cowhand as he tipped his hat. "Tony."

"Okay, Tony, better tell Robert Foxworthy. He takes a special interest in this area. I wonder if there's been other cross burnings."

"Well, he certainly wants to know what you're up to. Does anyone else know about me?"

"No. I think that's best."

"Any ideas on who might do something like this?" he asked.

"Not a clue. We have plenty of rednecks out here, but this takes racism to a whole different level."

I entered the phone number of the undercover FBI agent into my phone's contacts list. As he disappeared into the shadow of the house, I headed inside where I learned Zane walked James home. He would make sure the house was secure before he left James alone. Mom and Bill seemed hesitant to leave me, so I told them I was exhausted and wanted to crash land on my bed. Yet after they left, I stayed in the kitchen wondering of Zane would come back. He didn't, which failed to surprise me. He would think he'd embarrassed himself tonight. He probably had some terrible memory of a fire or an explosion in the night on one of his missions in Iraq or Afghanistan. I now had my own terrible memory of a fire in the night. However, my shock couldn't match the torment for James, an African American.

I awoke in a sweat at five, tumbling out of bed and stumbling toward the window. Rufus was surrounded by yellow tape. What was wrong now? I quickly dressed even as panic made my heart race. But for what? I was ready to dash out the back door, but I stopped myself. Think, feel, breathe. I stood still as I tried to empty my mind. After a few moments, I knew. I grabbed two keys and a scrap of paper from behind the cereal bowls, shoved my cell phone into my back pocket and rushed out the front door. On James' front porch, I rang the doorbell then knocked. Nothing. After I knocked again, I unlocked the door and the dead bolt with the keys I brought then punched in the security code listed on the paper. I called out to James, but heard only a rustling sound from down the hall. I sprinted to the kitchen.

James lay face down on the floor.

Chapter 2

I grabbed his wrist, ready to flip him over to start CPR, but his pulse seemed normal, though not strong.

"Uhhh." He tried to move his head but couldn't.

"James, where are you hurt?"

"Wha—?"

He started to move his right arm and leg, but his left arm stayed still.

"H-hep me over," he said.

"Turn you over? You're not injured?"

He tried to push with his arm and leg, but he seemed weak. I moved one of the kitchen chairs out of the way then looped my arm under his good arm and pulled back. He pushed with his leg until he was on his back. He breathed hard, hissing through clenched teeth.

"Best, um, better," he slurred.

His distress confused me, but not enough to delay me from calling for an ambulance.

"I'll be already…all right. Just get me up."

"James, my dear friend, I love you, now shut up and let me take care of things."

He managed a limp smile. I called Bill and Mom then I did what I could to make James comfortable, or at least presentable. He wore light blue and white striped pajamas with a navy robe he forgot to close. He had wet himself, so I tied his robe. I straightened his left leg, which was bent strangely to the side under the kitchen table. I was afraid to do anything else. I wished someone would get here to help me. Just then, cowboy boots charged across the entryway, down the hall, and onto the linoleum. My uncle knelt down next to me. My mom placed her arm on my back as she leaned over me to look at him.

James looked at Bill and said with lips that didn't seem to want to move, "I fail. No, ummm, fall."

"Did you say you fell?" Bill asked.

He nodded.

I whispered to Mom, "I'll ride with him in the ambulance. Would you go get my purse and lock up my house? Oh, and the floor needs a cleanup. Might want to check upstairs before you come. Oh, and he'll need his wallet. I'm going to call Derek and Vonny now."

As I eased away from James, Mom took my place. She had the words of comfort I couldn't seem to find. I walked into the family room as I rang Derek then Vonny, waking and shocking both of them. Derek lived in Scottsbluff, so he'd arrive here in a couple of hours. Vonny had the longer drive from Denver. The Sidney ambulance siren blared as it approached the house. That was overkill as they probably hadn't encountered much traffic at dawn on a Monday. When a county deputy appeared at the front door, I waved him in.

In a flash, James was on a gurney and I was seated in a familiar ambulance. I even recognized one of the paramedics.

"Hello, Ms. Docket," said a smiling, chubby-faced man in aviator glasses. "Sorry to see you again."

"Likewise," I said with a nod. "James has high blood pressure. He takes a thiazide diuretic."

"Thank you, that helps us," said the other paramedic, a middle-aged woman, who started connecting James to portable machines. He was well-wired by the time we hit the interstate.

James looked at me with eyes that didn't seem to focus. "Sawm twiffy—"

"Psalms Twenty-three?" I asked.

He nodded and closed his eyes. He'd recited the scripture for me on two occasions. I did fine till I missed the line about anointing heads with oil, which made me back track before I finished it. He gave me a nod, yet kept his eyes closed.

Fifty thousand minutes later, I followed James and the paramedics into the ER. An orderly stepped in front of me.

"Ma'am, only family," he said.

Prepared for this hitch, I said, "I'm his attorney and I will represent his son and daughter until they arrive."

As the orderly pondered my answer, I stepped around him and moved to a corner of the ER room. The doctors and nurses hooked James up to machines as they asked him questions. A nurse held a clipboard while he slowly signed his consent to treatment form. A few minutes later, they wheeled him away for tests.

Now alone, I let myself slide down the wall to the floor. I pulled my knees into my chest as panic rose from my kneecaps then radiated through my guts and chest. This place had too much history for me. I'd even been treated in this room after I killed Salt Eldritch. Of course, I didn't even remember my trip here last month, as I was unconscious from a knife wound that killed my unborn baby and almost killed me. I'd been here as a visitor when my father died, then again when Mom was rammed off the road last June. Davey, RT, and Dobbs all ended up in the morgue here.

Now James…in the ER. Oh, God. I'd known him since I was a tot. His slurred speech, his left side weakness, his preexisting high blood pressure all smacked of a stroke. They can kill. Would we lose him, too? I flushed warm and my hands started to shake. I needed my mommy.

I found her and Bill in the waiting room, along with Patty, my elderly friend Bear Lake Beulah, Zane, and Brian my ex, as well as a slew of other Dexter residents and area ranchers, who continued to arrive throughout the morning.

"Megan, did you know you're only wearing one sock?" asked my mom with a smile.

I looked down at my ankles. "Oh. Hmm. I was in a hurry."

"I gave them his health insurance card—they always want that," said Bill as he glanced at my ankles. "I'll give Derek the wallet when he comes."

"I wonder if he's back in the room," I said. "I promised Vonny I would stay with him."

When I checked, the ER room was still empty, so I returned to the waiting room where an elderly volunteer, with lavender-gray curls, was handing out coffee. A few minutes later, Derek burst through the waiting room doors and strode to my side.

"He's not in the ER," said Derek.

He was tall and lean with a square head and a pink lower lip. He looked like a former jock, but he was actually a computer nerd employed at a computer security company in Scottsbluff.

"They took him for a CT Scan and an MRI," I said.

Derek nodded and shoved his hands in the pockets of his khakis. He greeted Patty as she walked up.

"I think it's interesting that Megan here decided she needed to visit her neighbor at five in the morning with his house keys," said Patty. "You knew, didn't you?"

"I knew where to go and to be alarmed about it...that's all."

"'That's all'? He could have laid there for hours," said Derek.

I shrugged, sat down, and answered Derek's questions about James' condition. An hour later, Vonny arrived.

Trim, tall, beautiful, and a bookworm, she worked at a finance company in a Denver suburb. She hugged me and Derek then clenched my hand tightly when we sat down. A few minutes later, a physician came into the waiting room. James' children were easy to spot as they were the only African Americans in the room and probably in western Cheyenne County. As the doctor led them to the hallway,

Vonny grabbed my hand and pulled me along. I went willingly.

The corpulent doctor paused when he saw me. "Glad to see you looking so well, Mrs. Docket."

I didn't care whether he knew me from my prior visits, so I broke in before he could address me further. "Did he have a stroke?"

Now speaking to Derek and Vonny, he said, "Your father did have a cerebrovascular disorder, a disturbance in brain function. One type of such disorder is a stroke. Your father's history of high blood pressure is probably a factor in the problem."

Some people cannot answer a yes or no question.

"Now a stroke involves the cessation of blood supply to the brain. Irreversible brain damage occurs. Now the MRI and the CT scans indicate no major blood clot or hemorrhaging in the brain."

"Did he have a stroke?" I asked again.

"Now I want Yvonne and Derek to understand—"

"It's a yes or no question. Then you can explain. Thank you."

He cleared his throat. The stitching in his white coat indicated his name was Doctor Dearborn; he should've gone into obstetrics.

"No. Mr. Wilson's neurological event was a Transient Ischemic Attack, a TIA. The symptoms are the same except with a TIA, there's no brain damage as there is with a stroke. And his symptoms may be temporary and reversible—we'll need to wait and watch. However, the chance of another TIA or a stroke is greatly increased."

"So what now?" asked Derek.

"Well, he needs to get his strength back. We're treating his heightened blood pressure aggressively and administering medication to prevent blood clotting. He was certainly fortunate to be found and treated as quickly as he was."

Vonny wrapped her arm across my shoulders.

"Doctor Dearborn, can trauma cause a stroke or a TIA?" I asked. "And I apologize for being testy with you. I haven't had much sleep."

He nodded. "We have no hard data indicating it does. Of course, we've all heard about the cross burning last night. So cruel."

"It seems like an extraordinary coincidence."

"We don't always have the answers. Mr. Wilson should be coming out of sedation. He's in ICU, room two. I know half of Dexter is in the waiting room, but visitors are not in his best interest today. I'll check back with you later."

As the doctor waddled away, I said, "Well, this is better than I expected."

Derek and Vonny just nodded and stood motionless as if they were still processing the information.

"Why don't you two go on to your dad's room? I can go tell the crowd in the waiting room. They'll certainly get the nutshell version."

Still dazed, I pointed them in the right direction for the room then headed for the Dexter mob. I did my best to explain the diagnosis.

"What was that fancy word?" asked Beulah. "Ah, I'll never remember it. Maybe I'll just tell folks he had a mini-stroke."

"Yeah, that would work."

"How long does he haveta stay here?" asked my elderly friend.

"We don't know. He needs rest for now, so no visitors. Sorry."

"But he could have another one you say," said Beulah as she wrung her veiny hands together. "He's gotta be watched. Heh. Man like James wants his independence."

"The family will need to figure some things out."

Soon some of the people left, others stood around discussing the news. After chatting for a few minutes, I took Zane's hand and led him into the hallway.

"I was hoping you'd come to me last night," I said.

FIRE IN THE WIND

"It was late and you never let me stay over," he said.

"Well, my divorce from Brian isn't finalized and I don't want to come off like a tart."

He stood stiffly, looking forward, which meant over my face.

"Talk to me. I thought we could talk about stuff. Was there a fire or something in Iraq that you remembered?"

He nodded, but said nothing.

He'd closed me off—I recalled how he'd do that to me when we dated in college.

"Well, the ball's in your court," I said.

I turned and walked down the hall. He would have expected me to stay with him, probe him a little more. But damn, I'd had my fill of drama for the day. Just then, Brian emerged from the other waiting room door.

"Whoa, shit! Megan, I can't believe this. Do the doctors think he could have a stroke anytime soon?" asked my soon-to-be former husband.

"They have him on heavy drugs right now. I don't know what happens when he goes home. He'll probably need a nurse."

"I don't even remember James having a cold. That he could have a stroke just blows my mind. Sixty-five isn't that old."

"No, it's not," I said.

I dropped my head, tired with sadness. Brian brought my head to his chest then wrapped his arms around me. Zane walked past us down the hall. I wondered what he was thinking. I hoped he was alarmed or jealous or at least ready to talk.

"I want to see James," I said. "I don't know if they'll let me. It's a little obvious that I'm not family."

I stopped outside the nurse's station, where I was told he was absolutely forbidden visitors. I texted Vonny and told her I'd try tomorrow, but she could call me anytime. We were wrong to use our cell phones in ICU, but I intended to remain available to the family. Besides, I was an incorrigible rule-breaker—why stop now?

At home, I ate a late breakfast, showered, and then went to work. Just after three o'clock, the memory of a cross on fire startled me awake. I lifted my groggy head from my cherry wood desk; I'd even drooled on the Uniform Commercial Code.

James, the burning cross, Zane's shut down—in two days my world had been shaken. All when I was still reeling from the death of my daughter and the collapse of my marriage. Was I never to experience peace?

I wiggled my mouse then scrolled down to the next case on my list. Ah, hell, I hated auto injury claims like this one—a dent the size of my fist in a rear bumper and twelve grand in chiropractic and physical therapy bills. Sometimes I enjoyed giving worthy people a hunk of money, like that family with a toddler in a body cast or the young man who'd lost the use of his arm. I felt bad for them and knew they deserved ample compensation. But not this unemployed bimbo—I was glad she hired an attorney so I wouldn't need to listen to her whiney babble again. Usually insurance companies sent their own adjusters to handle personal injury claims, but I'd established myself in the courtroom and as an able negotiator, so they often requested my assistance with cases in my remote area. I could cough up the additional five thousand and settle it, but I usually played the bulldog in bogus cases like this one. Yet the ground felt shaky underneath me. I'd fight—but tomorrow.

Chapter 3

WHEN I arrived at the "big house," my spacious red brick home, I discovered Vonny texted me again. Her dad's spirits had improved, though he'd spent most of the day sleeping. I tried to sound encouraging in my reply. She and Derek must be worried about their father's recovery and his future care. However, the notion of sleeping all day was so appealing that I crashed on my bed till Patty summoned me for supper.

Patty and I shared our meal of salmon and asparagus with Mom and Bill in unusual silence. It has been a wild few days and we were tired. I wondered if Zane would call. While I intently and absentmindedly examined my strawberries, Bill cut into the silence.

"Jack was tending the horses and he saw Rachel McNeill. She must be on the State Patrol crew examining the fire."

"Makes sense," I said. "She knows the area as well as any of the troopers."

"I didn't think you'd want her around."

"Oh, who cares? Let her help."

Rachel had become my friend last summer, but that ended even before I killed her boyfriend. RT was a crooked DEA agent who was dealing the meth he was supposed to be investigating. Then he and Chief Dobbs killed the autistic young man, Davey, who innocently repeated the information that led to the arrest of RT's minions. I accused Rachel of either aiding the meth operation or being too stupid to figure it out; in time, I believed the latter was true. She'd fallen hard for RT, impairing her judgment. Yet my disdain for her softened last month when she aided in the search for the bodies of Mary and Julie Quinn, victims of a murderous attack in 1968.

"Oh, hey," said Bill. "I talked to Hank and Lew...they just got back here this afternoon. They like the idea of buying and fixing up the old Bolger house. They're also disgusted about the cross burning and sad about James."

"I wondered if they would want to live in a house where Ellie Bolger blew her brains out," said Patty.

"Nah, they hated that old witch and don't mourn Bert, that murderer, one bit," said Bill.

"They want to reestablish the Eldritch legacy in this area, so this is their chance," I said.

"Ah, they did wonder if they could come visit," said Bill. "I said I'd be over here and that I'd ask you."

"Sure, give them a call."

Before the Eldritch crew came over, I sat on the patio with Mom under the shade of the big oak. The south wind kept the heat tolerable. For several minutes, we just stared at the yellow police tape, the burnt grass, and the heap of rubble still atop Rufus. Most evenings I would have wandered out there, but the land now held a sense of repulsive horror to it.

"You're worried about James," Mom said. "In lots of ways. He hears...doesn't he?"

"His father and Beverly. I wish you could have known her. But if he is too disabled, he won't be able to get out here."

"Do you...does he hear the voices inside?"

"No, so you see, it's not just the wind, it's the land, too. I never heard anything all those years I lived in Omaha. I came out here yesterday, but never heard her. That's something special I have with James. I'm afraid of being alone, well, um, without someone else who understands. I know I used to hear Scottie...maybe I just projected your voice because I longed for you. I don't know. But I felt Scottie. I've never researched it, but they say twins often have a connection. Sorry, I'm babbling."

She smiled. "Does anyone else hear?"

"Lew, but promise you'll keep that to yourself. He listens for his mother, and maybe others...I've never asked him. You know how he is."

"He's a good guy, but he might be the world's worst poker player."

"It's good we don't use money. That always disappointed Rachel, probably because she was really good."

Patty announced that Lew, Hank, and Linda were here. Linda was a beautiful, reserved, full-blooded Lakota woman whom Hank planned to marry once I could complete her divorce from a low-life named Milner. Before I joined my guests in the family room, I checked my smartphone. Zane hadn't even texted me. I told him it was his move, so I wouldn't be the one to contact him. I wanted to be with him, but I was too proud to grovel. Maybe we were over. Great, more sadness.

"It's good to see you again, Lew."

"Ah, thankee ma'am," he said as he squirmed.

"Beth."

"Yes, ma'am...Beth."

I squelched a laugh. Lew was a lovable hick with poor social skills, particularly around my mom, whom he probably thought exotic and beautiful, with her dark skin and black hair. Lew was fifty-six, a year younger than Bill; Linda was sixty-three, with the more outgoing Hank eleven years older at seventy-four. He'd been living with Linda for eighteen years in northwest Nebraska. The lean bodies of the three reflected their hard lives of toil and tragedy.

After Bill handed out glasses of the traditional Docket bourbon, Hank expressed his regrets for the befouling of our land and the illness of James.

"And I'm mighty pleased with the offer of the old Bolger house. It's a big house, but Lew and I can fix it. Need to hire out any plumbing and electrical. We'd also like to buy that land to the north along with the house."

"No, I think the Dockets should keep it," I said. "I want to make sure that land never gets sold to a Burger King or some other obnoxious business. The only way to prevent that is to maintain ownership of it."

"But we would never sell it," he said.

"Oh, I know that," I said. "But you can't control what happens when you're gone. Sorry to be so blunt, but I'm younger and can oversee it longer. So keep your money. You would have full use of it, of course. I'm looking forward to exploring it. You guys probably played out there as kids with Clay and Andy Bolger."

"Yeah, we did...lots of fun," said Lew, "as long as Bert wasn't around. Oh, sorry, to say his name, Megan, so sorry."

"Oh, don't worry about it. I shot him dead and he deserved it and that's that."

Still, the ensuing silence hit us hard. Bert Bolger also killed the child in my womb. That was twenty-nine days ago. Physically, I improved steadily; but emotionally, I wondered if the wound would ever heal.

Bill tried to revive us by changing the subject. "I hear the town council has rejected all applicants for Chief of Police and they can't convince Bo to take the job."

"Art Meyer also wants one of us to take his spot on the town council," I said to my uncle. "I keep saying no. I'd need to act respectful." I took a swig of my bourbon. "No thanks."

I felt my butt vibrate. I checked my phone then I rose from the sofa.

"It's from Derek."

I went into the kitchen to talk to him. When I returned, a card table was being set up for poker. Mom and Linda were chatting on the sofa. Everyone froze to hear my report.

"James is doing better, but he's still weak. He's still sleeping a lot, but Derek said I could visit tomorrow over lunch."

I played a couple of hands of poker then began to long for my pillow. So in the third hand, I went all in on a pair of Jacks then laughed when I won. I distributed my chips then excused myself and trudged up the back stairs for my bed.

At eleven the next day, I left work and headed to the hospital. In the lobby sat someone who surprised me. Rachel McNeill, in her two-tone brown State Patrol uniform, leaned forward in a chair with her head down. Good-looking and thirty-three, she didn't have the manner of an officer on duty. She looked up at me—in a flash, her face changed from sadness to anger.

"Megan, we're going to catch the bastards who did it. If I had my way, we'd string them up and shoot off their balls."

Her eyes were intense, which pleased me. They would catch them.

"Save a ball for me," I said.

She grinned and rose. "James was asleep when I checked. They plan to move him out of ICU. I better get going."

Rachel went out the front doors. She was one of the investigating officers at the auto crash site that killed Beverly Wilson six years ago. I headed down the hallway. When I peeked in the open door, Vonny waved me in. I paused to squirt my hands with hand sanitizer. She and Derek looked drained. As James slept, I approached his bedside. An oxygen tube was loosely fitted under his nostrils and he was hooked up to a machine that kept flashing his blood pressure in bright green and his pulse rate in red. For a few moments, I trembled with my memories of ICU. After taking a few deep breaths, I motioned Vonny and Derek to follow me into the hall.

"Wow, he looks so much better," I said.

"Really?" asked Derek.

"Well, I saw him while he might have been in the midst of the attack. His color is so much better. He looks like your dad again."

"Yeah?" said Vonny, whose face brightened as she regained her posture. "The doctors don't tell us much, except to wait. Later, they're going to see if he can stand."

"His left hand is much weaker than his right, but he can move his fingers all right," said Derek.

"Well, that's a big improvement," I said. I didn't mention that his left side was completely limp when I found him. "Have they said anything about when he'd go home?"

"No, but they talk about him needing a nurse," said Derek with a wince.

"Well, there's about fifty levels of nursing care," I said.

"How do you mean?" asked Derek.

"Well, he may need some intensive help or he might just need a companion to make sure he takes his meds and doesn't leave the stove on or maybe some kind of help in between."

Derek turned to look down the hall at the approach of Officer Merritt. "Maybe he's got some news."

Merritt asked permission to see James. Afterward, he met with us in the hall.

"We've been checking, but there's no other report of cross burning in the whole Midwest in the last few years or even beyond that," Merritt said. "So it's probably localized."

"But it sounds more like the KKK in the Deep South a century ago," I said. "What else have you discovered?"

"We didn't find tire tracks, but the gravel was kicked onto the highway from the old Hexam road. Bill checked with his cowhands and nobody has been up there."

"So that was the escape route," I said.

"Probably. We did find some boot prints that went north to and from the road. They got tired and drug the beams for a while—they left grooves in the dirt. The dogs followed it pretty easily."

"How many were there?" I asked.

"Three plus the footprints of someone wearing trainers with small feet. But hers didn't go that far north. One dog went off running around the Seven Dwarfs and then up Big Leo."

Derek and Vonny chuckled.

"Oh, great. Will that dog chase me if he meets me?"

"No, we're working on training them not to follow your scent. Bill loaned us the riding boots you had in the barn. I think you're safe. Anyway, we're running tests. It will take awhile."

"Like the kind of wood used for the beams and the kerosene or whatever they used to light it up."

Merritt grinned at me. "Yeah. It would have taken some know-how to plan and pull this off. They had to know the right kind of base to build and how to assemble it quickly in the dark and get out of there fast. But we'll keep on it."

Merritt walked down the hall then turned back.

"Megan, could I have a word?"

I walked to where he stopped.

"News has it that Tate McNeill is applying for the Chief of Police job in Dexter."

"McNeill?" I asked.

"Right, Rachel's ex. They divorced last April. Anyway, he's a deputy in Ogallala. Decent guy. Knows his stuff. Could be interesting since Rachel has been assigned to the investigation."

"Yeah, I just saw her. Right. Interesting."

The next weekend, my mom's family from Omaha visited. Her recent wedding to Bill in Dexter had involved a small group—me. So, this was her family's chance to celebrate with us. Late in the afternoon on Friday, two minivans and a sedan arrived at my house with part of the Simon clan. I'd been around them a few times; yet, something felt different.

I sensed him before I saw him. Danger was on my doorstep. He came in the front door last, behind my mom and uncle, two aunts, two uncles, and five cousins from Omaha. Then he stepped into the foyer. Like my mother and aunts and uncles, he was full-blooded Lebanese. Unlike them, he was movie-star handsome, with suntanned olive skin, thick, black hair trimmed short, and oh those eyes— I'd never seen light brown eyes like these. They sucked me in and quickened my pulse. We shook hands; they were warm, but hard and strong, as if he wasn't a man who had lived a quiet, comfortable life. My Uncle Peter, a Methodist minister from Omaha, called a week ago to tell me about him. This man, Raz, brought peril—but to whom?

Still, the Simon family brought a robust levity to the house—they were natural huggers and laughers. Each of my aunts and uncles quietly expressed their grief over the death of my daughter, but other than those moments, they were a blast. A cousin or an uncle would start in on a story only to be corrected by another family member whose version was even more preposterous. Did they really play kickball for six straight hours? And who really cared what happened on the great trip to Vancouver? The sharing of the memories mattered greatly to them—veracity was an unimportant detail.

In their own effective way, their jocularity enlivened me. If one sister started laughing, the other two quickly chimed in with their infectious laughter, as close to giggling as three middle-aged women could muster— something they probably never did with anyone else. Most of the time I never knew what they thought so funny, for one merely needed to begin a sentence and the other two got going. One particular tale started with "Remember when Bobby Richards ate that—?" I never did hear what he ate, for it sent them into hysterics. It was impossible not to laugh with them. I'd need to ask my mom in private to get the full story about Cindy Lawson's watermelon.

In the company of the women, I enjoyed myself. Yet, this Raz person disquieted me, with his buff physique and gorgeous eyes surrounded by long lashes I envied. Still, our day–long party to celebrate the wedding of my mother and my uncle was filled with fun and food.

Before they left for their hotel in nearby Sidney on Saturday, I cornered my Uncle Peter, who looked like a giant teddy bear with his dark skin and stocky build.

"Have you told me everything you know about Raz?" I asked.

"This morning he told me he's been hired by Cabela's, so he'll be moving out here. He'll need help finding housing for him and his sister, Nori."

"I don't suppose that's her real name either."

"I don't know."

"Is she in hiding, too?"

"I think he's just protective."

"She'd be safer away from him. Anyway, I have an idea of where they could stay. It's a duplex with two bedrooms. Can you tell me anything about her?"

"I don't know much. They keep it pretty close. She's twenty-eight, no, twenty-nine…younger than Raz. She'll be looking for a job, he says."

"I still don't understand why he wants to live out here."

"He's never been clear on that. Anyway, they'll get packed then arrive late in the day next Saturday. Thanks a ton for helping out."

I called Art Meyer. He'd hired my dad as an associate lawyer back in 1989 when he brought me out to the family homestead from Omaha. Art, retired for many years, spent winters in Arizona with his wife, Laura. He answered the phone and I made my request on behalf of Raz. His answer surprised me.

"Why don't you just buy the duplex from me? It's getting to be a hassle I'd like to do without."

It would be a good deal. Sidney, twenty miles away, was bursting with growth and suffering from a housing shortage. I could easily rent or sell any property I owned. I told him I would consider it; meanwhile, he agreed to rent it to Raz. I'd need to hire an inspector, but I didn't really want to deal with any of that now.

The next day, I stopped at Zane's duplex. He answered the door, still in his Cabela's shirt.

"Look, I know I haven't called—"

"I'm not here to talk about us, so save it for another time," I said. "Now listen, you'll have a neighbor moving in this weekend. His name is Raz Peters. His sister's name is Nori. I know those aren't their real names. He has come here to lay low. He snitched on the Hezbollah for the CIA. They're Arab Christians. He is not related to my family, but my uncles and others from the Lebanese and Syrian communities in Omaha have been helping him."

"Why is he out here?"

"No idea, but he did get a job at Cabela's. So, if there's trouble, don't be a hero, we don't owe him anything. I thought you should know since you'll be living next door to him. And I'm probably going to buy this building from Art Meyer."

"Why?"

"It's a business investment. I'm buying some other property, too."

"You haven't told me about any of that."

"Like I said, it's business. I need to go. See ya." I stepped off the stoop.

"Megan."

I looked back at him. He opened his mouth and shut it. Ah, hell. I headed toward the street and my Acura SUV, the Barracuda. I wanted to be with him, but he had issues. He needed to know that I wasn't going to play Miss Lonesome and wait by the phone. I was powerless to help him if he wouldn't talk to me. If I couldn't be with a man of strong character, then it was better to focus on other matters, like the Wilsons and my own family. His PTSD was a thousand times worse than what I experienced. But he needed to fix himself—I couldn't do that for him.

Chapter 4

JAMES continued to improve during the week. He regained normal speech though his left side was still weak, forcing him to walk with a limp. Derek and Vonny each made trips home, but were back on Friday when their father was released from the hospital.

On Saturday afternoon, Jackson Draper, our friend and a Lakota elder from the Pine Ridge Reservation in South Dakota arrived for a brief visit. I made sure I was present when Jackson was visiting James, who lounged in his recliner in the late afternoon. James wore a light brown T-shirt and brown pants. With his brown skin he seemed to disappear into this brown chair, at least until I made an unusual request.

"Derek, would you give us a few minutes?" I asked.

He looked surprised, but nodded then left the room, leaving me alone with James and Jackson, the silver-haired sage.

"I knew something was going to happen the day of the cross burning," I began, "but I knew only vaguely that it would be in this area. Monday was different. I didn't sleep well, but I did awaken suddenly that morning. I was ready to start calling people like I've done before, even jump in my car to drive around until I found the event, the tragedy. But I stopped and I tried to clear my mind as well as I could. Then I knew where to go."

"It was lucky for me," said James.

"But I don't understand...it," I said. "James, you hear out there—have you ever known about something that's going to happen?"

"No, I haven't. I do hear, but I don't feel like you do."

I looked to Jackson. He was slowly nodding his head.

"I don't have these senses like you do, Megan," said Jackson. "Long ago, as a young man, there was a woman in our town. She knew when illness would strike a family before that family did. She said she just knew. Everyone befriended her, hoping she could help and warn them. No one ever understood how she knew. When she jumped to her death, we all assumed she saw her end coming."

"When Davey was murdered, I knew something bad was coming. When it happened, Brian drove and I knew where to go, but not till that moment."

"Maybe you are developing some insight, some special kind of focus," said James.

"I wish I could know more clearly beforehand. The State Patrol could've caught the devils that set that cross aflame."

"Maybe next time, you'll know better how to focus, how to see with your mind," said Jackson. "I think you must shut down your smart brain to see, to feel clearly. When you know, then you will know how to act."

"Shut off the brain, fire up the senses," I murmured mostly to myself.

"Megan," said James, "promise me you'll never move away."

I chuckled and kissed him on the cheek. "I'm not going anywhere." My phone buzzed and I walked into the kitchen to answer it. I returned a few moments later. "Well, I lied. I am going. My new tenants are here. Remember I told you about Raz and his sister Nori?"

"Right," said James.

"I'll go let them in. Then I'll see you two at supper. You'll meet them then."

"I'd like to meet them," said Jackson. "Full-blooded and from the Holy Land where Jesus walked."

That did sound cool, but when I was around Raz, I wasn't thinking holy thoughts.

FIRE IN THE WIND

A silver Nissan XTerra with a U-Haul trailer was parked in the single driveway of the east side duplex. I parked behind a white Honda Civic in the street as Raz and Nori walked around the yard. They approached the Barracuda when I exited. I swear he looked better than when I first saw him. I mentioned that my boyfriend lived next door. Nori was personable, of average height, attractive, with the expected dark hair, eyes, and skin. I showed them around the duplex, passed out their keys, and pointed out the garage door opener on the kitchen counter. Though the paperwork on the sale wasn't complete, Art authorized me to act as landlord. The cleaning crew I hired seemed to have done a good job. Raz and Nori promised to take a break from their unpacking to stop by for supper.

Raz walked me out to the Barracuda. I stuck out my hand to shake his, but he took my hand in both of his and thanked me for my kindness. As I climbed into the car, I still felt the warmth of his hands on mine. Yet, that strange sensation I felt when I first met him was as strong as ever. Was it danger? Was it that simple? I looked back over at the west duplex in time to see Zane move away from the front window. I missed Zane, though it was Raz who filled my head.

At supper, we hosted a large group. However, it had to be obvious for anyone with eyes and ears that Raz paid me a great deal of attention. Vonny gave me a wink and Patty gave me a pinch. His cologne made me want to rip the buttons off his shirt; still, I tried not to return his favoritism. Maybe he was humoring me because he assumed I was a hick, living out in the middle of nowhere. No, Zane was my boyfriend, though he still hadn't called me. My divorce decree from Brian wouldn't be issued for another month. Above all, I didn't want to come off like a bint.

Late on Monday morning, Pastor Ryder, the minister at my dinky Presbyterian church, called to tell me that Max Zimmer had died during the night after a vicious fight with emphysema. The Zimmers were clients of mine, and of my father before me. They were ranchers drowning in debt even before Max became gravely ill. He'd sold off his herd for cash just to make it through the winter, even as the county bank prepared to foreclose. His wife, Lynne, would need to file for bankruptcy, a task I would be handling without ever seeing a cent. Of course, I planned to jump right on it.

When Pastor Ryder stated he was driving Lynne out to the Sidney funeral parlor to pick out a casket, I concocted a plan then informed him of my conspiracy, which I knew he'd keep to himself. Pastors and attorneys knew the importance of keeping secrets. Then I called the funeral parlor; I'd done business with them after my dad died, so I knew for a fact that the owner and the manager, father and son, looked like Vincent Price and Boris Karloff, respectively. After I told Boris I'd cover the cost of the casket and their "other" services, which I didn't really like to think about, I called the Burton funeral home here in Dexter and told them to hold a lovely service and send the bill to me. Both Boris Karloff and Jim Burton agreed to say the costs were covered anonymously by "Dexter community donors."

I rescheduled an appointment then drove out to the Zimmer home. The yard was dirt and gravel, and full of chicken poop. Lynne invited me in, intent on keeping good form. She'd cry in the arms of her friends; she knew my job was to give legal comfort. The cramped house creaked with every step, and the chairs moaned their use. She'd tried hard to keep the house in good shape, but had given up that battle when Max became unable to work. Her face was lined with toil; she looked older than her fifty-two years. She'd formerly tried to keep her body in good shape, but lost that fight to poor nutrition and complacency. As she went to get me a glass of iced tea, I looked around at the wallpaper peeling off the walls after two or three attempts to glue it back on. The brown carpet was worn down so badly it lacked color in the oft-traveled spots. In the kitchen, the yellowing linoleum curled up at the edges, and the cabinet doors hung askew.

We chatted for a few minutes, her tough Midwestern nature held up well. She left me for a few minutes then returned with a box.

"Max always said I should give this to you," said Lynne. "We even wrote it down on that list you gave us at the back of the will. Oh, and the wills are in the box, too."

I opened the box, which held both wills, a book with a beat up leather cover, and an old Colt pistol.

I picked up the pistol and said, "This looks familiar."

"You have the other with your Civil War collection at your office. Your dad took it as payment once. That book is an old diary from a family livin' on the Potomac when the war broke out. He said they were distant cousins. Years ago I read it, well, what I could. The handwritin' makes for tough readin'. But Max remembered it a couple of weeks ago…thought you might like it for your collection, too."

"Yes, I'd be honored." I picked up the diary and opened it at the middle. "I see what you mean, not that I should criticize…it's better than I write." I placed the contents back in the box. "When do you expect your daughters?"

"Soon…anytime." She hung her head.

I took her hand. "Max was a good man."

She lifted her head, inhaled hard, and quelled the tears. Looking to seize an opportunity, I stood when a car pulled up on the gravel.

"We'll need to meet next week to talk things over," I said.

I wished Lynne well then expressed my sympathies to the elder daughter as I met her on the porch. I sighed in relief once I got into the Barracuda. She'd feel obligated to offer me lunch, a thought that made my throat constrict with emotion, for I knew we'd be eating food sent by the Dexter food bank, of which I was a substantial contributor. She'd asked me once why they still received electricity when they were so behind on payments. I told her that it was probably an oversight by the power company, and she should let it go. Of course, I knew Art Meyer had been paying the bills for the last year. Likewise, I was certain the community would come through in her time of need. By suppertime, Lynne would have ten casserole dishes and a dozen fruit salads. The generosity would persist for weeks. In proof, Glenda drove by me as I was leaving. My receptionist was the baked-goods maven of the county. She'd be back with two more cake pans by morning. I smiled and waved at her, and then headed for Custer's.

Yet, something nagged at me. I needed to go home, so I drove north on Highway 51 to Harney Street. I skidded to a halt as I passed by the Wilson house. Shit!

Proceeding to my house, I ran into the garage for a saw then sprinted across our wide yard into the Wilson front yard. I whipped out my smart phone and took several photos of it. Fortunately, the front curtains at the Wilson house were closed to keep out the southern sun. I hoped neither James nor Vonny had seen it. I cut through the rope of the noose.

I drove to the police station, where I found a middle-aged deputy from the Cheyenne County Sheriff's Department. Until we found a Chief of Police, a deputy covered the shift. The deputy swore under his breath when I pulled the rope out of a plastic bag and dumped it on a table. We printed the photos from my phone and laid them out on the table.

"Yeah, I know I should've left it where it was—but then it would've become a circus and James and Vonny would see it," I said. "I just couldn't leave it. Do we even need to tell anyone?"

"I'll write out a report, of course," he said. "But no, it doesn't need to become community news. And there's nothing distinct about this rope, so we could investigate it, but it wouldn't go anywhere. There wouldn't be footsteps to track, not on Mr. Wilson's nice lawn."

Fire In the Wind

"I'll check with Patty, but I doubt she saw anything because on a hot, sunny day like this the southern blinds would all be closed. You can check, but Paul Ritter would have been at his store and Kayla has started classes."

He nodded. "I'll stop by Ritter's Hardware, to make sure."

"Damn, this makes my blood boil. Paul will keep this quiet if you ask him."

I was in a foul mood by the time I reached Custer's. I was also tardy in meeting Mom for lunch. As I walked up to the entrance, a handsome stranger with brown hair and blue eyes held the door as he was departing. He nodded to me as I walked inside. Something strange stirred in me. He wore neatly pressed khakis and a black shirt that emphasized the light skin of an office worker. He certainly wasn't a rancher or cowboy. I did catch a whiff of soap, as if he'd just showered. Where else had I smelled it? Oh, well. I proceeded into the diner then turned to look across the street in time to see him climb into a black Honda Ridgeline pickup.

I slid into the Docket family booth across from my mom.

"I'm sorry I'm late," I said. Then I leaned forward. "Did you come from your house?"

"No, I was visiting Raz and Nori."

"I'll tell you later," I whispered.

She nodded then Carol, the waitress, took our orders. My mom studied me for a few moments then Beulah wandered over to our table, her flip-flops clicking.

"Say, that Raz fella is a looker. Yep. Kinda like a young Omar Sharif. But not a relative, you say?"

"No, just a friend of my brother's," said Mom.

"It's a shame about Max Zimmer," I said, eager to change the subject.

"Yep, yep," said Beulah. "That poor man's been goin' downhill for a long time, jest like the ranch. That emphysema is a nasty way to go. I was at the hospital yesterday afternoon...so sad...so horrible really...listenin' to him wheeze and gasp for air. Damn cigarettes—they're nothin' but a long, slow trip to suicide."

I thought that was a bit harsh, but she was right.

"What's Lynne going to do?" asked Marva Gush, from the next table. Marva was the town Avon lady and a newly-elected town council member, our first female in that post.

"Probably go live with her sister in Alliance," said Beulah.

Beulah chatted with folks in the immediate vicinity then turned back to us.

"Say, who are those two men in that booth by the door?" I asked.

"That dark one's Mick Spittle. Ain't improved since I've known him...got a real dull bulb in that noggin'. Sorry to see him back."

"He does look a bit like a Neanderthal," I said.

And he did. He had a protruding, squat forehead, with dark hair on his head, face, arms, and upper body that hung over the edge of the neck of T-shirt in the front and the back. Now I preferred my men with a hairy chest, but this guy looked like a troglodyte with a beer belly. I knew the name, for Dom Spittle was a client of Gus's. The family recently took over the Pizza Shoppe, which was now called "Spittles'," the world's worst name for a restaurant. Because Dom was generally known as a moron, the town council rejected his request for a liquor license. His son looked to be in his mid-twenties.

"Who's the other one?" I asked.

"Oh, that's Jake Waters," said Beulah. "He comes in sometimes on Sunday after church with his mom and dad for Frank Docket steaks. You know his dad, the State Patrol officer."

"Yes, I do. He's been around for a few of my incidents," I said.

"Heh! Is that what you call 'em?"

I shrugged and started on my sandwich. Jake Waters looked barely eighteen, tall and lean, with shaggy blond hair and light eyes, blue, maybe. As it didn't look as if he even needed to shave, he seemed the opposite of his moron companion. In the table across the aisle sat the Webster brothers, Nick and Brett, local troublemakers.

"Jake didn't follow his brother to college. Now Dan is a good kid...studyin' engineering at Nebraska Lincoln. But people say Jake likes his video games more than anythin'."

"Where do those guys work? I don't see them around town." I said.

"I don't know that they do much work. Jake lives at home with his folks in Sidney. And Mick might help out at the restaurant, but I don't know."

"I'm not partial to the new place." said Mom. "They have issues with quality control."

"Spittle's just stinks," I said.

Beulah chuckled approvingly.

"You missed the other one," said Mom. "He looked older and cleaner, but I'd never seen him before."

Zest—that was the soap smell of the stranger. Uncle Bill used it.

"Nope," said Beulah. "Don't know him, never seen him."

"If he comes back, chat him up," I said to Beulah.

Both women stared at me.

"Trouble?" asked Mom.

"Maybe. Hard to say."

"I got my orders," said Beulah. "Will do."

Chapter 5

I sat alone in my study that evening, working on the Zimmer case. First my dad, then I had fought many battles for them. But Max had lost—his health, his ranch, and now his life, leaving Lynne alone.

Loneliness stung. I should be with my baby, well, at least still pregnant with her. Brian wasn't here. Zane wasn't here. Mom and Bill were home, a block down the street, enjoying each other's company after years apart. I envied them.

Patty and I brought over dinner to Vonny and James. They seemed different—wounded and not just by James' health scare, but also by that damn burning cross. What soulless vipers did it? I told Mom, Bill, and Patty about the noose, but we'd keep that confidential—we all hurt for the Wilsons. Derek and Vonny couldn't continue to keep a watch on James forever. He didn't even like that a nurse came to check on him every day. The peace James and Beverly sought in moving here from the crime of the big city was now cruelly destroyed.

I had volunteered to sleep at the Wilson house to help keep watch on James. In fact, I'd slept there many times—it was the house my dad and I first lived in until my grandparents died. My father had separated me from my twin and my mother then told me lies. That was tyrannical, but I forgave him. So many of us were wounded—Brian was alone, banished from me for cruelty; Zane was alone, separated from me by his troubles. I missed them both. And Raz wasn't real, for he concealed his identity to hide from danger, from retribution. Maybe we were all hiding from the next blow.

I mostly spent my evenings working, filling my time with divorce, bankruptcy, and personal injury cases. It was taking its toll. I already existed under the cloud of grief over the death of my daughter, my Sweetie. The rest of my day was spent on other people's tragedies. I needed to find a way to shift more of my energy to estate planning; though it was difficult, for I was in high demand, especially for divorce and injury cases. The more trouble I got into, particularly the shootings and adventures, the more popular I became. I wasn't known as the ruthless divorce lawyer; in fact, I was sought because I pushed counseling and reconciliation. Judges in five different counties requested my services to represent the children of parents in vicious divorce battles. Those kids broke my heart, time after time. As my business flourished, my personal life floundered.

Raz and Nori visited the office the next day. I showed them the Civil War collection for a few minutes before I was interrupted by a phone call. They were facing away from me as I returned to them.

"Hey, Rana, look at this old cap," said Raz.

I slowed, certain I'd heard their first slip. I veered away to stop by Glenda's desk.

"You can see where sweat has made the brim stiff."

Raz moved to the next wall case as Nori turned at my approach.

"Look over here," I said. "This piece is new this week. It matches this Colt pistol my dad took as payment for a debt years ago."

Just then the door opened and Brian walked in.

"That's the man I'm divorcing," I whispered to them. Then in a louder voice, I called Brian over. "This is Brian Culhane. He's the brains around here. This is Raz Peters and his sister, Nori Peters."

The four of us exchanged pleasantries for a few minutes then Raz and Nori left. Brian followed me into my office.

"Are they relatives of yours?" he asked.

"No. He knows my uncle. Raz has a job at Cabela's."

"Why would he move out here? Is he after you? I don't trust something about him."

"Why, because he's an Arab? He was born in Duluth."

"Whatever. Hey, how come you always push for counseling for your divorce clients and I haven't heard a thing?"

I closed the door to avoid being overheard then went back to the side of my desk and said, "Rich Dewey should be sending you Judge Shelton's waiver of mediation."

"What? Why?"

"I told the judge of your violence and drunken behavior. This divorce will charge on to termination. The judge will sign the decree next month. Then our 'Irretrievably Broken' marriage will end a month after that. Dewey can't do anything to stop it or stall it."

"You bitch."

"Verbal abuse—another reason Shelton released me from a bogus attempt to reconcile. You've been cruel. Do you think the death of our daughter somehow hurt me less?"

"No, but you're being so hard-assed about it. You won't even talk to me about anything."

"Should we talk about how you tried to crush my face in? I'm never going to forget that."

"Then you can't forgive me," he said in a voice I formerly loved.

"It's not about forgiving you—it's about fearing you'd do it again."

"Fear, huh? Look at it from my side. You do reckless, dangerous stuff. People die. That's something to fear."

"If we fear each other then we shouldn't be together. You're a smart accountant, but a stupid, aggressive male and you do stupid immature things when things don't go your way. The thing is—I don't love you anymore. Is that plain enough?"

"So you get rid of me so you can marry Zane. How convenient."

"I haven't heard from Zane in a while. He had some kind of meltdown at the cross burning. James wasn't the only one wounded that day."

"Whoa, shit. That's too bad. I like Zane. I don't want him to take my place, but that sucks."

"Yeah."

"Does this Raz know Zane is out of the picture? No wonder he's sniffing around you."

"What'd you say? 'Sniffing'? Get the hell out of my office."

I walked by him and whipped open the door. I didn't look, but I'm sure Melanie, Glenda, and Joy were now staring at Brian. He strode out of the room with his head down. I shut the door quietly, though I really wanted to break something.

The next morning, Raz called. His report stunned me. First, a burning cross, then the noose, now this. I suggested he meet me at the police station. There, Raz handed the county deputy the boots from the paper sack he carried and told him where he had found them. The cop looked at him blankly.

"The boots were placed soles up," I said. He still didn't get it. "Showing the bottoms of your shoes to someone from the Middle East is an insult. Raz didn't want to make a fuss about it, but I said he should because we have a series of hate crimes in the area."

"Oh, I get it," said the deputy. "Well, you'll want to fill in this report, Mr. Peters. Here's a pen."

While Raz completed the report, I took notice of the scruffy man standing at the other end of the counter. He wore a crumpled white T-shirt, baggy jeans, and dirt-crusted cowboy boots. He was probably some cowhand on one of the ranches who had spent the night in jail. Deputy Bo could usually settle down the rowdies, but this drunk must've busted up a table or a head. Now he was in trouble and he'd missed a morning's wages.

I didn't do criminal work, but I knew the jail cells were located on the other side of that thick, steel door and down the hallway. I'd never seen them, never wanted to. Alone, behind bars and a thick wall. How terrifying.

Raz and I walked out to the parking lot. I told him goodbye then climbed into the Barracuda. Raz came to the side of the door, so I rolled down the window. Without a word, he leaned into the car and kissed me softly. Then he pulled back a little then kissed me again, longer and with enthusiasm. He smiled at me, keeping his face close to mine, and then he backed up and went to his Nissan. I wasted no time in getting away from him, from that place.

What was wrong with me? Why did I kiss him back? He was a marked man—one day the Hezbollah would catch up to him. It was stupid to get involved with someone like that. He muddled my brain.

The next evening, Mom and Bill, along with Vonny and James joined us for supper. Just before we sat down to eat, Raz showed up. I assumed Mom invited him, so I led him to the dining room. He explained that Nori was working at Wal-Mart that evening. After we ate, we shifted to the family room where I gave Mom the Civil War diary Lynne Zimmer gave me. She studied a few pages. Bill turned on a baseball game.

"This doesn't look so bad," said Mom. "They were still writing with quill and ink, so there's lots of smudged letters." She flipped to the front of the book. "They're originally from Pittsburgh, but here they're living along the Potomac River."

"Beth, what's the starting date?" asked James.

I didn't hear Mom's answer because Raz sat down next to me on the sofa. It would've seemed awkward, but it was the only open place to sit. Mom and James were discussing the book, but couldn't hear over the flush of warmth that rose from my chest into my face and ears. Vonny was the only one who noticed me. Maybe she even observed that my nostrils flared as I inhaled his cologne. I tried to focus on the game, but mostly I wanted him to leave. His presence disquieted, aroused, and confused me.

"Raz, when did you live in Beirut?" asked my mom.

"After college I went to live with a cousin. I stayed for nine years."

"You would've dodged a few bombs," I said.

He nodded. "Many people accept it as their life, their world, but it eats at you…the fear. It's hard for an American. You want to change things, some people even try."

"Did you?" I asked.

"Yes, and it got me in trouble."

I simply nodded—he was in hiding, so I knew better than to ask more questions.

"But you've had your own trials," he said to me. "How do you feel? Your Uncle Peter says you like to run."

"I'm still working on it. And I have started running."

It's a long way back from death. My spirit, my fight hasn't made it. No, I wasn't back. Maybe Sweetie's death broke something inside me.

I looked at the game; Raz knew that ended the conversation. Bill and Patty started preparing root beer floats as Mom handed out the Jim Beam Black.

"So are root beer floats and bourbon a western Nebraska tradition?" asked Raz.

"No, just a Harney Street way of life," said Bill as he set a large foaming glass of root beer and vanilla ice cream on a coaster set out by Mom.

James passed on the bourbon, for he was still on heavy meds, but Vonny imbibed. If she wasn't such a reader, she'd be going stir crazy, sitting in the quiet Wilson house. She enjoyed the Denver night life, even though she worked long days. I needed to ask about their plans for caring for James, though I dreaded the topic.

When the group broke up to go home, Bill offered to drive James and Vonny home so they wouldn't need to walk through the yards in the dark. James looked down as

Vonny accepted. Existing in his new world of weakness wore on him. Patty and Raz stood behind them in the foyer. The home phone rang, so I said my goodbyes then went to answer it in the kitchen.

Kayla proceeded to tell me about the grueling workout schedule for cross country. I had encouraged her to run while she was still enduring the agony of her parents' divorce. When her mom died, I suggested she run even more. I should start doing the same. After I hung up, I discovered the front door closed and the foyer light turned off. I started the dishwasher then turned off the rest of the lights and went up the back stairs to my bedroom. Once I brushed and changed for bed, I went back into my bedroom.

I stopped, suddenly aware of him, though I didn't see him. His hand lightly touched my shoulder as the other one drew my hair back from my other shoulder. From behind me, he kissed my neck, slowly, softly. I needed to stop him. This wasn't a good idea. Then he kissed the other side of my neck and my shoulder. I was held to the spot by the touch, the smell, the enticement of him. Then he ran his hands down the sides of my satin nightie. I was in trouble. Then his caresses were everywhere, still slow and thorough. Then he was in front of me.

"I'm here to help you live again. I won't fail like others have."

His lips were on mine, first softly, then harder and wetter as he pulled me close. This delightful torture made me pull back, take his hand, and whip back the bed covers. I couldn't wait to get under his hot flesh. Before I could crawl onto the sheets, he scooped me up and laid me down gently on the sheet that warmed in a flash to the heat of me, us. More heat. More excitement. Explosion. He rolled away, but I followed. I wasn't going to let my seduction end this quickly. No chance. I made him work till he collapsed in exhaustion. I suppose that was my counterattack. I fell asleep smiling.

Chapter 6

I awoke angry and alone. Lust made me an easy target. Lust could disguise itself as danger. Neither lust nor its satiation could bring me back to life, but indignation could.

After a shower, I sat at the table eating a bowl of Life. What did men want from me? What did I want from them?

As for sex, Brian, Zane, and Raz were all studs. I think they sensed the need to step up—a quickie poke wasn't going to cut it with me. With Brian, I wanted to share my life, but he wasn't up to the task. I wanted to be with Zane, slowly and carefully, as wounded people should, but he'd backed off. Maybe he knew he wasn't up to the task. Yet those two men cared for me—I even thought Zane loved me—but maybe love had its limitations. Could I deal with someone who could shut down so completely? At least Brian had some fight in him.

I didn't love Raz. Would it stay that way? Did he only want a conquest? Why the hell was he here in this desolate part of the world? The reach of the Hezbollah would find him here. I didn't see any evidence that he was prepared to defend himself. For a man with a death sentence on his head, it was strange that he didn't even carry a gun. But what was I to do with him now? Was something better than nothing? He was interesting company because of his varied background, but was I overemphasizing sex? Looking back, I'd done that with Brian, but at least I'd loved him. Yet Raz was still a mystery that intrigued me. Well, I'd deal with him later.

I stared at the remainder of my cereal as it became mushy. No more of this passive, wounded crap. Danger was still around. I would break its balls, thereby protecting my family and friends. Before I left the kitchen, I called Rachel and Merritt to set up an appointment with them.

This was step one.

At my first opportunity at work, I called Lew. He'd recently finished building a gate in one of Big Joe McCready's fences. He affirmed that Hank and Linda were also with him. A few minutes later, I was sitting with an iced tea in the front room of Lew's rental house. I explained my concern regarding the possibility of another crime, even another cross burning.

"Now this is what I need from you and Hank and Linda, if you want to help. I need a good map of that area north of the new Eldritch house, especially roads, good hiding places, ditches, and other dangerous areas. Check out the area along the highway, in particular."

"Why there?" asked Hank.

"Showing hate with a burning cross won't do any good, if nobody can see it. So, along the highway makes sense. But keep on the lookout—whoever is doing these acts of hate may be dangerous."

"Do you want us to guard the area?" asked Hank.

"Not right now, though I may ask if I think something is happening. How soon could you move into the house? I called to get the plumbing and the electricity back on."

"Bert woulda kept stuff workin', that's for sure," said Lew.

"I wouldn't mind movin' out there soon," said Hank. "We're crowding Lew with all our stuff."

"It needs a thorough cleaning," said Linda.

"And central air," I said. "Johnson Heating and Cooling from Kimball is installing air conditioning this week." That brought smiles from them. "I recommend changing the locks and installing dead bolts."

"But we ain't bought it yet," said Lew. "Do we pay rent?"

"Don't worry about that right now. Make those maps…that can serve as rent till the sale is complete. Somebody has declared war on Dexter and its people. I want to catch them."

This was step two.

At Custer's, I stopped to talk to Beulah at the cash register. Mom and Patty were already at my booth. The stranger was seated at the counter, finishing his lunch. He gave me a nod.

"Can't tell you much," said Beulah. "The stranger's name is Rob Faust. Says he's from North Platte. Don't look like a cowboy, don't act like one…talks better…like he's smart."

"Did you find out where he works?" I asked.

"Says he's in sales. He does seem to know those idiots at the back tables."

Mick Spittle and Jake Waters were seated at a table at the back of the diner, near the doors to the kitchen. Once again, the Webster brothers sat at an adjacent table. Spittle and Waters rose from their seats.

"Carol's been putting 'em back there…won't let 'em sit in a booth 'cause they don't tip."

I thanked her then started for the Docket booth.

As Spittle walked past my mom and Patty, he said loudly, "Goddamn! An A-rab and an Injun. If that don't beat all." He laughed till he saw me ahead of him.

I waited till they were both looking at me then I plunged my hand into my purse. They jolted to a stop. They knew who I was. They knew I killed a man a few weeks ago.

"You guys aren't causing any trouble are you?"

"N-no ma'am," said Jake.

Spittle shook his head.

"And you've been tipping Carol every time?"

"Oh, Mick, we forgot that today."

When the two men walked back to the table, the Webster brothers laughed and chided them. Spittle dropped some bills on the table then they left by walking down the aisle along the counter. I stood in the aisle till they exited the front door. Then I pulled my left hand out of my purse—I held a small mirror that I lifted to look in for a moment. I looked over to Maggie McCready and Marva Gush who occupied the booth where I stopped.

"I guess they think I'm a leftie," I said as I shoved the mirror back into my purse. That brought on a new round of laughter from the women and others.

Just as I slid into the booth next to my mom, I glanced over to the counter. The stranger Rob Faust was grinning at me. I enjoyed humbling those two jerks, yet a sense of disquietude buzzed around my head like wasps ready to attack.

"I know you're interested in those guys," said Mom. "So I took photos of them with my phone. They're not very observant. I even got the stranger at the counter."

"I've created a monster," I said.

Patty laughed.

"The stranger almost caught me."

That alarmed me—I'd set my plans, one of which was to keep family and those close to me away from the investigation and danger.

I'd also learned from the Quinn investigation the need for stealth. So when I met with Rachel and Merritt, I'd already sent Patty home. They came after their shifts in civilian clothes. Merritt parked his SUV at the Eldritch barn then Rachel picked him up, left her Subaru at Strider and Rohan's barn, and then they walked over to my backyard. I met them on the patio with a bucket full of ice and Heinekens. Both humored my wishes, though nobody thought any of it was funny.

The three of us sipped our beer and exchanged small talk as we stared out at Rufus. The rubble and the yellow tape were long gone, though the grass was still charred. I'd spread some wild grass seed in cooler weather. Now two weeks later, the media finally let the story die.

"So far, we don't have any strong leads," said Merritt. "We haven't even tracked the wood. They used common lighter fluid, a ton of it, but we haven't located a single location for a large purchase."

"The wood was in sections, so it could be easily transported," said Rachel.

"And hidden," I said. I was disappointed in the investigation. "So we need to figure out if somebody local is in on it. They obviously targeted James."

"They probably assembled the cross up on that Hexam Road," said Merritt. "That would take awhile. Then they had to drag it all that way, light it, and run back to their truck or trucks."

"Somebody or some group is mocking us with vile racist insults," I said. "Why? Is that fun? It seems like a lot of work just for kicks. And they're gloating because they haven't been caught, or even questioned. What about that moron Mick Spittle? He doesn't seem to work, but he's buying steak everyday at Custer's."

"Mick Spittle is a dolt," said Merritt. "His only conviction is from vandalizing a cemetery in Sidney eight years ago. He spent a little time in juvenile detention then got probation. The thing is, he doesn't have the brains to pull off that cross burning."

"No, but he could be the dumb labor," said Rachel.

"He's been eating lunch with Jake Waters," I said.

"Oh, man, that's touchy," said Merritt.

His father, State Patrol Officer Randall Waters, seemed the straight arrow, a former Army Ranger and sharpshooter, but that didn't mean his son was reputable. Maybe the State Patrol wasn't the best means to track Jake Waters.

"The Webster brothers have also started showing up," I said. "They always sit at a table next to Spittle. And there's a stranger in town named Rob Faust. Yeah, I know, unlikely last name. He's been seen in the company of Spittle and Jake, but he doesn't always sit near them."

"You're sounding xenophobic," said Rachel.

"Maybe, but the timing is interesting. Beulah says he's well-spoken. I don't think he's a clod like Mick. Smells better, too."

Rachel chuckled. I handed them each a photo of Faust, the one my mom took. They both shook their heads.

"Listen, when the cross burning happened, I knew something was up and where. Whoever's doing this might get bold and try it again. You have the maps from the Quinn excavation. Next time, exits need to be covered. I've bought land to the west of the highway—I think that area is a strong possibility since it can be seen from the highway."

"Do you think something is going to happen?" asked Rachel.

"Yeah...can't explain it...so don't ask...but I'm right time after time."

"Well, if you can pinpoint it at all, can you tell us where it's happening?"

"I will, if I can. Okay, so near my house or the Wilson house, like Rufus or the Seven Dwarfs or Big Leo, let's call that my 'Backyard.' To the east of Big Leo, that's 'Old Eldritch,' and, um, to the north, that's 'The Beast.' Let's see, far north toward I-80, that's 'Quinn' for names. I still need to explore the area west of Highway 50, so let's call that 'West 50.' I suppose they could get really ballsy and try something between here and the town, so that's 'South Harney.'"

When Merritt finished scribbling down the names in his notebook, I continued:

"If it's a cross burning, we should expect that it's going to be where it can be seen from the Wilson house. It doesn't have the same message anywhere else in this 'whitebread' corner of the world."

After they left, I stood out on the front porch, watching the sun set into watercolor waves of yellow and lavender. A Nissan Pathfinder was parked next to Derek's car in the driveway. Zane came down the Wilson porch steps. I walked over to meet him. He should have been with me last night, not Raz.

"Finally come out of your shell?" I said as we met midway between the houses.

"That's not fair, you know I'm—"

"In a crisis? Join the club. By the way, my baby died last month. Did you remember that? Or are you just so self-centered that you only see your own woes?"

"I'm sorry I haven't been to see you," he said.

"You haven't even called for a chat. We should be able to chat, but you shut down and shut me off—you've always been like this—it didn't take a war to create self-centered immaturity. I mean, it's not like we need to discuss the meaning of life, a few comments on the Cubs or Cardinals would be fine."

He shoved his hands in the pockets of his cargo shorts.

"Are you still in therapy?"

He shook his head.

"What? Why the hell not? You're in a crisis and you decide that's a good time to avoid getting help?"

He looked away from me. Why were men so damn stupid? I went from Brian to this? I'd traded one numskull for another. I walked back to the house. By the time I arrived at my porch, Zane was backing out of James' driveway. Meanwhile, a silver XTerra turned off the highway and drove my way. Zane passed the Nissan, slowed then stopped. Raz parked in my driveway. When Raz took my hand, Zane's taillights flashed off and he coasted to the highway and turned south. He didn't come back for me. He didn't fight for me. We were done.

"How about a drink?" I said to Raz as we walked into the foyer.

"That's fine," he said.

"Nah, it's too hot. I need a bath. Wanna help?"

"That's even better."

The next day, I started step three. At twilight, I took Strider, my lightning-fast black stallion, out into my backyard. We covered the rough ground and stayed out till after dark. Back at the barn, I taught him a new command. I'd taken him out in the dark just once before, and he'd done quite well, but I wanted him to know the importance of silence. So when he started to make a noise, I pulled on his mane then put my hand over his mouth. It only took a couple of nights for him to learn it. I rewarded him with carrots or sugar. Over the weekend, we started exploring the old Bolger land. I studied the maps Hank brought over, but I wouldn't be able to use them in the dark, so Strider and I needed to feel that land to learn it.

One evening, I met with my posse, Hank and Lew for the land west of the highway, and Jack and Bud, Bill's trusty cowhands, for the land east of it. I went over the area names I developed with the State Patrol. We discussed escape routes and practiced texting each other as we hid the cell phone light. We needed silence and the disguise of darkness.

The next night, we checked our flashlights then we cleaned and loaded our weapons. Later we discussed gun safety—God forbid we should shoot each other. I also cautioned them to shoot low, unless they fired on us. We couldn't shoot to kill unless we were likewise in danger. If the scum were only trespassing and were unarmed, we could only maim to stop their flight.

"But I still don't get how we're gonna catch them in the dark," said Lew.

"We'll see them," I said.

Setting before them a box I brought from the house, I opened it then handed each man a pair of night goggles.

"Holy shit!" said Jack.

"We're gonna be a kick-ass Night Posse," I said. "But these take a bit of practice, so try them at home then outside. I'm going to wear them when I work with Strider tonight. We'll see if he trusts my new night vision."

"Megan," said Jack, "if Strider starts to fall, get your feet out of the stirrups and try to jump and roll clear."

"Yeah, don't get trapped under him," said Bud.

Strider was a beautiful horse, black from hoof to nose, without a pinch of white on him. He was a mix of quarter horse and Holstein, a breed of German army horse, and stood a full seventeen hands. He was a horse meant for the likes of John Wayne—I'd hate to get crushed under him.

Chapter 7

OVER Labor Day weekend, John Tremaine visited. A good friend of my dad's, he was our paid counsel for the firm and my former Creighton Law School estate planning professor. I consulted him regularly on probate, wills and trusts, and other estate planning issues. Sixty and on the chunky side with receding gray hair, he possessed deep wrinkles in his forehead and brow that gave the impression he was always deep in thought.

John—I had trained myself not to call him professor—left after his last class and arrived at the big house in time for Bill's grilled steaks. After I got him settled in the guest room, we went to the kitchen to check on the status of supper.

"Hello, Liz," John said.

"Hi, John, good to see you," replied my mom.

Dang, I forgot they would have known each other from Omaha. He would have been at Mom and Dad's wedding, and known me and my twin Scott as babies and toddlers. I wondered if he knew my mom and my uncle had an affair after my parents separated. I'd never bring up the issue, for I dreaded rehashing the events of that time. The knowledge that I'd been taken from my twin and mother was still a painful issue for me. Although evening passed quietly, I remained disconcerted until sleep took me.

The next morning, John accompanied me to the office, even though it was a Saturday. We went over several complicated trusts, including two for special needs individuals. Word got out that I had written a special needs trust for Davey Shuster, so now I was considered the expert in the area. I also handled the conservatorship and guardianship filings for special needs and other incapacitated individuals. I dreaded the nasty scene on Tuesday morning when a couple from eastern Cheyenne County, who were also in the throes of a divorce, needed to sign the final documents for a guardianship and a conservatorship. The wife was bringing her own attorney, which was fine, but we probably needed a bouncer to keep the warring parties from going at each other. I wish I could duct tape shut their mouths long enough to get their signatures. If they both lived through the meeting, I could still file the documents with the court and proceed with the divorce.

After John met with Mark "Gus" Gustafson on a couple of files, we went back to the big house for a late lunch and a game of chess. Like Judge Dean Shelton, and most men I played against, he was over-aggressive in his tactics. I read his plan then picked off key pieces before I began my attack. It took three hours, but I finally beat him. He took defeat well, even though it probably pained him to lose to a shrimpy former student.

Before we visited James, whom John had met on prior visits, I covered the facts of the cross burning minus my premonition of evil during that day. James seemed to have stalled in his recovery. The strength in his left side still hadn't returned, though he worked hard on the therapy exercises. From his home office, James was forced to supervise the work now done by strong young men he hired. Tom Sedlacek, who had worked part-time with James for the last couple of years, supervised on site. Tom also constructed a rock slab walkway from the Wilson house to my front sidewalk to make it easier for James to visit.

After supper with Bill and Mom, John was eager to chat about my investigation of the Quinn murders. Later, when we were alone, John downed a second bourbon and mentioned my admission of our family secrets in the Dexter Gazette, a newspaper I created just for that purpose. Maybe he thought I'd hesitate to offer a third glass of bourbon, so he went into the kitchen and brought back the bottle. He poured us both a generous portion, even though I hadn't finished my first glass.

His speech began to slow and he looked drowsy, then he uttered a shocker: "You know, Frank was always worried that Bill was your father."

Oh, big shit!

"Of course, he told me that he had separated from your mother, but it did surprise me that she took up with Bill. He was ready to grant her request for a divorce, but then came the news of the pregnancy."

I downed a big swig. I knew Uncle Bill and Mom had dated, but Bill said he wasn't the father because the timing was wrong.

"So Frank felt lucky to have custody of you while your mother stayed with Scott."

"My dad threatened to put Scott in an institution. My mom refused to permit that—he forced her to make a choice between her kids."

"Well, he never told me that. But he was eager to get out of Omaha."

"To keep the truth from me…so I wouldn't go back. He lied and told me my mother was dead and he never mentioned I was a twin. I had to figure it out on my own. Uncle Bill backed the plan out of guilt. I didn't learn any of it until after my father died."

"Hmmm. I see. Well, I'm bushed. I'll see you in the morning."

And just like that, he rose and ascended the front stairs. He'd turned my world upside down then shrugged it off. Did my father really worry I wasn't his? Why would John lie about it? Was Bill my father?

I stared at nothing for eleventy hours then I started the dishwasher, downed a handful of Rolaids, and then sat on the edge of my bed in disbelief. Part of my brain was numb, the other half was reeling.

I wanted to feel like I'd come all the way back to life—now this.

John left after church. I took Strider for a long ride on a path along the south pasture where my stallion could unleash his speed. The thrill of the ride and the force of the wind in my face made other thoughts impossible.

Monday at lunch, I still felt walloped. The biggest regret of my life involved my messy, mysterious family. I was told my mother had died; I didn't remember Scottie, my Totty, from our first three years of life—but he had always touched me, haunted me—so maybe I did somehow know of him. So now I had the fatherhood mystery. Other regrets, yeah, they ate at me. I wished I was going into my sixth month of pregnancy; I wished I was still married and growing older with the right person; and I wished things had worked out with Zane. But this was the second time we'd dated and parted. That should tell me something.

I looked up from the menu I wasn't reading to find Beulah standing next to the booth.

"I guess I shoulda announced my arrival with a horn," she said. "You look distracted. What's eatin' you?"

"It would be easier to list what's not. Oh, but you'll be glad to hear that James is coming for lunch. Too bad he picked a day with a thunderstorm."

"Well, that's great. I'll be lookin' for him. Been waitin' for him to show up one day. So, you gonna share anythin' with your Best Friend?"

"How about a dead baby, James, and troubles with men? That would sum it up."

"Oh, Lordy, Megan."

"But there are good things too—Mom and Bill, James back on his feet, the first rain in what—four weeks?"

"Oh, here he is," she said. "Oh, by the way, that Rob Faust you were asking 'bout is always pushing me for information on folks."

"And you love to share. Who has he asked about?"

"Ever'body who walks through that door."

James shuffled through the entrance with Vonny at his side. James received pats on the back and "Great to see you" from several of the Custer's denizens. Vonny got greetings and tipped caps. Bud jumped up from his booth, approached Vonny then he held out his hand and said something. She smiled and handed her umbrella to him. He shook the rain off the umbrella outside then returned it to our table with Vonny's thanks.

I took a quick look at the table where Bud was seated. He was with Jack, Drew, and Tony, the FBI undercover agent posing as a cowhand, still in the area investigating meth trafficking. Both Jack and Bud were sworn to secrecy regarding our clandestine plans, and I trusted them. I told Carol to bring me their check. Cowhands in Custer's on a weekday created a strange sight—they usually worked through any sort of weather, but lightning was a wise exception.

As James sat down and Vonny slid into the booth next to me, I noticed that Tony's gaze was fixed on her. After a few minutes of small talk, Tony approached our booth and thanked me for paying the bill. I introduced James and Vonny to him. It was the first time I'd seen Tony in daylight. He resembled the Marlboro man, before he got lung cancer, with his chiseled good looks. He said goodbye then held his eyes on Vonny that extra second before he left. She kept her eyes on him till he walked out the door.

"Too bad…" whispered Vonny.

I nodded then wrote on a napkin: "SECRET—FBI Denver," which I placed on her lap.

She looked at me with raised eyebrows.

"There's Brian," said James.

I waved him over. James scooted over to make room for him. Brian glanced back at Deputy Bo and a man who entered the diner with him.

"Oh, that's our interim Chief of Police," said Brian. "He was talking with Gus when I left the office."

A stocky man of about forty years with sandy brown hair and a goatee looked odd next to the younger, lanky deputy. The two policemen stopped at every table. Bo would introduce the man then the new chief would gush with congeniality. Clearly, he meant to play the good ole boy role. He arrived at our booth.

Bo introduced Tate McNeill to us. McNeill shook each of our hands.

"Call me Chief Tate," he said.

As he moved to the next table, Rob Faust sat down at the counter. Meanwhile, I passed around a bottle of hand sanitizer. James chuckled about it, but we all used it. How many hands had Chief Tate shaken that day? Ick.

"That's Rachel's ex," I said. "He was a deputy in Ogallala. Officer Merritt thinks well of him. I'm sure that helped convince the town council."

When we finished our sandwiches, Vonny said, "Well, we have news. Derek is moving here. He's persuaded his company to let him work off-site. He didn't have much trouble, I mean, it's all computer stuff so it wouldn't matter where he worked."

"That's great," I said. "He told me about getting engaged to Tina. But he won't be married before they come out, right?"

"Actually, they will be. It'll be just a minister and a witness. They'll postpone a reception till later."

I was so pleased. James' health scare was terrible, but I'd enjoyed seeing Derek and Vonny so often. Now my old friend was moving home.

Late that night, I lay next to Raz in bed. Since the first night when it was all about conquering and counter attacking, we started to have fun. Mr. Tall, Dark, and Handsome only came over two or three nights a week and that was all right with me. He became more talkative, more affectionate, more playful, and more creative—I'd never even thought about making love on the kitchen table.

Yet I was always alert, never able to completely relax with him. He never stayed past eleven, and I never questioned him about it. In fact, I encouraged it. My divorce, though complete in my mind, was not official. I was committing adultery, and it nagged at me. Sensing this lovers' romp was temporary, I never let him in, never let him get too close. Marriage suited me—I wanted to be with someone over the years, watching each other's arches fall and complaining about stiff backs and ugly bunions.

Still, I enjoyed his companionship. Raz didn't care about watching sports, but a man could have worse faults. And now that he was more relaxed, I discovered his great sense of humor. The guy was downright funny, more so than Brian, the mopey, or Zane, the damaged. Raz was getting under my skin. What was I to do with him? He would leave then I'd be alone again. Yet he took the sting off Zane's absence.

Did Raz make me feel like I'd come back to life? Nobody could do that for me. A life died inside me; when Sweetie died, part of me died, too; replacing her was never considered. In fact, the thought of becoming pregnant frightened me in the dark, terrified recesses of my wounded soul. Also, no worthy father existed in my life for a baby. I'd failed at marriage; I'd failed to keep my Sweetie alive.

Humbled.

Guilty.

Wounded.

Chapter 8

FRIDAY morning I jolted awake, my guts churning and my head swimming with a sense of portent. Lord Almighty, what would happen today? Would they come back to burn another cross or do something else horrible? I scampered out of my sheets and knelt on the carpet. God help me. I suddenly felt bad that I had enlisted the help of others. I didn't want anyone to be injured, especially the good guys and my magnificent horse. I should've just gone out there with my Glock and my night goggles to face the consequences. But I really wanted to catch those evil bastards. Oh, sorry, God. I just wanted justice, and well, to avenge James. That last part wasn't Christian of me, I suppose, but the police weren't even close to making any arrests. Maybe my throbbing head could be more effective than their methods.

At work, I tried not to raise a stir, but Melanie, my paralegal, kept staring at me. That woman was much too observant. I think she must've told Brian, because I looked up to find him standing in the doorway.

"What's up?" he asked.

"Something."

"Whoa, shit. Just tell me what to do."

"I don't suppose you have time to go home and get your Glock?"

"That would be easy. I moved into Lew's old rental across the street, now that they've taken over the old Bolger house."

"Okay, great."

"So, what do I do?"

"I don't know—but I'll tell you and the police when I do."

I tried in vain to work; instead, I stared at all the tragedy on my desk—probate, somebody died; divorce, some family was breaking up; bankruptcy, somebody was drowning in debt. So, after my three o'clock appointment, I went home, shocking Patty.

"What's up?" she asked.

"Something."

"Oh, no. Do you know what it is?"

"Not yet."

"Well, I'm calling your mom. She's over with James."

"No, I don't want to alarm James. Text her, tell her to go home for supper and to make sure Bill comes home. I want to know where everybody is. You can tell Vonny, but don't scare her. I'm going to have protection at all the houses."

"Then it's here. Oh, and Vonny left. Derek is there now."

"Oh, that's right. Well, I need to figure out some things. Can you stay this evening to handle phone calls? I'll tell Brian to come over here."

"Yeah. And I think I'll sharpen the knives this afternoon."

I changed into my black jeans and a black T-shirt. In the study, I called my FBI connection in Denver. Robert Foxworthy answered right away.

"Got any news for me?" I asked. "Are you involved in the cross burning incident?"

"Yes," he said. "How's James?"

"He's holding his own, but not really improving. So do you have wind of anything?"

"That's probably what I should be asking you."

"It's today."

"I'm calling Tony."

"Send him to Strider's barn at twilight. Tell him to act like he just happened to show up. No need to blow his cover unless he has to. And yes, I'll be talking to the State Patrol soon. I've talked to them in the past about it—possible locations, escape routes."

"Who have you talked to?"

"McNeill and Merritt."

"Not Waters?"

"No, Jake Waters has been seen hanging with Mick Spittle, and the Webster brothers—the group I think is probably behind the cross burning."

"Oh, that's a problem."

"Yeah, no kidding. The thing is…the people I've talked to say Jake's lazy, but he's never been in trouble and he's not been seen with this group before this summer. By the way, do you have someone else out here?"

"Why, what makes you think so?"

"There's a stranger in town and he doesn't make my stomach turn over."

Robert chuckled softly then said, "Megan, take care now. I think the police should take over."

"Just send Tony for now. I promise I'll call them. But there's nothing to tell them yet."

I then called Jack and Bud, who would meet me at Strider's barn. Lew agreed that he and Hank would be on the lookout on their land near the highway.

Next I called Zane at work, something I didn't like to do, for he should be making a good impression.

"Megan, what's up?" he asked.

"Something."

"Well, damn."

"Can you go over to Bill and my mom's house about twilight? Bring your gun."

"Megan, what are you going to do?"

"I have a general idea. I'll keep in contact."

I went out to my backyard. If someone meant to cause trouble, they'd wait until darkness could hide them. But I needed answers. I skirted Rufus to the west then headed north forty yards to the first of the Seven Dwarfs, small rocky mounds referred to as buttes. I sat down in the September shade of Sneezy, stretched my legs out to the edge of the curly gray-green wild buffalo grass.

What? Where? Think, no clear my head, feel. Just feel. Feel anger, feel the need to protect. Think where. No, clear head. Abandoned. What? No, just feel. Breathe.

Here. Right here.

Come on, bastards. Come and get all that you deserve.

I ran back to the house to call Lew. I asked him to come across the highway and keep watch in the Wilson backyard with Hank as soon as dusk hit. I didn't want to reveal my guess to anyone except Jack and Bud, or the police would converge on the area and scare them away.

I tried to eat, but found it hard to swallow the lasagna Patty made. My hands became sweaty with anticipation. My heart beat hard and steady through the early evening. Finally, I got so antsy that I wrapped my Glock and my night goggles in my black hoodie and set out for Strider's barn by cutting through the field between my house and Bill's where I turned north. Out in the rough ground, I crept through a maze of rocky ridges. Zane had taken a position next to a scraggily old oak, the only one left intact by the tornado that leveled Bill's house my first summer back in Dexter. Just as the setting sun was lighting the western horizon, I dashed to Strider's barn.

Excited, fearful, resolute, I waited for the others. Jack and Bud came first. They also wore all black, including their cowboy hats.

"You two don't look like the good guys," I said.

Bud smirked then pulled his goggles out of his coat then he looked toward the door.

"Just checking on the horses," said Tony, who yanked shut the door behind him.

"We've got it handled, so you can leave," said Jack.

Tony looked over to me.

"Actually, he can't...he has his orders," I said.

"Megan, we can handle this on our own," said Jack.

"Maybe, probably," I said. "Look, um—"

Tony nodded to me.

"Tony is FBI out of Denver working on the meth problem," I said. "I have a friend out there and he ordered Tony to help. So, he's with us."

I called Brian to ask him to watch over to the big house and to make sure no backyard lights were on. Meanwhile, the men snapped into action. Bud saddled Strider and Jack saddled Rohan. We checked our flashlights, cell phones, and handguns. I told them of the guards at the three houses and my expectations. Then we peered out the windows of the barn as twilight became night.

"Okay, remember, we're only shooting at legs unless they shoot at us. We want to catch them with the cross or whatever, but stop them before they can erect anything or start a fire."

A cross on Big Leo would be incredibly bold and difficult. They'd need to haul those heavy beams up the side of the bluff, though the east side wasn't steep. No, I thought they'd go back to Rufus, just for spite. But maybe they didn't plan for a cross, maybe just a fire. If that was true, they'd want to get close to one of the houses.

Jack positioned his night goggles, hung binoculars around his neck, and then set out on Rohan, the only horse besides Strider that knew the rough land. He was to cut south, around the rough ridges east of the barn, then ride north as the scout. Bud set out to wait behind a rocky ridge northeast of the barn.

I mounted Strider. "Danger, Strider, danger."

We trotted west toward Rufus, but stopped short of it. Tony followed on foot. I used Strider's body to block the light from my cell phone to tell Tony where I was. They'd picked a moonless night to stage their malevolence. Time passed. I checked the time on the cell phone, nearly ten. My house was lit only by an interior light, probably from the kitchen. I wondered if Patty was standing with Brian, a sharpened butcher knife in her hand. More time passed. I let Strider graze.

What if I was wrong? What if they never came? I'd feel like a fool and my credibility would be shot to hell.

The cool September wind lashed at us. Was Bill my father? No, focus. Then my heart started to pound—I was right. My cell buzzed.

The text was from Jack: "pu west of eld barn. 3 men beams going sw."

They were parking the getaway pickup closer this time. They probably assembled the cross near the Eldritch barn and were headed my way. Bud would wait on me. I'd let them come close then chase them back. My heart hammered my chest. God above, please let them not be armed. I started Strider slowly forward. I gave Tony a quick flash of light from my cell. Then I called Merritt and Rachel.

My cell buzzed. Bud reported men had passed him on foot.

From Rufus, I headed northeast. Then I saw their flashlight beams, three of them. I veered south to stay out of their light. I tugged on Strider's mane to assure silence. Now, I could see them. They were dragging the cross, and none of them was Simon of Cyrene and they weren't on their way to Golgotha. We slowed as I stared for a moment at the cross. They planned to use the most sacred of God's symbols as a vile tool of hatred. Rage swelled from my kneecaps and rose up past my thundering heart.

I dug my heels into Strider and we charged.

Strider was so quiet he was nearly on top of the first man, before I shot out the legs of bastard number one. He wailed and writhed on the ground, the cross fell on top of him.

"Go!" A man yelled.

You pathetic son of a bitch, as if you could outrun my steed. The man picked up the flashlight he dropped, but not before I saw the shine of metal in his hand. His shots rang out even though he hadn't spotted me. I fired at his body.

He was running now, the flashlight beam landed on us but swept on by. I urged Strider onward as I fired again. The man stumbled as I kept firing. He went down screaming like a fourth grader. I rode eastward, anxious to get away from more gunshots. A figure ran to the man. That would be Tony. Someone grunted. I circled around and rode back. I hit the two men with a blast from my flashlight.

"I got him!" yelled Tony. "Go after the other one!"

Two shots were fired. I turned Strider and charged toward the sounds. In the distance, I saw the red and blue flashing lights from two police cruisers near Bill's house. When I flicked on my flashlight, it illuminated a man on the ground next to Bud, along with Jack and Rohan's approach.

"Jack!" I yelled.

"We got this one. Did we get the others?" asked Jack.

"Oh, yeah."

"Megan, better call for an ambulance."

"Okay." I dialed emergency.

After I flashed my light on and off a few times toward the cruisers, one of them veered to the south. Another cruiser drove through the area between my house and the Wilsons. Tony shone his light toward that police car.

"Is he hurt badly?" I asked.

"Nah, took off a chunk of his calf," said Bud. "I was gonna tackle him, but it sounded like someone was shooting back at you so I figured this guy had a gun, too."

"He was. I bet he's worse off. Tony's with him. I shot the first guy and the cross fell on him. Strider was so quiet he nearly ran him over before he knew we were there."

The danger was gone, but now my heart pounded with adrenaline. "Strider was great. Didn't even flinch when I fired. Hey, guys look."

Bud and Jack both shone their flashlights on us.

Just as we practiced last June, I stroked Strider's neck then yanked back on the reins. His front feet left the ground and his body rose high into the light beams. He held it long enough to kick his front feet in the air before he dropped to the ground as Bud and Jack whooped.

"Jesus Christ," said the man on the ground.

I jumped off my horse and ran over to the man. Bud lit his face.

"Jesus Christ! Is that what you said?" I rammed the cold steel of my gun into his throat. "And you were getting ready to burn his cross, you devil. If you've never feared God before, you better learn to. 'Cause He'll show you no mercy now."

The cruiser came to a stop near us. I shoved my gun into my rear waistband and stood.

"Rot in hell."

I walked over to Strider and stroked his neck, glad it was dark so nobody could see how badly my hands were shaking.

My mind darted back to my thoughts a few minutes ago—the feeling of neglect as a child and the need to protect. Was that it? Was I over-protective because I had been abandoned? But I hadn't, not really. Torn away? Yeah, from my mother and brother, a father who died guilty, later from my husband, who started the separation. Me, torn into with a knife, my baby, torn away, murdered. Yeah, I had something powerful going on.

Torn.

Chapter 9

SOON the night was teeming with stiff-brimmed State Patrol officers and county deputies. We were taken to Strider's barn where Bud and Jack tended to the horses. Merritt and Waters soon joined the officers with us.

"We choose not to speak at this time," I said.

"Tell us what the hell you were doing out there," demanded Officer Waters.

Bud and Jack followed my lead and remained silent. Waters got into my face, well, he looked down into it. I'd been around him on a number of occasions, but he seemed different, as in threatening and unprofessional. In fact, he scared me. Though his face turned red and a vein in his forehead popped out, I held my ground. He only turned away when his cell phone buzzed. He paused for a moment, mouth slack, and then stormed out of the barn. His cruiser roared into the night.

When Rachel arrived, I told her and Merritt the whole story. Bud and Jack gave their accounts. Then Tony stepped forward from the doorway and confirmed my account, adding that he handed the second man's gun over to a State Trooper.

"Megan, did you do all the shooting?" asked Merritt.

"No, the second guy shot at me. After that, I was able to hit him on the second try. The plan was to aim at their legs to stop them. But after that guy shot at me, I aimed for his body. I had to bring him down or he'd shoot one of us."

"Do any of you know who you captured?" Rachel asked.

"I could probably guess, but I never saw any of them well enough to identify them."

"But you were all wearing night goggles."

"They do work, but your vision is funky and everything is green."

"Megan, you shot Mick Spittle in the left testicle, as well as the abdomen and left leg. Nick Webster just got it in the right lower leg. Then the cross fell on him, fracturing his collarbone."

"I was lucky to hit anything. You try shooting across your body from a running horse."

"Bud, you got Brett Webster twice in the left leg."

Merritt stepped forward with a canvas bag and requested that we surrender our guns and night goggles. I expressed my displeasure, but complied.

"Jake Waters was the driver of the pickup. I caught up to him...it was easy after Zane shot out two tires," said Rachel.

"I wondered if Jake Waters was in on it. That's why I didn't want to talk to his father."

"Randy Waters is a good guy, a good cop," said Merritt.

I didn't say anything.

"What?" he asked.

"Nothing. Just keep him away from me and these men. It has all changed for him."

"He'll be taken off the investigation. Why did you think Jake might be involved?"

"He'd recently started eating at Custer's with Mick Spittle."

"That's all?"

"That's all. I wasn't sure who we would meet out here or exactly what they'd do."

"So how did you know they'd try to do this tonight?"

"Just did."

"Did you hack any computers or use any other kind of surveillance?"

"No, sir."

Merritt folded his arms across his chest as he stared at me, wondering about me or waiting for me to explain or maybe both. But the less said, the better.

"Hey, can we go to my house to talk? It smells like horseshit in here."

Rachel grinned at me. As we left the barn, she whispered to me, "Too bad you only got one ball."

As we walked across the field to my house, I lagged behind to send a text to Patty, telling her to hide Lew and Hank's night goggles in the basement and to tell them not to say anything about being in the Night Posse.

Back at my house, a crowd was gathering. Patty nodded to me when I entered with Rachel, Jack, and Bud. She was dishing up root beer floats with my mom and Bill.

Mom turned to me, "Megan, that was very dangerous."

"But worth it. Maybe James will sleep easier, I know I will."

Zane entered the kitchen to get his root beer float. He leaned toward me and said, "I could have been of help to you out there."

"I know." Actually, I didn't know. "But I called on you to protect my mom and uncle. That was very important."

He nodded.

My mom handed Rachel a root beer float. Merritt walked into the kitchen. Patty handed him one, too. He looked a little unsure.

"Go ahead. Your shift was over hours ago. Mom, I think you should give Jack, Bud, and me bourbon floats. Those guys really earned it. Is Tony here? Give him one, too."

"You know Tony?" asked Bill.

I nodded.

"You should see her in all black on that horse," said Jack to Bill. "Pretty damn scary."

Brian stood in the doorway, grinning at me. "Derek's here. He wants the story from you. And we all want to hear it complete. We've only heard some of it."

I found Derek in the family room. His hug lifted me off the ground. My mom handed Raz, who was standing against the bookcase, a root beer float. She must have called him, for I hadn't even thought of him.

"Thanks, Bill, for calling me," said Derek. "We knew something was up when Lew and Hank stood at the edge of the backyard. Then Bill called to tell us those...ah...men had been captured. My dad knew right away who was behind it."

I smiled then launched into the story. Jack and Bud added their roles in the capture. Tony said he just tagged along. Lew and Hank remained silent.

"And one of the guys, the driver, was Jake Waters," I said.

"Waters?" Bill scratched his whiskers.

"Yes, the son of Officer Randy Waters," I said.

"Oh, that's too bad," said Bill.

"So Officer Waters won't be a part of the investigation, so nobody, and I mean nobody, has to talk to him. Of course, we'll cooperate fully with Officers Merritt and McNeill, and any other state or county officers. But Waters needs to leave us alone. He ought to be finding a good lawyer for his son, because hate crime is a felony."

"Won't they claim the right of free speech...aside from the trespassing?" asked my mom.

"They can try to argue free speech, but they won't get far. Ten years ago, the Supreme Court ruled that states have a right to ban cross burnings—as Nebraska does—that are intended to intimidate observers. These laws don't violate free speech rights because cross burning has an extensive American history of gruesome violence."

"Thanks to the KKK," said Mom.

"So once those guys get out of the hospital, they'll go to jail and then to a trial they will lose or maybe they'll cop a plea bargain. Oh, and Mick Spittle shot at me, so he's in really deep."

Rachel was smirking, so I rose.

"Well, I need more ice cream. Rachel's dying to tell you something. By the way, I think we should celebrate at the Cowpoke tomorrow night."

When I left the room, it was buzzing with chatter. Once in the kitchen, I downed a couple of swigs of bourbon. But the booze lacked the strength to glaze over the hum of adrenaline still coursing through me, from my tingling scalp to the tips of my big toes. I had three studs in my house and I was dying to get next to the heat of one of them. Tomorrow I'd feel sad about my lack of love for any of them, but right now I was hyped and frisky. I'd get knocked down another day, but tonight felt like a victory.

I took another swig then I heard his voice behind me, close to me, now against me. He pulled back my hair then put his face into my neck.

"You smell like a horse barn."

"I wonder how that happened."

Brian put his hands on my hips, turning me around. He planted a kiss on me that I hadn't felt since last June, before we'd lost so much.

As I slid my body from between his muscular hulk and the counter, I said, "I need to go back to my guests," I said.

Back in the family room, I said good night to my gang of supporters, asked Patty to lock up before she left, and then went up the back stairs to my bedroom and a shower.

I awoke to Brian sleeping next to me. Damn you. If you'd been a better man, I'd be sleeping next to you every night. Did he know about Raz? Brian hadn't been asking to come back—maybe he was just staking his claim in the faces of his two rivals. He generally disapproved of my dangerous undertakings, so he wasn't hot for me because of that. He was competing.

I carefully slid out of bed, took a quick shower then went into the office, ignoring the seven reporters camped out in front of my house. Work wasn't terribly pressing, though I often worked on Saturdays—I simply wanted to avoid Brian and the pathetic soap opera of my love life.

Around two, I started to feel hungry. As I was cleaning up my desk, I heard a knocking at the back door. I peeked out Brian's office window before opening the door to Raz, who looked angry.

"You hardly even spoke to me last night," he said.

"I helped in the capture of four felons and all you can think about is you? They probably gave you those upturned boots. Maybe you were their next target. They probably think you're Muslim. And a ton of people were there. I couldn't have personal conversations with twenty people. Besides, the cops hung around a long time. It's best not to blab too much in their presence."

He stood with his hands on his hips. I opened the fridge and took out a container of orange juice. The law firm building was originally a house, so it had a full kitchen. I took two glasses out of the cupboard. I poured a glass then offered it to him. He just stared at me, so I drank it.

"And you slept with Brian."

"I slept with my husband because you never came. I don't know from one day to the next if you ever plan to come back."

"You don't realize how hard—"

"Why is it hard?"

He took a step back as he shoved his hands in his pockets. I put away the juice as the acid hit my empty stomach.

"I'll be right back," I said.

I powered down my computer, locked up my desk, and returned to Raz.

"Look, why don't you and Nori come to the Cowpoke tonight for supper? A bunch of us will be there."

"Brian?"

"No, he got kicked out after he kept getting drunk and starting fights…um…after Sweetie died."

"He was upset."

I nodded.

"What about Zane?"

"No, he says it's too loud for him."

"Right, because of the war duty, the shock of it. Ah, I don't know."

"So how come we never go out? You come to my house, we talk, and then we have hot sex."

"You think it's hot?"

"Yeah, I do."

He smiled, flashing his amazingly white teeth. He must get them bleached. I hadn't done that since the week before my wedding two years ago. I should probably do that again.

"What time do you go?"

"About seven."

"We'll see." Then he walked out the door.

I stood and pondered the strange conversation as I waited for him to leave. I didn't want to go out too soon in case he wanted to talk more. A part of me wished he had broken with me. If I was alone, maybe I could be at peace.

Though at home, I found no peace. Brian called soon after I got home.

"That was cruel the way you just left me," he said.

"I'm sorry if I hurt you," I said. What could I say? That I just wanted a warm body and sex? "Look, I don't intend to get back with you."

"I see. You just wanted some."

"That's a cold way to put it. It's hard to be alone...sometimes."

"But you've got Raz."

"He's just—" Hmm. What was he?

"A screw."

"Okay, we're done. Goodbye."

"Wait, that's it?"

"Brian, we're just not suited for each other. Making love was probably what we did best. But that doesn't make a relationship."

"Then you're really going through with it?"

"Yes, I am. In a couple of weeks, Judge Shelton will sign the decree. The divorce is final thirty days after that."

"You are such an unforgiving bitch."

"If I was standing there with you, would you try to smash my face in? Huh? Nobody should ever put up with that kind of abuse."

His silence was predictable. I hung up.

Chapter 10

BILL drove Mom and me to the Cowpoke. Vonny arrived in time to come out with Derek and James. Johnny Two Rivers, the Nez Perce owner, had set up a long table for us. Even though families often came for dinner then left before the music and the drinking began, it was the first time Paul Ritter, our neighbor across the street, permitted Kayla to join us. Kayla was fourteen and a special friend. I represented Paul during his divorce then became close to the family after Sheila died from a meth binge comedown. Kayla paused to look around at the bar and grill then rushed to get the open seat by me.

"I heard what you did," she said.

"And?"

"I think you're scary," then she laughed. "I told Emily and all my friends about it. They want to come see the horse. Did you take a selfie with you in all black?"

I laughed. "No, but the cops took a bunch of photos."

"I wish I could see one."

"Maybe I can get one from Rachel."

"That trooper? I thought you guys were enemies."

"No, we're okay. She's a friend of James'."

I looked around for a couple of minutes as Kayla did. It felt strange to me—I hadn't been here without Brian and as a single woman.

"I've never been in a bar," she said.

"Well, it's more of a restaurant till nine or ten when some people start drinking. All the families are gone by then."

"It's, like, nicer than I thought."

"Did you think it would look like one of those saloons from an old Western?"

She laughed. "Kinda. But there aren't any spittoons."

My mom laughed from across the table then said, "Oh, here comes James."

As James, Derek, and Vonny worked their way through the well-wishers, Kayla got my attention.

"I go over to his house after supper and read to him. He says he gets too tired to read late in the day."

"That's really nice of you."

"He was really nice to me, like, after my mom died."

"What do you read to him?" I asked.

"Right now, The Help. It's about African American women who took care of rich white kids in the South, back in the sixties. It's really good."

"I bought it, but I haven't read it," I said. In the past, I'd read quite a bit. If I swapped books for men, I'd be happier.

I stood as James approached the table. He walked up to me and gave me a big hug, causing a big lump of emotion to ram into my throat.

"We got 'em," I said.

"Sounds like you did more than that," he said.

I shrugged. As James sat down, Raz and Nori came in and stopped to greet my mom. I introduced Kayla, Vonny, and Derek to them. They were cordial to my friends, but then they sat down at the end of the table. I gave Mom a questioning look. She shrugged and picked up her menu. I recommended the burgers to Kayla, which Johnny Two Rivers and his cooks grilled in a smoker behind the bar. Just then, I felt the strong, but slightly palsied grasp of a hand on my shoulder.

"Heh! Here's the Ghost Rider," said Beulah. "How come this derring-do comes after my bedtime? Oh, and James. How you gettin' on, youngster?"

Beulah shuffled over to him, pressed down on his shoulder to keep him from rising then greeted others at the table. She chatted with him for few minutes then sat down just as Lew, Hank, and Linda arrived.

"Blue, I didn't think you drove at night," said Hank, her old friend.

"Oh, Zane brought me and Patty," said Beulah. "Yep, we're old travel mates." She gave me a wink.

Zane, who sat down by Raz, had driven the two women out to Colorado in July where I had been life-flighted after Bert Bolger stuck a switchblade in me. I nodded to Beulah, to let her know it was okay to mention the event. In truth, it caught me off-guard, so I took a drink of water to hide the warmth that flushed into my face. I hid my emotion successfully, except from my mom, who gazed at me intently.

We placed our orders then the topic shifted to the capture of the "The Four Bastards," as they had been dubbed. Even Nori, who had been sulking, became interested in the details. During the meal, Jack and Bud arrived. The men took off their cowboy hats to James, who shook their hands as vigorously as he could and thanked them. I happened to look over at Kayla, who was twisted around in her chair to look at Jack and Bud. Then she stopped eating so she could watch the cowboys who began to fill the tables at the back of the room.

"This is Jack and Bud, they were part of the Night Posse," I said. "This is Kayla. She's fourteen."

Kayla gave me a funny look then turned back to the cowboys.

"Nice to meet you, Kayla fourteen," said Jack as he tipped his hat to her.

After they left, Kayla finished her burger.

"Hey, is that a jukebox?" she asked.

"Yeah, it's an old-fashioned one, but it works," I said.

"Dad?"

Paul reached into his pocket and handed her a couple of quarters. She popped out of her chair and headed for the machine. I glanced at my mom, both of us predicting the same thing. I walked over to Zane, Raz, and Nori to chat, though I kept Kayla in sight. Within twenty seconds, a cowboy rose from his chair and ambled over to the jukebox. A pretty girl, she had long blonde hair and was fairly tall at five foot seven.

"Bill," I said then looked over to Kayla.

Paul had already risen from his seat.

Bill said to him, "I'll handle it. He's not one of mine, but I know him."

As soon as the cowhand saw Bill Docket approaching, he backed away from Kayla. Bill followed him to his table. Bill addressed the four tables of cowboys.

"He'll give those guys a lecture," I said to Paul. "And they'll listen. They know a complaint from Bill Docket to any of their bosses means unemployment. He fired one of his own cowboys once for saying 'good morning' to me when I was about her age."

Paul sat down and I walked over to Kayla. The stranger, Rob Faust, sat on a stool at the counter, sipping a beer.

"Find anything good?" I asked.

"He just said hello," she said.

"But you're not old enough to date, so that's what my uncle is telling them."

Kayla sighed then selected two songs. The stranger appeared on the other side of the jukebox.

"Hey, Kayla, why don't I see you back at the table?" I said.

She looked over at the handsome man, smirked, and then left.

I looked across the jukebox at him.

When Kayla's country ballad started, he said in a deep voice, "Lots of twang here."

"Too much," I said. "And it used to be worse. Last year I went to Sidney to hear a bunch of college students play jazz. I thought I was in heaven."

He smiled. Almost in unison, we moved around the corners of the machine so we were next to each other.

"I've been told your name is Faust."

"That's right."

"Did you sell your soul to the devil for knowledge or power?"

"Both, but you recall Faust won his wager against the devil."

"But he needed the help of some angels," I said.

"We all need a little help sometimes."

"True, but your name isn't really Faust," I said.

"Well, no, but Mephistopheles is too hard to spell."

I smiled at him. Even in the dim light, I could see his deep blue eyes.

"And you are Megan Docket, Esquire, also known as the Ghost Rider. Your name and face have been plastered all over the newspapers for the last year."

"I try not to think about it."

"You never give interviews."

"I'm not interested."

"What does interest you?"

"Whether you're FBI or CIA."

"I'm in sales—security systems."

"Yeah, right. Are you one of the bad guys?"

He smiled and shook his head.

"Then you better confess. I need to know whether or not to shoot you."

"Will there be shooting?"

I shrugged. "Trouble seems to find me."

"But you don't mind a bit of danger."

"I try to protect those around me."

"I don't mind a bit of adventure myself."

He slid his card across the jukebox screen. I read it then palmed it, sliding it into my front jeans pocket.

"I didn't know the State Patrol used undercover cops."

"Sure. And I'll ask you to keep this secret."

"Oh, I'll spill this to all the reporters I talk to."

"Call me the next time something comes up, Ghost Rider."

"Regarding the meth we must still have in the area?"

"Or about anything."

"Are you working with Tony?"

"Yeah, some."

"I suppose I better select a song, Jason."

"It's Jay and allow me," he said as he put a quarter in the slot.

"How about B-7?" I said.

"Now you're talking."

I punched the button for Janis Joplin's "Me and Bobby McGee."

"See ya, Faust," I said as I turned back to our table.

Zane, Raz, and Nori were gone. Once I sat down, I slid Jason Andrew Young's card into my purse.

Kayla leaned over to me and said, "I'm glad you caught that Spittle guy. His sister Louanne is, like, the meanest girl ever. She calls me," she whispered into my ear, "'Nigger Lover'."

"What a scummy brat," I said. "I haven't been going to their restaurant because the food's lousy. If I went there now, they'd probably poison me."

"It's getting' late, kiddo," Paul said to Kayla.

Then a song came on that brought people out to dance on the wood parquet floor. Paul glanced down the table at Patty. He squeezed the edge of the table with both hands till his fingertips went white. He happened to look my way. I nodded, which made his eyebrows rise. He looked back down to Patty then stood. He walked down the table and asked Patty to dance. She smiled and rose. Kayla watched them intently.

A few minutes later, Tony walked across the room and stopped behind Vonny's chair, leaned forward and held out his hand. She took it and they walked to the floor. This stole the attention of most of the room. Nobody had ever seen Vonny dance because `no whitey had ever found the nerve to ask her. If Tony wasn't educated and from an urban area, it probably would have remained that way. Uncle Bill taught Vonny, Derek, and me the two-step as teens.

Vonny and Tony made a fine pair and others joined the dancers, including Bill and Mom.

In time, Paul and Kayla left and we ordered pitchers of beer for our table. I danced several times with Faust, and even a couple with Jack and Bud. I broke away from Bud when a slow song came on, but Faust, or maybe he was Jay now, caught my hand before I could get off the floor. Blue-eyed and buff, he held me respectfully close as I inhaled his cologne. With the departure of Raz and Zane, and the absence of Brian, I could relax and enjoy myself.

Being single was suddenly fun.

Sunday afternoon, I went over to visit the Wilsons. James sat in his recliner watching football with Derek, and looking tired.

"James, my friend, bad things happen to good people," I said. "I don't know why life is so unfair, but if I ever get to heaven, I'm gonna ask."

"I'm sure you will, but the Bible says it rains on the good and the bad, the rich and the poor."

"It just doesn't say why."

"Because it rains," he replied.

Vonny brought in iced teas for us then sat down.

"Dad, I've been wondering…do you have any enemies?" asked Derek. "Did you ever have a problem with the Websters or the Spittles?"

"Well, Tom Sedlacek and I put in a retaining wall earlier this summer behind the Spittle restaurant. Mike, the father, and I disagreed on the materials—he wanted wood, but it rots. I convinced him to use rock. He seemed pleased with the result and paid us when we billed him. It was such a minor dispute, I never thought much of it. And it didn't involve his son at all." He paused to take a drink and catch his breath. "Believe me, I've been trying to think of things, disagreements, insults, anything. That's all I can come up with. I've never had any dealings with the Webster family."

We sat in silence for a few moments, Vonny and Derek had been called various names growing up, including the N-word, but only by stupid kids. The Docket and Wilson families endured much together, along with my efforts to unravel the mystery of my mother and the existence of a disabled twin. They were my chosen audience to air my latest concern.

"I have something," I said.

I must have borne a certain look on my face, for any wisecracks were stifled.

"You remember John Tremaine, my dad's friend?"

"Yeah, he works as a consultant for your firm," said Vonny.

I nodded. "He was here recently. After a bit too much bourbon, he let slip that my dad always worried that Bill was my father and not him."

James' jaw dropped while Derek and Vonny stopped breathing.

"My God," said Vonny after she resumed normal respiration. "I thought we were past all of this."

"But your dad wrote a will leaving his assets to you, his daughter…didn't he?" asked Derek.

"He wrote a will before Scott and I were born that gave everything to my mom then to his children if she didn't survive him. The divorce terminated my mom's claim. The strange thing is that he never drafted another will naming me and Scott as his kids. He put my name on all his assets, including the house, and made me senior partner of the law firm. All the land is held jointly by me and Bill."

"So that means what?" asked Vonny.

"The leaving his estate to his unborn children would fail if I wasn't his daughter. So he simply put my name on everything."

"But he could have updated his will and put your name on it as heir, right?"

"Yes, as beneficiary." My hands felt clammy. "Bill told me he didn't think the 'timing' was right for me to be his daughter, though he and Mom dated after Dad and Mom, Frank and Beth, separated."

"So, financially, it's all the same, right?" asked Derek.

I nodded.

"What has your mom said about it?" asked Vonny.

"Nothing to make me think it was unsettled. And I don't like the idea of bothering her about it, especially after she finally married Bill. I know your next question—Frank is listed as the father on my birth certificate."

James cleared his throat then said, "Frank always acted like your father. And he provided for you, Scott, and Beth financially."

"Yes."

"Megan, hon, what does it change?"

"The truth. I don't like the question hanging over me."

I really wished John Tremaine had kept his mouth shut. But if Frank wasn't my father, why had he died apologizing to me? He had borne the guilt of separating me from my mother and twin, and for abandoning his son. Over time, had he convinced himself that he truly was my father?

"But you're right—Frank always acted like my father and Bill acted like my uncle." I rose. "I'm sorry to have burdened you with this. You three have plenty to figure out."

"No, no, sit down, Megan," said James. "You have a right to worry over your parentage. I don't know what to tell you."

"I suppose a paternity test is the way to find out," said Vonny.

"But I sure wouldn't want to bother Bill with it…he and my mom seem so happy."

They truly did appear happy, so the idea of stirring anything up was abhorrent to me. I sat down and stared blankly at the game. If Bill was in fact my father, then he was the one who abandoned Scott and Beth. And he would know that he'd let his brother steal me from him. It would set him on a guilt trip that he would take to his grave. As for my mom, she would learn that she needlessly parted with me; she must have believed Frank was the father or his threat to put Scott in an institution was unsubstantiated. My nagging uncertainty would be minimal compared to the upheaval it would cause them.

When I looked over at the three of them, they were staring at me, so I said, "I think it's best if I leave it alone."

The room sighed in relief. We all relaxed and watched the Bears and Packers.

"Hey, what's with you dancing with a cowboy, Sis?"

She looked at me and smiled.

"He's FBI out of Denver looking into meth in the area," I said.

"Well, damn," said Derek. "I thought that crap was done."

"No such luck," I said. "Hey now, Vonny, tell the truth…would you have danced with him if he was just a cowboy?"

"Well, he's a looker, but a long distance relationship with an uneducated cowboy…no, I needed your tip-off, Megan."

I thought for a moment she was going to ask me about Faust or Raz, but she decided against discussing my messy love life in front of her father. And I was grateful.

Chapter 11

SUNDAY night, I went for supper at Bill and Mom's house. His house was rebuilt after it was leveled by a tornado my first summer here after law school. The twister could have killed Bill, but he was able to hide as Nebraska possessed soil that enabled the excavation of basements. So with homeowner's insurance and life insurance money from his brother, Bill was able to build another ranch style house, now larger and with a red brick front. One of the first things my mother did as new wife was to decorate—as a bachelor, Bill left his walls bare except for an occasional wall clock and the paintings I bought for him.

Bill and Mom also invited Raz and Nori to dinner. Raz and I exchanged smiles when we could do so without being too obvious. Yet, I kept thinking about Jay's square jaw, dimpled chin, and gorgeous blue eyes. Nori ate very little of Mom's spaghetti and meatballs, and said even less. As the meal progressed, I became aware that Nori kept staring at me. If I looked her way, she would avert her gaze. Maybe she didn't like me. Maybe she didn't like that I was dating her brother. Did she think me inferior because I was only half Lebanese? I didn't know and didn't really care, apart from the fact that Mom noted her behavior and resented it. Nori started to pay attention to Bill's tornado narrative when he told of how the part of the house collapsed on him. She went back to toying with her noodles when he told how I was lowered down into the basement to give him first aid. Up till now, she'd been cordial to me. Fine, be a bitch, though she better not insult my mother or uncle. Good grief, I just realized Uncle Bill was now my stepfather. How bizarre.

I helped Mom clear the dishes after the meal. While I was rummaging through the Tupperware, Raz walked into the kitchen.

"I don't think Nori likes me," I said to him.

"She says you think too highly of yourself," said Raz.

"Well, I am pretty awesome. I'm so great that I carelessly got myself in danger with a murderous lunatic, who killed my baby and nearly killed me. Yeah, I'm so great that I'm getting a divorce before I've even hit thirty. Actually, there was another lunatic, he had a shotgun, but he missed. I was stupid and got him mad at me. Yeah, I'm wonderful. Oh, I found it." I held up the coveted bowl with the blue lid. "This is just perfect for that salad. See how special I am?"

Raz grinned at me like he was ready to ravage me on my Mom's kitchen table. Of course, that would have gone far beyond tacky and a disaster for the apple pie my mom meant to serve later.

By the time Mom and I finished the cleanup, Nori was debating Bill on the civil war in Syria.

"Obama is so worried about his damn health care law that he's clueless about Syria," said Nori. "He shouldn't delay. The West must help the rebels."

"I believe President Obama is concerned about aiding Al Qaeda," said Bill.

"That's just hot air. The rebels will unite." Nori now glared at me. "I suppose you oppose helping the people of your heritage."

I wasn't going to play her game, so I simply said, "It's a difficult situation."

"What? That's all you have to say?"

"No. Bill, do you think apple pie would be better with bourbon or brandy?"

"That's all you people care about—your own small world."

"Mom, how's that song go—'It's a small world after all…it's a small world'—oh, that's all the lyrics I know."

Nori's face turned red.

"What do you think about Omaha's plans for the tri-faith center?"

Nori just stared at me, or was she really Rana, as Raz called her when they thought they were alone?

"The synagogue just opened and the mosque and the church will be completed in a few years. They'll share a common courtyard and a community center. It's the only place in the country where the three faiths—Christians, Jews, and Muslims—intentionally plan to build their houses of worship together."

I sat down next to Mom then resumed staring at Nori.

"You don't know about this and you've been living in Omaha? Or have you just been living in your own small world?"

"Well, I...I've heard something about it...I've also been in Nevada some."

"But you make a point," I said. "It is easy to get complacent when life is secure. The war is spilling into Lebanon from Syria. The Christian population in the Middle East is shrinking by the day. How would you like to be a Coptic Christian in Egypt? When I go to worship on Sunday, I don't worry that a militant group is going to bomb the church."

Nori just looked at me. I'd rendered her speechless by agreeing with her. Wanna try again, bitch? I'll take any argument you can throw at me and wrap it around you till your head spins.

"I'd go with the brandy," said Bill.

"Megan, why don't you help me serve the pie?" said Mom.

I rose with her. "Do you have five snifters? I only have four."

Raz stood. "We should be going. Thank you for dinner, Mrs. Docket."

Raz shook Bill's hand and they were gone.

Bill exhaled loudly. "C'mon, let's have that pie."

Wednesday night, Mom and I stayed with James while Vonny went out on a date with Tony. James sat in his recliner and listened to Mom talk about the story of the family from the Civil War diary from Max Zimmer. The family was from Pittsburgh, but they lived on the south side of the Potomac River in Virginia, operating a ferry boat across the wild mountain river.

"One of the big problems for the family was that they were Union sympathizers, but they lived on Confederate soil. In fact, the son was fighting for the Federals as a private."

"What's the date during this time?" I asked.

"It's early in the war...the summer 1862," said Mom. "The son is south of Richmond, where they were fighting a series of battles."

"I believe that's the Seven Days Battle, or something like that," said James. "The Union Army tried to march on Richmond, the capital of the Confederacy."

Mom nodded then continued. "And the son, Matthew, gets injured in the arm, so after a battle, they stop to tend the wounded, but the Confederates march on their camp. The son escapes and helps his injured lieutenant escape by wagon. Meanwhile, a battle comes close to the Barton house, that's the family name, and they end up tending to several wounded soldiers from both sides at their home."

"But all their neighbors are Southerners, right? So are they against this family?" I asked.

"One Confederate sympathizer does try to set the storage depot and ferry on fire, but this daughter, Kate, the one who's writing this diary, takes the ferry out to the river away from the dock and saves it. She nearly drowns swimming back to shore in the strong current."

"Was there a mother there?" I asked.

"She died shortly before the diary starts. I think this is a second volume because of the way it just picks up."

"Yes, and you have a huge battle coming up not too far away from that family," said James. "The battle that takes place at Antietam near Sharpsburg, Maryland is the victory for the Union that President Lincoln was waiting on before he issued the Emancipation Proclamation. It's also known as the single bloodiest day in American military history—22,000 men died."

Just then my phone vibrated. I answered the call from the Cowpoke. Mom stopped the story as I walked into the kitchen to take the unexpected call. I soon returned to the Wilson family room.

"Well, that was Johnny Two Rivers," I said. "I guess Zane is drunk and causing trouble. I'm going down there. Go on with the story, you can fill me in another time."

When I got there, Zane was sitting at a table across from Jay. I took a seat between them. Johnny gave me a nod from behind the counter. The crowd was sparse; I'd never been here during the week.

"So, what's happening here?" I asked, trying to keep the tone light.

Zane scowled at me then said, "Oh, are you here to rescue me? You try to save everybody. It can't be done. It can't."

"You tried. You said you built schools in Afghanistan. You tried to help. I'm just here to see if I can help."

"You think you can help me? Fat chance."

"You helped me when I was in trouble back in December and then after Sweetie died. But you need some specialized help."

"I'm sure not gettin' it from God. Where is he? Anybody know? He lets us be so miserable…do such terrible things to each other."

"It's called free choice. We get to go our way, do good, do evil, make mistakes, accidentally shoot a boy."

"Damn you, Megan," he hissed. "That's a secret."

"Faust won't say anything."

"And what the hell kinda name is that?"

"A fake one. I'm investigating meth in the area. But I'll ask you to keep that quiet."

Zane stared at Faust for a moment then nodded.

"It's Jay."

Zane reached for his drink, but I snatched it first.

"Do you mind? I'm thirsty." I took a swig of his whiskey, then another, finishing it. "Have you eaten?"

"Yeah."

I looked to Jay, he nodded.

"Then let's get out of here."

Jay and I stood. Zane slowly rose. Johnny approached the table, but I met him and told him I'd handle Zane's tab next time I came in.

"Wha? I gotta pay."

"Johnny said he'll bill you. C'mon."

Jay helped a wobbly Zane to my Barracuda. Jay put Zane in the back seat and sat next to him.

"Is that your Nissan SUV?" I asked Zane.

"A Pathfinder, yeah, took a while. Smokey found it for me. I send money to that family every month. That's another reason I can't be with you. I'm so goddamn poor and you're rich. You even own the place I live in."

I jerked the car to a halt. "Rich? Yeah, I've got some money. It's called life insurance. I'd rather be poor and still have my dad."

"Sorry."

Damn drunk. I drove out of the parking lot to Zane's place.

"Okay, I'm fine now. You can go."

"I want to see the place."

I walked up the sidewalk followed by Zane and Jay. Zane fumbled for his keys, dropping them on the concrete porch. He scooped them up and unlocked the door. The place was a mess, with trash on the coffee table and pillows on the floor.

"Dang it, Zane." I said, letting my purse drop to the carpet. "The place is a mess and you've been smoking. Since when did you start that nasty habit?"

He plopped down on the couch. "Just sometimes."

I walked into the kitchen, it stunk of an overflowing trash can and dirty plates in the sink.

"Zane, this is disgusting. This isn't you. What's happening?"

"Well, we don't all have a maid like you."

"She was my nanny, as you know. And she kind of came with the house. So, if I hire someone to come clean, will you stop smoking?"

"Yeah, I know it's disgusting. Why don't you go next door to your—"

"To my what? My Arab? You could have kept that from happening, but you didn't fight for me."

"Yeah, I'm a wuss like Brian. I thought I'd better bail out before I disappointed you."

"That is so lame and a conversation for another time." I glanced over at Jay, who stood against the wall with hands in his pockets. "But what you can talk about is when you're going back to therapy."

He looked down at his hands. "They've done as much as they can."

"So what should you be doing to help yourself?"

He shrugged.

"So the answer now is public intoxication? And blaming God."

"I'm not an athe—ah, atheist. That's it. God just doesn't care."

"So God doesn't fit your ideal. James would tell you it rains on the rich and the poor and that God never promised us a life that's fair or just."

"James got a raw deal. Now just leave me alone. Go take your…next door."

"My what? You pathetic piece of shit!"

Jay caught me around the waist before I could get to Zane. I hadn't planned on doing anything except get in his face until he apologized.

"Oh, were you going to hit me? Isn't one of the reasons you're divorcing Brian is because he hit you?"

I pushed Jay away and said, "It's amazing what you can find out when people let booze loosen their tongues—or their fists." I took a deep breath. "This is a non-smoking building. It's in the lease you signed. So cut it out or I'll evict you."

As we walked out to my SUV, I couldn't help but glance over at the other side of the duplex. The lights were on in the front room, but the curtains were drawn. Jay looked over, as well.

"So Zane thinks you're just dating Raz because he's out of the picture and Raz is available. Of course, it's always more complicated than that. And obviously Zane has some issues with communication."

"I don't plan to discuss my love life with someone I've talked to twice," I said as we climbed into the car.

"You lost your baby less than two months ago. Yeah, I've done my homework on you."

"Goody."

"Plus you're in the process of a divorce. Popular opinion says you'll go through with it."

"And you're a busybody, Jason Andrew Young, and a walking acronym."

He laughed. "And you're right—God lets us make choices and gives us comfort…but he doesn't drink Jim Beam Black and watch baseball with you or heat up your sheets."

"You're impertinent. But thanks for helping me with Zane."

"Clearly, you're still hurting, but the men in your life have disappointed you. They're not nearly as reliable as your horse. So you're hesitant about men, but not willing to do without them."

"As in join a convent? I'm not Catholic."

"Men do have a purpose."

"Don't get fresh."

"I play chess."

"I don't like being investigated."

"Got something to hide?"

"Nope," I lied. "It's just that people think they know you because they've talked to a few people and read a few newspaper articles."

"Have you Googled yourself? It's fascinating."

"It wouldn't amuse me."

"I like trying to figure you out. When you're done with Raz, give me a call. We can discuss Goethe."

"'Tell me of your certainties, I have doubts enough of my own.'" I pulled into the parking lot of the Cowpoke. "That's my one Goethe quote. Feel free to be impressed. I am supposed to be a hick, you know." I glanced over to see him smiling. "By the way, does the local State Patrol know about you?"

"No, and I'll ask you to keep it quiet."

I stared at him by the dim light of the lamppost. How strange—he was investigating in the area without the knowledge of the state troopers.

"If I call you, it won't be for bourbon and chess. Catching the Four Bastards has solved only one problem in the area."

"How do you know?" he asked.

"Because you're still here and so is Tony."

"And do you feel something?"

I stared at him. Who would talk to him about that?

"Time to say goodnight," I said.

Jay stepped out of the Barracuda and said, "Goodnight, Ghost Rider."

I watched him get into his black Honda pickup.

Why did he make me so nervous? I didn't like how much this stranger knew about me. Yet, he spoke like he was a Christian and well-read. An intelligent, Christian stud ranked as high on my list as a man could. Come to think of it, I required those traits in anybody I dated. Still, my life was messy and I wasn't ready to risk my heart on anyone right now.

Chapter 12

THE next day, I arrived home early enough to ride Strider before supper. We dashed along the trail at full speed. It was sad to think Strider was my most reliable male right now. Oh, I loved Uncle Bill, but at times, I did resent that he took my mom away from me just when I was in a crisis. So I was left with Raz. He often came by on Thursday nights, and I knew I would give him a bourbon and we would chat for a while and watch a movie or TV then I'd take him up to my bed. It was so easy with him—I never needed to worry about his character or if he had marriage and fatherhood potential. He meant sex, and it numbed my pain. Or was there more? I liked his funny stories about his childhood. Yeah, I cared about him, but not enough.

So both Brian and Zane knew about Raz. Who told on me? Maybe they drove by my house, which was out of the way for both of them, and saw his car. Perhaps they even knew Raz came and left in the night. Yet, neither of them fought for me. None of them prevented the sting of loneliness.

Rachel stopped by after supper. She requested and I obliged her with a visit up Big Leo to my Fort.

As she peered through my binoculars at the Joker, a bluff to the north, she said, "I was with Merritt when he was talking to the new county prosecutor. This Larry Peake thinks you're a dangerous vigilante who needs to be reined in. Maybe he resents your popularity with people across the state."

"Does he dispute my ownership of the land I was defending? Dang, I was protecting the reputation of the whole panhandle. Omaha thinks we're all a bunch of white, ultra-conservative hicks."

"We are."

"Speak for yourself."

We laughed.

"The editorials in the newspapers are strongly in your favor. Folks think you rescued our reputation. But really, that new prosecutor is a real hard-ass. If you're going to shoot someone, get out of the county."

"I wasn't planning on it, at least not today. Hey, what do you think about our interim Chief of Police?" I asked.

"Oh, he'll be all right. He acts it, but he's not really a hick. Good with evidence, interrogations. Plays it by the book."

"You talk well of a man you just divorced."

"We've been separated for three years. His sons are a couple of teenage hellions. I don't miss them. He lost his first wife to breast cancer. I never quite lived up to her, I guess."

"That's a tough order."

We climbed down the bluff and laughed at our dirty clothes. Raz and I would be bathing tonight.

"So, we still have meth in the area," I said as we wandered through the Seven Dwarfs.

"An upkick, to tell the truth. And more cocaine."

"And it's not just passing by on the interstate?"

"No, there's a dealer or dealers close by, but we can't find them. It's like they're invisible."

We were quiet for a few minutes.

"So, what's the deal with the Four Bastards?" I asked.

"Love that name. Oh, they've all clammed up. Jake Waters is the only one out on bail. Judge Shelton set a stiff bail. I was surprised Randy Waters could plunk down twenty grand so easily. And he's hired some hot shot attorney out of Omaha."

"I feel bad for Officer Waters."

"Hey, I heard you're dating Mr. Tall, Dark, and Handsome," she said.

"I guess."

"You're not sure?"

"Oh, life is such a mess right now."

"I don't understand why. Just because you recently lost your baby and your husband and Davey in the winter and your twin and father before that. C'mon, lighten up."

I smirked and gave her shoulder a shove. We both looked at the Wilson house to the southwest.

"And you worry about James. I know he's special to you."

"My father was a cold man. So James was very much like a father to me. It's really a shame...because he loved walking out here. But the ground is too rough. I've seen him standing at the edge of his lawn looking sad. Hey, I wonder if Smokey sells four-wheelers."

"That would get him out here. I'll check his sales lot on my way home. I'll even go halves with you."

"Deal," I said. "By the way, are you seeing anyone?"

"Yeah, he works at the county bank in Sidney."

"Do you know anything about Raz and his sister, Nori?"

"No, but I've seen them."

"Well, he's in hiding. He befriended my uncle in Omaha. Raz supposedly helped the CIA, which didn't make the Hezbollah happy. The thing is...I've never seen any threat or seen him act like he's on the defensive. Does he expect his assassin to walk down the street in a kaffiyeh?"

"Have you gotten yourself in the middle of something?"

"Oh, I hope not...that's all I need. I've never figured out why they're out here. Raz comes up with a new reason every time I ask."

"Maybe he's counting on you to save him," she said.

"I doubt that. But I wonder if he really has a death threat against him."

"Well, if Raz came out here looking for protection from the State Patrol or the county sheriff, he's an idiot. We're maxed out with the meth investigation. Hey, that looks like Vonny."

"Know any other tall black women around here?"

Rachel chuckled. "And who's that white guy?"

"That must be Tony. You know who he is, don't you?"

"FBI from Denver," she said.

We wandered over that way. Tony went back into the house. Vonny spotted us and walked our way.

"I see the Marlboro Man is hanging around," I said.

"Well, you can't befriend too many cops," said Vonny.

"So the first date must have gone okay."

"This place…I tell ya. We went to dinner and a movie in Sidney. Talk about stares."

"Well, this isn't Denver or even Omaha."

"No, there you have a chance. I mean, who really does?"

"Your folks," I said.

"Yeah, who else?"

"Um, WALL-E and Eve," I said.

"Buzz Lightyear and Jessie," said Rachel.

"Jane Eyre and Mr. Rochester," I said. "He ends up blind and cranky. Who else would want him?"

"It's easier to name those who won't make it," said Rachel.

"You mean besides me and Brian? How about Jason Bourne and somebody who doesn't like to travel?"

"Sherlock Holmes and Irene Adler," said Vonny. "Too many games. Could you imagine their kids?"

In that moment of silence, I bet we were all wondering if we'd ever find the right man, the one to grow old with, raise kids, and supervise lemonade stands.

"I'm heading back," said Vonny. "See ya."

"Hey, Vonny, wait. Rachel and I were thinking how sad it was that your dad can't get out here. He likes going over to Raccoon Creek. Would he ride in a four-wheeler?"

Vonny smiled. "Derek has already talked to Smokey…he found a good one in North Platte. We're supposed to get it this weekend."

"Don't forget helmets and some training," said Rachel.

"Got both covered," said Vonny as she left.

"Oh, I almost forgot, Warren Merritt got promoted to sergeant. He's a fan of yours."

"That's good to know," I said. "You can't befriend too many cops."

Rachel and I parted at my house, in agreement that we'd both do some checking on Raz, real name unknown, and Nori, also known as Rana.

The next day I stopped by the duplex. I entered Zane's side. The cleaning crew had done a decent job restoring the place; Zane must have resumed his tidy habits and stopped smoking as well. When I walked into the bedroom and kitchen, I felt overwhelmed with sadness for him, for us. He was functioning well enough to work, but he was a mess. He'd gone where I couldn't follow. I should've waited till my divorce was legally complete before we dated. I should've held off Raz, too. I could think of so many things I'd done wrong. Finding the stricken James and capturing the Four Bastards were two things I did right. Those were acts that came from the gut, not from the head or the heart—my wounded heart compelled me to seek comfort from Zane while I was grieving the loss of Sweetie and Brian; my lonely heart convinced me to seek comfort from Raz while I was feeling the loss of important people in my life. I glanced around at the orderly front room and resolved to clean up my own life.

But first, I needed to complete my inspection. Raz and Nori should both be at work, but I rang the doorbell anyway. I'm glad I did because Nori opened the door.

"Hi, I was inspecting Zane's half, I'd like to take a look at your side," I said, resolved to keep everything in a business tone.

"Why? What are you looking for?" she asked curtly.

"Your lease permits me to enter, so I plan to."

I pulled the screen door out of her hands, and nudged her to the side as I entered. I stopped in the middle of room, mostly because I didn't like her standing where I couldn't see her. I turned around to see her angry visage.

"Well, that's mostly what I need to know," I said truthfully. "Zane started smoking, which violates the lease agreement. But you and your brother don't smoke."

"No."

"Nasty, expensive habit. Any problem with bugs? The evenings are cooler, so they try harder to get inside."

"No, we're okay."

"Sinks draining okay?"

"Yes."

What she really meant was, yes, I'd like to choke you. What was up with her?

"Okay, call if you need something." I walked past her out the door, which was quickly shut behind me.

Two nights later, Raz came over. I wasn't going to dump him till I had more information. I made sure we took a bath, so that his pants were in the bathroom with me while he was still lolling in my bed. I snatched his wallet from his pants. His driver's license said his name was Raz Peters, but once I searched the many compartments, I found another driver's license and a credit card. I wrote down the numbers from the two cards on the back side of a box of bandages. Rariq Abboud. It was time to get some answers—but I'd never get the truth from him.

I slid in next to him. He seemed distracted.

"You're deep in thought," I said.

"I think I've been lucky…not getting caught. It can't go on. Starting to look over my shoulder more. I registered and bought a gun. It's just like yours."

Well, this was great—I'm spying on him and he's lying to me when we ought to be acting intimate.

"Mine was a gift. Do you know a lot about guns?"

"Yeah."

"What does Nori think?"

"She has a gun. She always goes on about danger and trusting the wrong people. She's lived a harder life. I've spent more years in the States than she has. In fact, I met her in Lebanon."

"Was she born there?"

"Why do you ask?"

"Oh, just wondered if she'd grown up in that environment—around bombs and just being scared."

"Yeah, she always seems tense."

"Especially around me," I said.

"Don't worry about it."

But I did. Like Raz, I didn't know if she meant danger or was in danger. I didn't believe Raz was a threat to me, particularly now as he responded to my caresses. If I planned to dump him, I might as well get my last bit of loving before I faced an extended period of cold sheets.

Now, I could take the next step. I called Rachel and gave her the information I discovered on Raz. Then I thought about how the State Patrol was investigating itself with Jay, if he was even legit. In fact, who could I trust? Rachel had gotten close to the meth problem by dating RT, the corrupt DEA agent—not that I foresaw any reason to connect Raz with the meth trade. Still, I felt uneasy, even though Rachel made a point of thanking me for trusting her with the information. So, I called Robert Foxworthy of the Denver FBI office. Strange, but he was always quick to take my calls. I started with an apology, for I didn't know if he'd even be involved. I gave him the information on Raz and Nori. He said he'd do some checking then advised caution. Then I sent out my own spy.

I'd overheard a phone conversation between Raz and Nori last evening, well, I assume it was Nori. She or whoever was to start a noon work shift. So I sent Melanie, my paralegal, out to wait and follow a white Honda Civic. I instructed Melanie to park on Hickory Street then follow the car on Highway 28, at a distance, then to go north to the Sidney Wal-Mart to determine if Nori actually went there. Melanie called me a half hour later—the white Civic started toward Sidney, but turned off eastward on a gravel road, the unmarked third turn. I thanked Melanie then asked her to buy a few office supplies to make the trip look legitimate. I didn't like involving someone else in my spying, but Nori would have recognized the Barracuda. I was pleased when Melanie arrived back at the office safely.

So, what did it all mean? I'd known early on Raz and Nori were using assumed names. Was Nori supposed to be going to Wal-Mart? Where did that gravel road lead? I went out into the lobby and asked to borrow Joy's cell phone. She complied with raised eyebrows. I stepped away from her a few feet then I called the Wal-Mart and was told no Nori Peters worked there. Did she work there, but was forced to use her real name because she lacked documentation for her phony name? I phoned my mom; she agreed to call Wal-Mart and ask for Rana Abboud. Again, the answer was a negative from the superstore. I then asked Mom to keep that information in strict confidence.

"Megan, are you getting yourself in another mess?"

"Oh, I think so."

Chapter 13

SATURDAY night, Mom, Bill, Patty and I went to the Cowpoke for burgers. Paul Ritter, who was probably there by arrangement with Patty, came by and Bill invited him to sit with us. Jay was sitting with Tony, Jack, and Bud at a table near ours. When the dancing started, I was surprised that it was Tony who first came to me.

He guided me to a corner of the dance floor. He took my hand and placed his other hand on my waist, yet we didn't move. His smiling face changed.

"I spoke to Robert today," he said. "He has a CIA connection. Raz has not done a good job of concealing himself. You need to be very careful. Robert promises he'll contact you as soon as he knows more. If you're not packing, better start. In fact, it's best to stay clear of him."

"He and his sister are coming to my house for dinner tomorrow after church," I said. "Won't it look strange if I cancel? Do you know how closely he's being watched?"

"I don't have any other information. I promise I'll get it to you as soon as I know. But I'd stay clear of him."

"But tomorrow was my opportunity to dump him," I said.

"Oh, well, that sounds like a good idea," he said as started dancing slowly. "Though it broke our confidence, thanks for tipping off Vonny."

"I'm normally good with secrets, but I knew she wouldn't see much future with a cowboy. Oh, and here's a couple of tips—if you aren't familiar with Toni Morrison and Charles Dickens, get that way."

"Bit of a contrast, wouldn't you say?"

"Yeah, that should be another tip—don't be too quick to peg her. She's an intelligent woman with diverse interests."

Tony turned around as Jay appeared.

"Someone's cutting in," said Tony.

"Okay, since I have you two together, Jay is legit State Patrol, right?" I asked.

Tony nodded.

"And Robert has vouched for you, Tony. So tell me, Jay, why are you investigating the local State Patrol? Too lax or too corrupt?"

Jay shook his head. "I can't say."

I smiled at his ambiguity. "Fine, then. I've talked to McNeill and Merritt...about things. Waters suddenly scares me. Is my gut feeling off? I need to know or it'll come back on me."

"I don't know everything, but I think you're okay. But understand this, we don't know everything, we're not even close."

"I'll leave you two," said Tony. With the absence of a hat, he touched his index finger to his forehead. "Ma'am." He backed away.

As a slow song started, Jay pulled me in close.

"Getting' fresh, young man," I said, but didn't pull away.

"You never called me," Jay said.

"Well, that's because I haven't broken with Raz, at least till tomorrow night."

"And then?"

"Then I need some air."

"Got it. Just don't ask for any right now," he said in a voice low and soft.

He backed me to the edge of the dance floor into the semi-darkness, dropped my hand, wrapped both arms around my back then bent forward to kiss me. Beams of light exploded from our heads and blasted through the roof.

"Now you've gone beyond fresh."

He kissed me again. The floors rumbled and the walls collapsed.

"This is sheer impudence."

His third kiss made my knees wobbly. I needed to run away. When he pulled back a little, he looked inside me and knew he'd hit the mark. As soon as he let me back away from him, I departed for our table. Mom and Bill soon joined me and we went home with Paul's assurance that he'd take Patty home.

No way. I wasn't ready to deal with Jay. Not now, maybe not ever. I needed peace.

At home, I sat in the nursery rocker, staring at the white walls of the vacant room. She should have lived here. Instead, she lay in a silver box in a small grave in the Docket family lot at the cemetery. In December, she should have been in the bassinet Lew made and Brian heaved through the window in drunken anger. In December, she should have been in my arms.

In the hall, I passed by Mom's old room, now the guest room again. I missed having her here. With Raz gone, Patty would start staying in the evenings to watch a movie with me. But right now, I wanted to be alone. I walked down the hall to my room, but before entering, I opened the door across the hall. This had been my dad's room. When we moved here from the house next door, he'd given him and me the largest bedrooms, each complete with a sitting room and a gas fireplace. In this great big house I felt small, no, diminished. In front of a cold fireplace, I sat down in a wingback chair, with my feet dangling a couple of inches from the floor. The only light came through my east window from Bill and Mom's porch down the street. Then the doorbell rang. That would be Raz, the last person on earth I wanted to see. He could wait another day to get dumped.

At two o'clock the next afternoon, the doorbell rang. Beulah and I had just finished setting the table in the dining room.

"Hi, ah, Nori's not feeling well, so she stayed home," said Raz from the front porch.

I hid my joy over her absence. "That's a shame. Come on back. Derek and James are watching football with Bill."

After our roast beef dinner was consumed and the kitchen was cleaned, we all went to the family room to digest and watch the NFL. With four trim women, Beulah, Mom, Patty, and I could all sit on the sofa together.

"That was a mighty fine meal," said Beulah. "Nice to be waited on."

"We're glad you enjoyed it," said my mom.

"Best Friend," I said, "When are you going to get some decent shoes? It's getting cool and you're still in flip-flops."

"Heh! You're motherin' me, you shrimpy girl."

"We know you'll wear those till December," said Bill. "You're a skinny bird with no insulation. Look at these arms, how do you stay warm?"

I grabbed her upper arm and said, "Just skin and bones. We better give you dessert and maybe some bourbon to warm you up."

She reached down and squeezed my knee with her bony, age-spotted hand.

"Ow! Still got a heckava grip. Must have some muscle somewhere."

"Most are in my brain, shrimpy girl. You're the skinny one. And walkin' around in thongs we useta call 'em...heh, ain't nothin' to the daredevil stuff you pull."

The chuckles around the room were cut short when Raz blurted: "I must speak."

We snapped our eyes on him. What the hell?

From his chair next to Derek, he looked intensely at me and said, "You take too many risks. Riding in the dark after those evil men. And I saw you today on your horse. You ride too fast. It is too reckless."

I smiled at him. "My, my. Well, I think Strider and I will just go on having our fun."

"I forbid it."

Stunned silence. Eyes went back and forth from me to Raz and back again.

I burst out laughing. "You come into my home and presume to tell me what to do? Get real. Who anointed you prince?"

Patty snickered.

"Derek, I think I'd like a walk outside," said James.

Raz and I continued to glare at each other as father and son exited out the back door.

When Raz stood, so did I. Oh, I was going to enjoy telling him to get lost. When he left for the rear hall toward the back door, I followed.

"What's with you?" I asked.

"A respectable woman would listen to good advice," he said.

I was quick. I was precise. I was pissed. And I was much too fast for him to have stopped my fist from hitting his nose, even if he expected it. His head snapped back and he gasped then grunted. The blood came. With a sense of satisfaction, I watched it run down his face and onto his shirt. Mom rushed behind me into the laundry room. She handed him a towel that he pressed to his face. He turned away then stomped out the back door. I took a step after him then alarm, no, terror kicked me in the gut. I stumbled backwards, ran to the study to get my Glock, and then dashed out the back door.

I caught up to him as he skirted Rufus to the west. He kept going. I needed to jog to keep up with his quick pace.

"Why don't you just go ahead and call me a whore?"

He turned north toward the Seven Dwarfs.

"What is going on?" I demanded.

He stopped and turned, the southwest sun shone on the blood that dripped from his jaw. I stopped in front of him. He wiped the towel at his face again.

"We need to talk," he said.

"I agree. I need to tell you we're done."

"Huh? I thought you—"

"I've known for a while. It's best, especially since I know you don't respect me. I should have ended this long ago when I knew I didn't really care about you."

He looked stunned. I felt the soft ground under my right foot. I stood on the edge of a freshly-dug prairie dog hole. All seemed calm—why did my heart pound so hard against my chest?

As I took a step to the left I said, "What did you want to say?"

From behind, I heard the sound of a shot. Raz collapsed to his knees, his mouth open, clutching his chest as blood ran through his fingers. When he fell backward, I dropped to the ground, gasping for air.

He'd been shot!

As I pulled my gun from my rear waistband, I rolled over so I could see behind me. A shot whizzed over my head. I couldn't see anybody, but I fired a shot westward into the dirt where I thought the shooter was hiding. Then I hopped to a crouch and ran to Sneezy, the nearest Dwarf, and hid behind the rocky mound. A third shot didn't come, but my breath came out in quick, panicked bursts. I waited a few moments, as fear clawed at my lungs, and then I moved to the edge of the mound.

My God, what just happened? Raz lay motionless, sprawled on his back. I peered around the corner, but no one approached. Then I saw Derek running from his backyard toward me, fifty yards away to the south. When I rose and held up my hand, he stopped. He stared at me for a few moments, looked over to Raz, and then ran back to his yard and into his house. I checked the area on the other side of the butte, but saw no one. I could do nothing but wait while my guts churned and my heart thudded against my ribs.

Chapter 14

EXTER Chief of Police Tate McNeill arrived first on the scene. This wasn't his jurisdiction, and he usually had Sundays off, but I was relieved to see him. He came running out from the east side of Rufus. He paused at the body, checked the pulse, and then walked over to me, scratching his weekend whiskers. I moved away from the east side of Sneezy.

"Two shots...from over west...I think from Raccoon Creek or Pooper's Canyon...I never saw him...but I fired a shot into the dirt just hoping to scare him away," I babbled.

"Pooper's Canyon?" Tate asked.

"Yeah, a dry gully, gets deeper as it cuts southwest."

I tried to hide my trembling hands then realized I still held my gun. After setting it down in a patch of buffalo grass, I walked over to Raz. The shot must have hit him in the chest, for his burgundy polo shirt had a hole surrounded by a circle of blood. His nose and chin were bloody; I regretted punching him for my sake.

"I don't get why he has a bloody nose," said Tate. "Looks broken."

"I punched him when we were in the house because he insulted me. We'd been dating, you see. I broke up with him just moments before he was shot."

"Any ideas why he was shot?"

"I'd been told that he had aided the CIA against the Hezbollah. He was supposed to be hiding out in nowhere."

"Looks like he got found."

"Yeah." I sat down on the ground and stared into my lover's face.

Two State Patrol officers approached us. I didn't recognize either of them. The redheaded one inspected the body and the other, a thick-chested baldy, asked Chief Tate for my story. Nobody from the house came out to us, so police must be holding them back. Derek probably warned them of a gunman in the area.

"The CIA? You believe that? Sounds like a lovers' quarrel to me," said Baldy. "And no evidence of another shooter."

Baldy walked over to me. I started to stand when I felt a thick hand grab my shoulder. In a flash, I was face down in the buffalo grass with a knee in my back, smashing the breath out of me. I didn't resist, I let him yank my arms together behind my back. Cold metal was snapped onto my wrists. I gasped to breathe, as my left ribs ached.

Triple shit.

"Hey! This is a respected attorney," said Chief Tate.

Surprised, I saw Lew standing off to the side, noticeably trembling.

"Who are you?" asked Baldy.

"Lew Eldritch."

"He's a family friend," I said then spat some dirt out of my mouth.

"Did you see the shooting?" asked Red.

"No, sir. But I was downwind. Heard three shots. That's all I know."

"All right, just stay here."

Baldy lifted me off the ground by my armpits as Red started reading me my rights. A shove got me walking toward their cruiser.

"You stay with the body," said Baldy to Chief Tate.

"Sorry, not my jurisdiction."

Two more officers converged on the scene.

I looked over to Tate. "Call Rachel for me, would you?"

He nodded as the officer yanked me past him.

"Hey, this will be our first murder collar," said Red.

"Yep," said Baldy.

It seemed unnecessary as I hadn't resisted, but the officers walked beside me, each clenching an arm as we approached my backyard. Mom, Bill, Patty, Beulah, and James stood in my backyard, in stunned silence. Derek was off to the side, being interviewed by a trooper. When he saw me, he ran toward us.

"Hey!" he yelled.

"Derek, stop!" I said. "Don't say anything. Don't do anything. It won't help me."

Thank you, God, for he stopped.

"Son," said James.

Derek looked at his father then back at me, his chest heaving in anger.

"Keep an eye on the hothead," said Baldy.

As we drew closer, I could see Patty and Bill were turning red in anger and Beulah was shaking. My mom looked the most composed.

"Somebody take Beulah into the house and give her brandy. Mom, Nebraska has parent-child immunity. You don't have to speak."

The grip on my left arm tightened. I winced in pain.

"If you're not going to confess, shut up," said Baldy.

"We know whom to call," Mom said.

I nodded to her as I was hustled toward their cruiser which they parked on the side of our house. The bastards probably tore up the grass. After Red shoved me into the back seat, Baldy turned on the siren. What a shithead.

Once On Highway 51, Baldy said, "What did lover boy do to make you so mad?"

Refusing the bait, I said nothing.

"Looked like a terrorist," said Red. "Do Muslims make good lovers, sweetheart?"

These guys were pathetic. I stared at the wildflowers along the road—prairie clover, white aster, pink smartweed. I gazed out over my land, rough, but protected, unlike me. We passed the Beast and the Joker, both high bluffs, and finally the white cross Bill and I had erected on the site of the Quinn murders.

As we neared Sidney, I felt my pace quicken. Would they put me in a cell? No, first other stuff, right, breathe, breathe deeper. Still, I trembled. Okay, think. Head up, mouth shut. Rachel would come. Maybe even Sergeant Merritt. Maybe he'd recall I gave him quality beer on our patio—twice. I'd solved the Quinn murders—surely he would consider that. He got promoted after the Four Bastards were captured—by me and my gang, though he probably got credit. I prayed to God that he'd remember.

They parked in front of the Sidney Police Department, which was on the south side of the courthouse. Baldy jerked me out of the cruiser though I came willingly. Then the two shitheads marched me up the concrete steps, all ninety thousand. People stared at me. I tried to look forward. Sergeant Merritt stood just inside the doors, looking angry.

"Let go of her! Now!"

The officers complied.

"Take those cuffs off her and get out of my sight," said Merritt.

He did remember.

"Megan, are you all right?"

"Yes…better now that you're here."

"Did you shoot him?"

"No. That's not my bullet in his chest."

Raz was dead and I'd been arrested. I wanted to cry. The lump in my throat choked me. Breathe. Deeper. And again.

People sat in cheap plastic chairs along the wall or stood in two lines leading up to a gray counter where middle-aged police officers sat behind bullet proof glass. Of course, everyone stared at me. Merritt led me to a side door where he punched in a code and we entered. Just inside the door, he gave me a cursory frisk then led me to a counter—no, I didn't have identification with me. I told the officer my family would bring it. Then my hands were pressed onto a blackened pad then onto a page. A clerk gave me moist wipes to clean my hands. I tried not to look guilty for my mug shot, but I probably looked scared. A few minutes later, I was seated in an interview room with gray walls and a speckled gray linoleum floor, drinking a cup of coffee a civilian brought me.

Merritt left me for few minutes. I needed to concentrate, to be clear and concise. Think, time to think. They'll take the bullet out of him and see it's not from my gun. But that could take days for testing to be completed. Would they still lock me up? I'd relished previous occasions when I sent men to jail. The prospect of going back there, to one of those cells terrified me.

Locked up, no escape. I pressed my hands together to keep them from trembling. Think, be calm. My arms and back hurt. Merritt would come back. He wouldn't leave me here. I'd be home later, I'd go to work tomorrow.

The door opened. He did come back, accompanied by Stan Spurlock, the middle-aged Dexter attorney who did the criminal work in town. I never really liked the man; he had an unctuous manner with combed-back unctuous hair, and poor posture. But holy shit, I was glad to see him.

He greeted me then leaned forward to whisper into my ear. "Gus went to find Judge Shelton."

I nodded.

"Do you want to talk?" Stan asked me. "You don't have to."

"I will. I'm ready."

"The detective will be right in," said Merritt. "Did you have bruises on your arms before you went out north of your house?"

"No."

"Did those State Patrol officers do that?"

"I'm not looking to cause any trouble or issue any complaints."

The door opened. A man of fifty with graying hair, a nice gray suit, and a big gut walked in. He possessed something familiar about him. He shook Stan's hand then mine.

"Ms. Docket, I'm Detective Dennis Moore," he said.

Of course, he must be the older brother of my insurance agent, not that it mattered. Again, I consented to the recorded interview. Then the detective methodically questioned me about my relationship to the deceased, the events of the day and of the shooting. I answered honestly. I even described the order Raz issued in the family room and the conversation that lead me to punch him in the nose. The interview seemed to take as long as the actual events, but it finally concluded.

Yet, before the Detective concluded, Sgt. Merritt identified himself and asked me to describe the arrest. I did so without embellishing. Merritt then asked me to show my arms and back. I held out my arms and lifted the back of my top and turned around as he photographed my bruises. I probably looked roughed up—I was still in my church clothes, a turquoise short-sleeved silk top and sand dress slacks, both probably ruined.

Detective Moore thanked me for my cooperation then left. Before the door shut, both Gus and Rachel were in the room. I was ecstatic to see them both.

"Tate told me your account," said Rachel. "You never should have been arrested."

"It's done," said Merritt. "The lieutenant authorized it."

"Now what?" I asked in a small voice.

"We wait for Judge Shelton to come through for you," said Gus.

"While we wait, could I use the restroom?" I asked.

"Yeah," said Rachel. "I'll take you."

"Will I get to come back here?" I certainly feared the alternative.

"I believe so," said Merritt.

I stood then grabbed my cup. No need to surrender my DNA. I crushed the cup then threw it in a hall trash can. Rachel gave me a smile—she understood.

"I'm surprised the lieutenant authorized the arrest," said Rachel as she led me down a gray hall. In truth, the whole damn place was gray. "He's actually a fan of yours, especially after you solved the Quinn murders. If you ever want to quit law, he'd hire you in a flash."

That didn't comfort me—I just wanted to go home.

On our way back to the interview room, Detective Moore stopped us in the hall. Gus gave me a smile.

"This is your ticket home," said Moore as he held up a piece of paper. "Judge Shelton issued an R-O-R, a release on your own recognizance, as long as you agree to appear in court for a hearing on Friday at ten. I've never seen one of these issued on a Sunday night."

"Yes, of course, I agree."

"He is leaving town for the week, so I guess that's why he gave you the R-O-R."

After I signed the form, he told me I was free to go. So I went, as quickly as I could, but not before thanking Merritt and planning a meeting with Gus and Stan for tomorrow.

Once back in the lobby, I was disappointed no one was here to meet me. Maybe it was too long a wait.

"Do you have change? I need to call for a ride."

Rachel smiled. "Keep going."

I walked to the double doors and felt a wave of assurance wash over me.

"Do you have any hand sanitizer?"

"Oh, yeah." Rachel took a bottle out of the back pocket of her brown uniform pants and gave me a squirt. "I wouldn't be caught dead without this stuff."

"Hey, thank Tate when you see him. I'll try to give him a call. I was so glad to see him. Those other two, Baldy and Red were brutes."

"What did they do to you?"

"Talk to Merritt. I just want to forget it."

"I will. Now go see your admirers."

I went out the door with Rachel, though she stopped once we were outside. Mom saw me first. She rushed to me then squeezed me harder than I thought she could. Uncle Bill's hug lifted me off the ground. When I reached the ground again, I felt Beulah's grip on my shoulder.

"Heh! Those fools!" she said with a wink.

As I was hugging Patty, I felt Beulah's bony hands grab my wrist.

"Hey, now. Look at your watch."

I looked down, it was scuffed with dirt. She took her flower-print blouse and began to wipe it clean. I grinned at my mom.

"See, better. Needs a good cleanin' when you get home." Beulah placed her wrist next to mine revealing the identical watch, one I bought for her last summer after we made up following a falling out.

I hugged James then asked, "You feeling all right?"

"Much better now," he said. "They roughed you up a bit."

I looked down at my clothes. "Well, some of it is my doing."

Derek stepped forward. "They can't get away with that. They were hurting you."

"This is not a time for me to be stirring up trouble. I did get arrested. I've been released on personal recognizance. Though, I know of a couple of troopers who aren't pleased about it." I looked over my shoulder at Rachel still standing by the doors. "Darn convenient of Sergeant Merritt to get promoted just in time to help me."

"Chief Tate was yelling at the troopers who stayed, ordering them to go search the area," said Bill. "They would have anyway once they heard what you said. So, uh, they booked you."

"Yeah. I have a hearing on Friday. Gus tracked down Judge Shelton. He's the one who got me out of there."

For the first time I saw Lew, who was standing halfway down the steps.

"Lew, thank you for coming forward," I said, knowing that it scared him badly.

"Glad to do it," he said then twitched.

"Just stick to your original statement. Don't try to add to it…they'll know."

Lew nodded then flushed red. "Damn that cop. He didn't need to throw you down like he done."

"Just forget it. Right now, I want to go home and take a bath. That place is icky."

Chapter 15

IT was nearly seven when I finished my bath. Before going down for roast beef sandwiches, I gazed out my window at the troopers who were still discussing, photographing, and measuring the site. Most of the activity focused on the area of the body and off to the west—just as I suggested. This group of State Patrol officers seemed to believe my account. A long band of yellow tape stretched as far east and west as I could see, cutting off the Docket and Wilson yards to the north. Both Merritt and Rachel had joined Chief Tate out in my backyard, which heartened me greatly.

I didn't have much of an appetite, at least at the start. Mom and Bill joined the informal dinner. Considering how much had happened, we were mostly quiet during the meal. While I was bathing, Mom visited Nori at the duplex, describing her as "distraught." That figured. Nori was talking to my Uncle Peter on the phone when Mom left.

I longed for my bed, but first I attended to my stream of visitors. Though I'd often been in crises, getting charged with second degree murder stunned most of them to near silence. Kayla just stared at me with big eyes.

"Don't worry, the police tests will prove me innocent," I said. "It just takes awhile."

"Did you have to go inside a jail cell?" she asked.

"No, just an interview room. Going into a jail cell would be scary."

"But I don't understand what happened," she said.

"Sorry, Kayla, but I can't discuss it…not until the charge is dismissed."

"I'm sure we'll hear all about it," said Paul. "Chief Tate is a talker and Bill says you told him what happened."

"And Beulah will talk nonstop all day tomorrow," said Brian, who leaned against a wall in the kitchen next to Zane.

"Well, don't tease her about it," said Bill. "She was pretty shook up."

"I should call to check on her," I said.

By the time I finished a call to Beulah and Vonny in Denver, who was ready to spit fire from Derek's account, Brian and Zane had left. Meanwhile, Jack, Bud, and Tony were consuming root beer floats in the family room. Nobody sat, except for me and James. The others stood at the family room window and tried to catch a glimpse of the state troopers. A little after nine, I announced I was going to bed. I thought I might be too rattled to sleep, but exhaustion made my brain limp and I slept till my blasted alarm roused me. As I rolled to the edge of the bed and dropped down, pain from my back stabbed at me in protest. I guess I should be glad Baldy hadn't crunched my spine.

Normally I would go for a run before work, but I was feeling self-conscious, so I went down to the basement to run on the treadmill. My basement was essentially a storage and junk room with racks of old clothes, bookshelves, furniture from Bill's former marriages, a half bath, a stack of landscaping bricks, and other odds and ends. I turned on an old TV to watch the morning news as I ran. A few minutes of the national news preceded the local, well, the Scottsbluff news.

The murder and my arrest were the lead stories for the Nebraska panhandle. Shit!

I tumbled off the back of the treadmill issuing a jumble of obscenities and fell on my butt. Now my butt and my ribs both complained. I gave up on the run. From the floor, I spotted the extra pairs of night goggles on a bookshelf near the back wall. Fine, they could stay there because I wasn't planning any adventures in the dark.

I lay back on the floor and stared at the wood frame ceiling. Oh, Raz. Why did you die? Why did you come here? Murdered. God in heaven, why? No, I never loved him—but dead. So cruel, so senseless. I wondered what Nori and his parents would decide about the funeral. First, the body would need to be released by the police. Truly, I felt very sorry for my woes, but he was dead. My lover. Just like that. Thirty-three years of age, his prime. Dead.

I arrived at the firm later than normal, dread slowing me to a snail's pace. Yet my staff arrived early, and popped up from their chairs when I walked into the lobby. Glenda gave me a hug. Employees didn't usually hug their bosses, but most bosses didn't get charged with murder. Melanie and Joy, my assistant, stood by unsure what to say or do.

Gus came lumbering up and said, "Let the felon breathe."

I laughed and that changed the tone. The women patted my shoulder and Glenda gave me another hug. No doubt Gus had informed them of all the details, so there wasn't much to say.

"Okay, then, let's work," I said.

They looked pleased to be told what to do, so they all gave me another smile then went back to their desks. Brian followed me to my office.

"How ya doin'?" he asked.

I'd nearly forgotten—Judge Shelton had signed the divorce decree on Friday. It would be in my noon mail.

"I feel dazed. I suppose work is the best thing for me."

"Sleep all right?"

"It was more like scheduled unconsciousness." I unlocked my desk drawer and took out a bottle of Advil for my ribs and butt, which, of course, I needed to explain to Brian.

"I didn't know they roughed you up."

"I felt like an unwilling participant in the WWF."

"Shitheads. Something needs to be done."

"Well, I don't plan to do anything, except behave like a model citizen till I get that charge dismissed. I wish Judge Shelton wasn't off in some remote part of Canada. Damn, it's all over the news."

"Yeah, now you'll need to hire another attorney for the firm," he said with a smile. "Every time you have one of your adventures, everybody in ten counties wants to hire you."

Glenda, the Good Witch of the North, scurried in with a plate and a cup of coffee. "I couldn't decide which one to make, so I made both of your favorites. And I figured you'd need a strong cup of coffee for today." She set a plate with a brownie and a cinnamon scone on the desk. "Now don't forget your ten o'clock appointment."

"Thank you, Glenda. You take care of me."

She smiled so hard her face flushed. She scurried back out.

I tried to focus on work for the next hour, but felt on edge. My morning appointment was one party in a contentious child custody case. Today, Doug seemed unable to spew his customary vitriol.

"Cynthia and I don't agree on much, well, nothing really, but we support you a hundred percent. Annie is very upset."

"Well, hang on, I'll write her a note since she'd be in school now."

I took out a piece of my letterhead and wrote a note telling the fourth grader that I was fine and everything was just a big mistake and would soon be fixed. I showed him the note and he nodded. I folded it, put it in an envelope, and then sealed it.

"Tell her you haven't seen it."

I handed him the envelope.

He looked down at it for a few minutes then said, "I guess I'd be willing to give up Thanksgiving."

Whoa! I should get arrested more often—this was the first breakthrough in four months with this family.

I wrapped up the appointment then Brian, Melanie, Gus, and I walked over to Custer's for lunch. Beulah was at the counter when we walked in. It seemed to assure her that I was in my work clothes and was here for lunch as if nothing had happened. But it had. Other patrons greeted me with awkward support. I bet many of them spent last night on the phone with their friends, checking the Internet and the ten o'clock news for information. But here I was, looking and trying to act like it was a day like any other.

Back in the office, I summoned a burst of respectable, industrious energy. By five-thirty, I felt drained, so I headed home. Mom, Bill, and Patty awaited me. After supper, Mom decided we needed a dose of Young Frankenstein.

The next night, they gathered in support again, but I surprised them.

"I need alcohol and loud music. Let's go to the Cowpoke."

"Is it open on Tuesdays?" asked Mom.

"Yeah, it's just closed on Mondays," said Bill.

Because Patty had prepared salmon for dinner, we ate and arrived at the tavern at eight. The place was only about a third full. Johnny Two Rivers hustled over to greet us. He shook my hand twice, unsure what to say. Five cowboys sat in the corner, trying not to stare at me.

"Those are McCready cowhands. Decent guys, been around a while," said Bill.

"Do you ever think of putting someone in charge and becoming the gentleman rancher?" I asked.

"Well, Jack and Bud do a lot of supervisin'."

"Maybe you ought to promote them."

"Jack would like it. But Bud always talks about being a cop."

"Really? He doesn't want to shovel my horse's manure for the rest of his life?"

Bill chuckled. "I'd hate to lose him. But I doubt he'll be leavin' anytime soon. He's started takin' some night classes at the community college."

"We ought to help him."

Johnny brought us a pitcher of beer. I called Jack. He was always easier to talk to, though Bud was the better dancer.

"Hey, I'm at the Cowpoke—why aren't you and Bud here to dance with me?"

They were at our table in less than twenty minutes, both smelling of shaving lotion. I doubted they bothered with more than showering during the week. Cattle just want to be fed, they don't care about appearances. But if one plans to dance with someone charged with murder, one ought to be well groomed.

As I danced with Jack, he said, "I've never danced with a convict."

"Well, how do you know? Women don't bring their rap sheets to the bar."

He chuckled then gave me a spin.

"You know, if there's something I can do...well, Bud and I would do anything for you."

"Of course, you're my Night Posse. But I really hope there's no need. I just want this to go away."

I danced the next several dances with Bill, Bud, or Jack as if it had gone away. Then my gang and I left for home.

The next morning, I awakened with a jolt, my insides twisting and roiling. Oh, God in heaven, what would happen now? I hustled into work, never telling anyone my distress. I sat at my desk, dread pulsing through my veins. Think. Focus. What was coming?

Just before eleven, Merritt and Spurlock came.

They sat down in the chairs in front of my desk. Gus followed them in and shut the door.

Merritt cleared his throat then said, "Megan, this isn't good. Ah, the preliminary tests on the bullet taken from the body of the deceased indicate it came from a nine millimeter Glock."

Shit. Oh, shit. Oh, sweet Jesus.

"The county prosecutor is pushing this fill-in judge from Kimball for another arrest warrant for you," said Stan. "Larry Peake, the prosecutor, told me he plans to argue that you possess violent tendencies. He cited the shooting of Webster and Spittle in August, as well as the killing of Bert Bolger, DEA Agent RT Martin, and Salt Eldritch, all within the last four years."

"I don't suppose it matters to the prosecutor that those deaths occurred in self-defense," I said.

"Peake will still point to a pattern of violence. This judge from Kimball is Dale Turvey. He'll cave-in to Peake, rather than ruffle any feathers. He's been working the afternoon hours here while Judge Shelton is gone. Larry Peake has it out for you. If he could find a way to charge you with first degree murder, he would. But you followed Raz outside, so it's hard to prove premeditation."

"But I can post bail, right?"

"Judge Turvey will set that."

I braced my hands on the desk to stop the room from spinning, but it didn't work. Gus started pacing in front of the door.

"So I'll be arrested this afternoon?"

"Yes."

I looked at Sergeant Merritt. "Will it be you?"

"I don't know," he said. "The warrant has to be issued before it is assigned to an officer."

"Should I turn myself in?"

"Again, the warrant hasn't been issued and we don't know what time Judge Turvey will issue it."

A ball of rancid fear began to percolate in my stomach.

"Thank you for letting me know. I better wrap up a few things here then I'll go home to wait for the officer."

Another arrest, this time with frightening consequences. God, help me.

Chapter 16

AT noon, I left work and went to the Cheyenne County Bank. The Finch family had worked here for generations, including Jeff, a friend and former classmate, yet I was glad he wasn't here—I didn't want to talk to anybody. I added my mom's name to my checking account and transferred from an investment account $100,000.00 to that account. Surely, the bail wouldn't be as high as a million, but I wanted to be prepared. But really, how does one prepare for jail?

When I arrived home, Patty was running the vacuum in the living room. I dashed up the back stairs to my room. What does one wear to jail? I put on jeans and a simple black cotton long-sleeved shirt, white crew socks, and my tennies. What does one take to jail? I dumped out my purse, and put my driver's license, two twenty dollar bills, anti-bacterial wipes, my toothbrush and toothpaste, a hair brush, lip balm, and a copy of a diminutive green Gideon's New Testament inside. I didn't go anywhere, not even out to Big Leo, without my smartphone, but I'd do without it now. Maybe they'd seize it, claiming it was evidence.

I went down to the kitchen and Patty's stare.

"Patty, would you mind sleeping here tonight? Leave the front porch light on, if you would."

"Megan, what's going on?"

"I'm going to be arrested and taken to jail."

"But the judge—"

"This is a different judge. Judge Shelton's on vacation."

"Hang on, I'm gonna call your mom."

Though I lacked an appetite, I made a sandwich and started to force it down—I needed to eat, simple as that.

Even so, the shock on my mom's face didn't help. Soon, Bill came stomping in, stinky from the feedlot and sock-footed, for he'd removed his boots in the mud room.

"What the hell?" he said.

I told them about the Glock bullet, the substitute judge, and the prosecutor out to get me.

"But they'll do more tests, right?" said Patty. "They can tell from markings on the bullet and the insides of your gun that the bullet didn't come from your gun. I saw it on TV."

"And Glock is a common kind of handgun," said Bill. "They'll get it right."

"I know," I said. "But that takes time."

"Shouldn't they set bail right when you get there and then you'll be out, right?" said Mom, half pleadingly.

"I just have a feeling that it's not going to go that smoothly," I said.

"What? How?" asked Mom.

I shook my head.

"Well, eat. You need to eat."

I looked at her then back at my sandwich. It was as if a simple ham sandwich was transformed into a burnt slab of liver and a vat of over-cooked Brussels sprouts. I even smelled liver. Mom and Patty launched themselves into finding something I would eat. Bill sat down at the table with me, but Patty shooed him away, claiming his stench wouldn't help my appetite. I finally managed to eat a container of yogurt, buttered wheat toast, and a banana.

"I don't want you to tell anyone…not yet anyway. I told Glenda I was gone for the rest of the afternoon, but I didn't say why. Gus will find out from Spurlock. If I can post bail and come home…then let's not make a big deal out of it."

Then we waited. Now and then, Patty would go clean something. Mom started organizing the organized Tupperware cupboard, fully aware Patty would put it all back the way it was. Bill sat and stared.

"I'm glad Dad isn't here to see this day," I said.

Bill looked at me with basset hound eyes, the ones my dad had when he thought I might take a job at a law firm other than his.

Time passed. Both Bill and I started pacing the hallways that ran the length of the house, he in the west hall, and me in the east hall next to the kitchen.

At three thirty, Patty suggested that I should eat again. I obediently sat down at the kitchen table. Again Patty and Mom began the task of finding food I would eat. I ended up smearing peanut butter on a hunk of chocolate. After I brushed my teeth, I returned to the kitchen. We all sat back down at the table. What does one say before going to jail?

Then the doorbell rang. It hit us like someone blasted a fog horn in our ears. My body jerked, Bill jumped from his chair, Mom's head snapped toward mine, and Patty gasped.

Mom grabbed my hand and squeezed it hard. "Head up. You're innocent."

"Will they have pillows?" Patty rushed from the room to the coat closet. She met us at the front door with my black Ghost Rider hoodie. "You can use the hood as a pillow."

Maybe in a year, I'd look back at this day and think it was funny. But at this moment, it was terrifying.

"Courage," said my mom, who stood beside me in the foyer.

I opened the door, hoping it would be Rachel or Merritt. It was Waters. A wave of menace wafted from the porch into the house. This straight-laced cop scared me, as he did in the barn after we caught the Four Bastards.

"Hello, Megan. I'm sorry to be the one," he said.

Was he really sorry? I doubted it. I'd helped to get a felony charged against his son. He also knew I would have shot out his son's legs if I'd needed to. Rachel told me Waters had taken out a huge equity loan to pay for legal expenses incurred from the hate crime charges. No, he wasn't sorry. He was a frightening, lying bastard. But he didn't handcuff me and gently helped me into the back of the cruiser.

As we drove away, I gazed back at my wonderful mother, uncle, and friend. Pain and helplessness were plastered on their faces.

I checked my watch when we arrived at the Sidney police station—it was well after four o'clock. Again, I was marched up the ninety thousand steps. For some reason there were lots of Sidney police, county deputies, and State Patrol officers milling around outside. My mom told me to keep my head up, so I tried, though my stomach quavered. I recognized a couple of troopers from the scene of my Mom's car accident when they'd helped her out of the overturned SUV. When Waters and I walked near them, both men touched their hats. That was nice and I was pathetically ready to cling to any sort of pleasantry.

Inside the front doors, Sgt. Merritt awaited me.

"Thanks, Randy, I'll take her back."

I was overjoyed to be out of the presence of Waters. We walked through the lobby and through the security door.

Merritt turned to me. "You all right?"

"Yeah," I lied.

He performed a quick search of my person. I handed him my purse.

"You pack light," he said with a smile.

We stopped at a desk where a clerk checked my driver's license. It was a bit like checking into a hotel, but with a grave, ominous feel about it. Merritt then took me to the interview room to wait for Stan Spurlock. After waiting alone for a few minutes, Rachel came in with a cup of coffee for me. I'd already put on my hoodie, for the whole building was chilly. Her smile helped me handle the otherwise daunting experience.

"Oh, Megan. I can't believe this. That prosecutor is such an asshole. He'd never get away with this if Judge Shelton was here."

"That's what I gather."

"Why it took all afternoon is beyond me. But your attorney should be here soon. I hope he's working hard for your interests."

"He should," I said. "My dad and I have referred a ton of business to him."

A few minutes later, Stan, Gus, and Merritt returned to the room.

"I'm sorry," said Stan. "Judge Turvey left without setting bail."

The silence shouted: Jail!

I didn't allow myself to babble my objection. I just took a deep breath.

"You've got to be kidding!" said Rachel. "What a crock of shit."

Head up, head up. Oh, God, I was going to be jailed. Two Sidney police officers in their navy shirts and navy pants entered the room. Merritt nodded to them.

I stood. It was no use being a pansy about it, no matter how terrified I was.

"I'll just walk down with you," said Merritt.

The two Sidney officers looked surprised, but didn't say anything.

"I am a ferocious criminal, you know," I said to Rachel, who gave me a smile. "Will you go tell my family?"

"Right away," she said.

"Thank you, Stan. I'll be seeing you."

He actually looked a bit emotional about it all. He just nodded to me. The Sidney officers escorted me out of the room. They stopped at a huge black steel door. It was ugly, but the only bit of the station that wasn't gray.

Codes, keys, more officers, some on phones, another long gray hallway. I half expected someone to yell "dead man walking," but the only sounds were our footsteps on the heavily waxed gray linoleum and my heart pounding so loudly that I was sure everyone could hear it. Chasing criminals in the dead of night on a horse on rough ground should be more frightening, but it wasn't. Head up.

I looked over to Merritt who walked beside me. "Do they give us meals?"

He tried, but failed to squelch a smile. "Yes, they do. It's the same food they serve us in the cafeteria."

Us. There would be others. Oh, Lord. Maybe they'd spend the night taunting me. Ha! Ha! Look at the attorney who got sent to jail. Yeah, so funny. Would I get put in a cell with some big bruiser who thinks I'm pretty? My blood iced over. I was trapped like an animal, innocent, but a prize catch for that son of a bitch prosecutor. I think it was the first time I truly hated a person who hadn't tried to kill me.

As we neared another black door at the end of the hall, Merritt squeezed my hand. I'm sure that was prohibited behavior on his part. I guess I looked scared. I gave him my attempt at a smile. As the keys and codes started again, I decided I shouldn't look scared to my cellmates—looking vulnerable would only open me up to abuse. I swallowed hard as the door swung open. I couldn't see much around the officers. Merritt stepped forward to talk to them and I saw even less. He returned to my side.

"It'll be just a minute," he said.

The officers walked into the room; one went to talk to the officer at the desk and the other disappeared around the corner. Merritt asked for my purse, so I handed it to him.

"Hey! What the hell?" said a woman's voice.

The female officer at the desk glanced over at me then walked toward the cells. Clanging metal and mutterings echoed against the concrete block walls. More gray. Someone who was mad. Lord above, please don't desert me. Then I heard one of the officers say something about a murder suspect.

"No shit?" said another woman's voice.

Yeah, that was me. Head up. Don't look vulnerable. One of the officers came back for me and I followed. Twenty feet from the officer's desk stood three cells spanning one wall to the other with black bars in the front and gray concrete walls in between the cells. One cell was empty with the door ajar and a hole in the floor where the toilet should have been. The center cell was also empty, but the desk officer and the other officer stood on each side of the door. Merritt handed one of the officers my nearly empty purse. He searched it and handed it back to me.

As I approached my cell, I studied the three women in the cell to the right. One young woman with dark, matted hair lay sleeping on a lower bunk. A chunky, middle-aged woman with greasy blond hair stood at the bars staring at me. Next to her was a tall, lean woman with unnatural red hair, probably forty years or so, with black and red tattoos running along her arms. Thank God they were locking me up alone.

"Hey!" said the chubby blonde. "I've seen her."

"Yeah," said the tall redhead. "She solved the Quinn murders. It was on TV."

The young brunette sat up. She wore a red top with silver sequins in a heart shape. "She killed that DEA agent. I hate those sonsabitches."

Merritt kept me moving toward my cell.

"Wait!" said the chubby blonde. "We want to meet her. It's Docket. I remember. What? You got something better to do?"

I couldn't help but laugh at that. No, I wasn't all that anxious to hurry into my cell and see that door close. Merritt looked down at me as I slowed to a stop.

"I'm Megan."

"I'm Kim," said the tall redhead.

Tough chick, lives in a trailer, and probably owns a Harley.

"Donna," said the chubby blonde.

Expired Twinkies and deep-fat fried anything.

"Celeste," said the young brunette.

Fancy name for a meretricious lush.

"Hey Loske, she's puny…better give her two blankets," said Kim.

"I'll bear that in mind," said the night guard.

Her name tag indicated she was officer Marty Loske. Unlike the others, she looked as if she'd bathed in the last week. I caught a whiff of their collective stench as Merritt led me into my cell. I turned around as the black bars grinded to a clank.

"Megan, you're going to be okay," said Merritt.

"Right, I know. Thanks."

He walked away with the two male officers.

The black steel door slammed shut, as did three metal bolts—the sound smashed against the concrete walls then reverberated within my skull.

Chapter 17

MY cell had bunk beds on each side with a sink and an uncovered toilet without a lid against the back wall between the bunks. I turned to sit on one of the beds, but the night guard standing outside my cell pointed to the bunk on the right, so I sat on it. It could've been worse—the bed was low enough that my feet could touch the ground, and I was short enough that I could sit up straight without hitting my head on the bunk above. Still, the mattress was thin and bare, and a thin cotton blanket was folded at the end of the bed; though, the pillow did have a zipped pillowcase. I hoped the paper cups at the sink were clean.

"Supper is served at six," said Loske.

"Yes, thank you," I said.

"The overhead lights go out at ten."

"Will there be any light?" I asked quietly, hoping to avoid taunting by the others.

"Yes, the light at my desk stays on."

Loske went back to her desk and flipped up the laptop lid and began to shuffle through a stack of papers. The open toilet gave the cell its stale, dank odor.

"So, did you murder someone?" asked Kim.

"No."

"Ah, c'mon."

"I have killed three men in self-defense, but I'm innocent of this homicide charge."

"They had a picture of that guy in the paper," said Celeste.

"What paper?" snapped Kim. "Ya gotta read the Omaha paper on the Internet now."

"That sucks," I said. "I liked having the real paper."

"Whatever," said Celeste. "I'm tellin' ya he was a look-er. Was that your boyfriend?"

"Yeah, well, I'd just broken up with him."

Why was I saying all this?

"That don't make sense," said Donna. "Then why would you kill him?"

"Right. There was no reason."

"So, you're in this shithole and you're really inno-cent...now that sucks," said Kim then she coughed.

I was getting their sympathy. Maybe they wouldn't har-ass me. And Kim had a smoker's hack. Thank God, I wouldn't be forced to smell that.

"Hey, those steaks at Custer's...Rick and me ate those once...damn good. Can't afford 'em though." Kim coughed again.

"The Frank Docket Steak," said Loske. "They're cheaper at lunch. We go there every Sunday. What is that marinade?"

"Bourbon...Jim Beam Black," I said.

"Now you're talkin'," said Donna. "Love some of that bourbon. Better than just plain whiskey."

"Ah, you're cracked," said Kim. "Scotch is the best."

The two women debated their tastes in booze for a while. I lay back on the bed and felt the edge come off my fear. I would live. Loske went back to studying her papers. She seemed to be cross-checking information on the com-puter with that on the forms. She frequently reached up to reposition her dark-rimmed glasses. She looked to be late forties, maybe early fifties with shoulder-length sandy-brown hair. I'd noticed a wedding band, so her kids were probably old enough to have mom away at night. Maybe they were even out of the house. Kim and Donna had moved on to red wine varieties. I didn't mind the chatter—it was the silence of the night that I dreaded. Celeste must have gone back to sleep for I heard her snort. That got Kim and Donna laughing. They acted like they could be drinking buddies.

"Have you ever had bourbon floats?" I chimed in.

"What's that?" asked Donna.

"You use bourbon instead of root beer with vanilla ice cream."

"Oh, that sounds good," said Kim.

"Too bad they don't serve those in the cafeteria," said Loske. "I know some cops who need to mellow out."

That got us all laughing. Somebody in human resources had done a good job with staffing this shift. I shoved my purse under my head—I'd been lying on my arm, but it had gone to sleep and was now starting to tingle. Who knows what had been on this pillowcase? Oh, shit, I needed to. I was normally a morning pooper, so why of all days was I out of whack? At least, I didn't have to poop in front of my fellow convicts. Maybe if I lay real still, I could hold out till dark. Nope. Damn. At least, they gave us toilet paper, though I soon decided it resembled sandpaper. Loske looked up once then kept her eyes on her work, which I appreciated. The two women had moved on to debating the best flavors of ice cream—at least till I flushed.

"Hey, lawyer, how'd you like shittin' in public?"

"Could be worse," I said.

"Yeah, like we have to crap in front of each other," said Kim with a touch of resentment in her voice.

I must have displaced her, so I said, "Well, they didn't want you fine ladies consorting with the likes of a murderer…afraid I might rub off on you."

Celeste snorted as Kim and Donna laughed.

"Hey, lawyer, I need one," said Kim.

"Sorry, I don't do criminal work," I said.

"Oh, yeah, too good for us?"

"When attorneys say they don't do a particular area of law, it means they don't know what the hell they're doing. I'd just screw up everything. Need a will? I'm good at those. If you get in a car accident, I do those. Bankruptcy, divorce…that's what I do."

"Well, if that bastard Rick doesn't drop his charges, I'm gonna be here all night. Then I'm gonna need a divorce lawyer."

"What did you do to him?"

"I hit him over the head with a bottle of tabasco sauce. Heh, heh. What a jerk."

"How could they tell the blood from the sauce?" I asked.

Silence. Uh-oh. I said something wrong.

Kim burst out laughing. "I hadn't thought of that."

"Well, he probably deserved it."

"Not as much as that Bert Bolger deserved it," said Loske. "That man was evil. He killed those two women back in 1968."

"And they just figured it out now?" asked Donna.

"Megan figured it out," said Loske. "Nobody could before her."

"And now you've got her locked up for a murder she didn't do…that's so effin' cracked," said Donna.

"He killed my baby."

Why did I say that? I need to keep my sob stories to myself.

"Oh, my God," said Celeste. "I remember that now. That was in, like, July."

Why did I say that? I needed to shut up. As if this wasn't miserable enough.

"How far along were you?"

I wasn't even sure who asked that. I rolled over to stare at the gray wall. Gray, the color of desperation. Gray, the color of my great humbling. God, I'm a sinner, we both know that. I've done my share of wrong. But am I supposed to learn something from this? I escaped punishment for my past sins, now I'm in jail for something I didn't do. I'd been committing adultery, for my divorce wasn't final till next month. I baited RT to grab his gun in anger then I blew him away as he turned his gun on me. Dobbs—I deserved to be here for him. I rendered judgment then impulsively shot him dead with RT's gun. I lied and put the blame on RT. Yeah, the sins were piling up. But I confessed and repented. God, I thought we were square on that. I'd done extra pro bono work, increased my charitable contributions, and tried to be a good citizen. Ah, it was useless—I didn't deserve mercy.

God had deserted me. Maybe he'd reconsider and reissue grace at another time. Until then, oh, shut up, someone was talking to me, I was fending for myself. Alone, without my Sweetie.

"Megan."

Oh, what the hell. Just leave me alone. I only wanted to see my mom. Did I? I'd sunk so low. I'd brought shame on her and Bill. Could I even look them in the eyes, tainted as I was? Better to just leave me be. I was Joseph K. playing out my Kafkaesque trial of judicial torture—unfair and unjust. Or was this my Edwin Drood story, a mystery forever to elude me: who killed Raz and why was I to blame for it?

"Megan?"

I hurled my purse as hard as I could against the bars. It clanged, silencing the room.

"Megan, stand up from your bed."

As Loske approached my cell, I rose.

"Megan, you need to calm down," she said.

"Right. Easy for you to say. Somewhere there's a murderer walking free while I'm rotting in jail. What if he goes after my family? Huh?"

"I know. But you need to keep your head. When you get out of here, you need to think and not let your anger overcome you."

I nodded.

"Now, if you can relax, we can serve supper."

"Okay. Sorry. I'm not angry with you or anyone here. I'll be calm. I don't mean to be a problem."

A few minutes later, I was sitting with a plastic tray on my lap, trying to shove warm mashed potatoes down my gullet. The roast beef was decent, but I struggled to find an appetite. The applesauce was warm by the time I tasted it and the carrots had cooled to lukewarm, which deposited an aftertaste in my mouth and made the whole meal gross.

Two officers leaned against the wall near my cell. They seemed to care little about the other jailbirds, for they were staring at me every time I looked up. Creeps. I wished they'd leave, but I guess I was a novelty, the Dexter attorney brought low. I set the tray on the floor and waited for instructions. Once the trays were collected, I lay back on the bed, lacking anything else to do.

I wondered if Mom and Bill were eating supper with Patty. I had certainly taken life for granted—a warm house, good food, family and friends who didn't stare at me like I was a freak. Well, okay, they had on a few occasions when I was feeling something. But I missed my comfy sofa and the satisfaction of a good, hot meal. I even missed bringing work home. I didn't even want to think how badly I'd miss my bed and my pillows. I just wanted the freedom to go home.

The officers wheeled the cart around the corner. The big, black door crashed shut. Then the bolts slammed across one by one, echoing though the room.

Since my outburst, the other women spoke quietly and only to each other. I started to feel lonelier than when we were talking.

"So, Donna, what are you in for?" I asked, hoping they hadn't decided to shut me out.

"Forgery…writin' bad checks," she said.

"Got a good lawyer?"

"Both me and Celeste got Rich Dewey."

"I know him. He's a good guy."

"Oh, you've worked with him?"

"No, always against him, mostly on auto accident injuries."

"You work on the other side and you still like him?"

"Well, he's fair…knows his stuff and he has a soul."

"Uh-huh. What does that mean?"

"It means he actually has compassion and listens to his conscience. But I thought he was trying to get away from criminal defense work."

"Don't know."

"Celeste, why are you here?"

"Possession."

As she was the scummy queen of bling, I thought she might have been in possession of a paying customer.

"Hey, can we get visitors in the evening?" asked Celeste.

"Not after five," said Loske.

After a couple of minutes of silence, Celeste said, "I'm sorry your baby died."

"Yeah."

"Yeah," said a third voice from the cell.

"Thanks, me, too," I said.

"Does it help knowing that you killed that murderer?" asked Loske.

"Not enough," I replied.

We were quiet for a while. The clock on the wall above Loske's desk said five after eight. I checked my watch. How cruel for a jail clock to run slow.

"Hey, when am I gonna find out if I get outta here?" asked Kim. "It's after eight."

Loske picked up the phone and talked in a low voice. After she hung up, she said, "Sorry, there aren't any releases scheduled for tonight."

I wasn't expecting one, but I still swallowed hard.

"Dammit it! That's it. I'm done with that shithead. Hey, lawyer…ah, Megan, got any cards with you? I'm getting rid of him."

"Sorry, no. But I'm in the phone book under Docket Law in Dexter."

It never occurred to me to bring business cards with me. I had a short list of objectives for my time here—head up and survive.

Kim began to pace back and forth in her cell, her shoes, which I hadn't noticed, scraping on the floor every time she turned around, which was often since the cells were only about twelve by twelve.

After a half hour of pacing, I asked her, "Do you really want to divorce him?"

"Rick. Yeah, he's a jerk."

"Now, divorce is serious shit, Kim. Do you have kids?"

"No, he don't want 'em."

"Do you?"

"Yeah."

I sat up on the edge of my bed. "That's a big problem. So here's a question for you—was today's action, the reason you hit him over the head with a condiment, a one-time deal? Or is it a pattern that shows his character?"

"Before I hit him, he shoved me to the ground then laughed at that. He's always bad-mouthin' me."

"You deserve better than that."

"I do?"

"Yes."

The bunk squeaked when she sat down.

"Would you be better off without him? Do you have a job? Friends and family to back you up? You don't need to answer, just think about those things. I have a horse— sometimes he's the most reliable male in my life."

Donna and Celeste sniggered.

"Kim, people don't improve. If your husband is a jerk, he'll become a total bastard at some point, short of a life-long, earth-shattering religious experience. It can happen. Is Rick a Christian?"

"Ha! No way."

"That's a shame. Without God, where is hope? Comfort? The chance to be a better person? I mean, I'm in this shithole and I don't know why, but God hasn't gone anywhere. Men leave, men cheat. Men do all sorts of terrible things—they can be as bad as women."

Even Loske laughed.

"But God stays. We're the ones who turn away from him. That's my lecture for the day…just some things to think about. By the way, I'm going through a divorce."

The room was quiet for a few minutes. The bunk creaked and Kim started pacing again.

"Hey, and you had a horse that got shot," said Donna.

"Yeah, he was a good one."

"Honey, I'll say this, your life ain't boring," said Donna.

"So true," I said as I laid my head on my purse.

Chapter 18

THE next hour passed with occasional small talk between me and my fellow jailbirds. I kept looking at the clock, thinking I didn't want the lights to go out. At a quarter till ten, I brushed my teeth and used the toilet. The sink dispenser contained only watery pink soap, but at least it contained that. Loske gave us a five minute warning then walked up and looked us over. She asked if any of us needed another blanket. I gave a small wave and she brought me another scratchy blanket. Small person, small wave, small brain to have ended up here, feeling smaller by the minute.

I pulled the blankets over my body and stared at the clock. When the lights went out, my breathing went shallow. The lamp on the desk drew my gaze as Loske sat down. I clutched my purse to my chest like it was my teddy bear Brownie and I was three years old on a stormy night. I worked to slow and deepen my breathing, but my innards were contracting into a ball.

Shouldn't I be able to handle this? I was scared when confronted by Bert Bolger and his switchblade; I was scared when RT reached for his gun; I was scared when Salt Eldritch chased me with a shotgun. But this was different—I was caged, I had no control except to choose if I wanted another blanket. Loske worked on at her desk; meanwhile, the other women were quiet. I was the only one who was frightened. What a scaredy-cat. Big me—give me gun and I had plenty of bravado, especially if I had others to back me up. But now alone, I trembled. I wondered if I'd sleep at all this night. At least I had these two blankets. What decade were they last washed? I pulled up my hood, tucked in my hair, and then laid my head on the pillowcase, unwilling to risk lice or any other icky substance.

Alone. I stared at the clock then at the lamp then back again. My friends and family were all comfortable in nice warm beds. I wasn't cold, not my skin anyway, but I felt cold inside. I wanted to sleep. Maybe Celeste would start snoring; I'd like to hear the sound of comfort, but all was silent. I couldn't even hear Loske turn the pages in her folder. Maybe I had dropped into a hole of silence and near darkness. Yet I kept staring at the light; just as it began to blur, Loske was standing, putting papers in a file, bending down to look at the computer screen. Another woman in a Sidney police uniform walked up to the desk. The clock showed midnight or just before. Loske closed her laptop.

"So, we've got the vigilante here tonight," says the new woman, with a round face and short dark hair. "It's all over the news."

"I have a feeling she shouldn't be here," said Loske. "You watch, when the truth comes out, heads will roll."

Someone in the next cell turn over in their bunk. As the women looked over, I closed my eyes.

"Any troublemakers?" asked the new woman.

"No, it's been fine," said Loske as she collected her laptop and files. "Here's the list. See ya tomorrow."

I jerked as the big, black door clanked shut.

The new woman studied the list for a few moments then walked toward the cells. I shut my eyes, not wanting conversation, especially with someone who was set against me. After a few minutes, I heard the desk chair pull out. I opened my eyes as the woman spread out her work and logged into her laptop. She glanced back my way, so I shut my eyes again and decided I would keep them shut.

Silence. Darkness, drifting into the black. Out in the open, the wind howling, alone, small, then I'm inside searching—no mother, no brother, no father, no faces. I go room to room, but they're all black as I search in the silence. Where is Scott? My Totty. His warm body, bent, twitching. I pull soft blankets over us and I scooch in tight. He coos, I tell him a story in the words I know. I try to straighten his bent body, but I can't, I strain and tug until he grabs me with his strong arms and pulls my head into his neck. I hear my father, he says what Scott is, but I don't understand. He is bent, I will fix him, I will keep him warm. Cooing, no words, never words, just smiles in a bright, warm room. My mother smiles at me. My father is gone. Then the blackness returns. No Totty, no mother. I'm lost, I'm alone, but I'm searching in the rooms and in the wind over rough ground of dirt and wild grass. She is dead they say, they lied, my father and my uncle, then my father is my uncle and my uncle is my father and they lie. They are in a bright room and they talk to me, but I am in a dark room. They fade away. Abandoned. I fall farther into the black.

The grating of the cell door jolted me to a sitting position. Not my cell. Two officers led a young woman into the other cell. I quickly resumed my sleeping position on my side. I heard her drag her feet. A drunk driver probably. She climbed the ladder at the end of the bed and flopped onto the mattress. The others muttered or turned over in their beds. The officers then talked to the woman at the desk. They left and the black door crashed shut.

I thought about my dream. Dark and light, Mom and Scott, loneliness and lies. My nightmare was the truth. It was after two in the morning. I began to drift away, but stayed long enough to watch the woman at the desk transform into Nurse Ratched. I jerked awake. The dark-haired woman at the desk looked over at me.

I turned to the wall and stared at the concrete blocks. The wall became a projection screen—I see Raz, bloody in the dirt, Brian, angry his fists clenched, Zane silent and staring away, Jay amused and smiling at me, says he likes adventure, too. Beulah cackles, holds up her wrist to show the watch I bought her; my mom adjusts the sling on her broken arm; Bill stomps across the floor as I bend over

James; I kneel over a stone in the ground with new grass over the dirt, "Sweetie" it says.

I opened my eyes to gray concrete. I wiped my eyes and tried to stay awake, but failed. At five, I rolled out of bed to use the toilet. The dark-haired woman watched me the whole time. I washed my hands then crawled back into bed. Stop staring at me, bitch. I squinted at her as she resumed her work at her laptop.

I awakened to sounds in the next cell. The clock read half past six. Thank you, God, for getting me through the night. I rolled over on my back, and the verse came into my head. "Be still and know that I am God." That was in Psalms somewhere. I shut my eyes and tried to feel him. Tell me the lesson I'm supposed to learn, God. You give life meaning, please make this horrible time worth something, I beg of you. I wasn't being "still," but it comforted me to think of God, who would get me through all of this.

The overhead lights popped on. I grinned when Celeste muttered an obscenity. The lights boosted my spirits. I rolled out of bed and brushed my teeth. Then I realized I'd slept in my eye make-up. I washed my face with the runny soap then used a towelette from my purse to clean around my eyes. Then I brushed my hair and tried to straighten my rumpled clothes. Then a thought made me freeze—what if the judge waited till my Friday hearing to set bail? Oh, God. Could I take another night here?

Officers, they weren't really humans to me, just indistinct men who thought all of us jailbirds as trash, wheeled in our breakfasts. One officer handed me my tray. It was two small boxes of cereal, Wheaties and Raisin Bran, why do they care if we poop more? A glass contained the milk and a Styrofoam cup contained coffee. Why did they want us stimulated? The officer took note from his pocket and set it next to my bowl. He was a middle-aged man who had probably lost his beat to a younger cop. He smiled at me, stunning me. What was this about?

"Please flush it," he said then turned away.

A few moments later the big, black door crashed shut.

I quickly read the note which said: "Keep your head up." It was signed, "Sidney & S.P. Admirers." I felt a sliver of hope. When the guard wasn't looking, I tossed it in the toilet and flushed it.

"You all right over there, lawyer?" asked Donna.

"Hangin' in," I said. "Had a lovely night in my lovely bed."

They were still laughing when the night guard walked up to my cell. Her name tag indicated her name was Trumboldt.

"What is this crap?" she said. "What did you say?"

"Anything I say can be used against me in court," I replied.

Snickering from my cellmates made her face turn red. She glared at me. I looked closely at her nose—I knew that shape—she was a Bolger. Suddenly, I knew I was an inch from trouble.

"I meant no disrespect, officer," I said.

She stood staring at me, with one hand on her keys, and the other on her night stick. The big, black door opened. She backed away from my cell and turned around. Sergeant Merritt walked toward us.

"Is there a problem here?" he asked.

"No, officer," I said.

"Open this door," he said.

Trumboldt unlocked the door then turned without a word and went back to her desk.

I flashed a grin at him as he led me out of the cell and out of the room. The big, black door crashed shut, but now I was on the other side. He paused in the hallway and handed me a breakfast sandwich. I gasped.

"I figured you wouldn't be eating well," he said.

I gulped down the sandwich as we walked on.

"How are you?"

I shrugged. "Tolerable. Not a place for a good night's sleep."

"Is it noisy?"

"No, just disturbing. By the way, where are we going?"

He smiled. He had become my new big brother; he was definitely looking out for me.

"You have a visitor."

My pulse quickened as I felt a burst of hope. He led me to a room, which to my shock was beige instead of gray.

"Your attorney will be permitted to see you later."

I thanked him and he closed the door behind me. Officers stood at each end of the small room with a table running the length of the room, meant to seat four on each side. Only one person sat on the visitors' side. Her smile warmed me deep inside. I sat down across from her then grabbed her hands—hands that were always warm.

"Hi, Mom, thanks for coming."

"Of course. This is the earliest they would let me come. Are you okay?"

"Yeah, anxious to get out of here, but who knows when that will be."

"Won't you be able to post bail this morning? And how do we do that?"

"Well, the judge doesn't report till one o'clock. And then it's up to him to decide whether to set bail today or wait for my Friday hearing."

"Another night?"

"It's possible. Now I put extra money in my checking account and I added your name to it, so you'll be able to post my bail, even if they accept only cash."

She must have seen something in my face for she flushed with emotion.

"Are you, um, doing okay?" She wanted some specifics and was hoping for something encouraging.

"I'm in a cell by myself. Sergeant Merritt fixed that for me. He's doing what he can for me. There are three other women, well, a fourth came in during the night. They've actually been a godsend. They're a rough trio, but we've had some laughs."

She nodded. I was proud of her fortitude, but I could see pain in her eyes.

"Mom, if this is supposed to be some sort of wake up call, what am I supposed to learn or do? What lesson do I take from being punished when I'm innocent?"

"I don't know. Maybe just endure…wait and hope."

"Wrap it up folks," said the nonhuman in the navy uniform.

Mom took a book from her lap and pushed it across the table to me. The officer closest to us stepped forward. Mom handed him the book.

"It's a diary from the Civil War," she said.

"Really?" The officer inspected it then said, "The handwriting looks hard to read." He set it down on the table in front of me.

"You'll get the hang of it," she said.

I picked up the book just as the other officer terminated the visit. I leaned across the table and we hugged. The door opened behind me. I held her gaze as I backed toward the door.

Merritt was waiting for me in the hall.

"Rachel wishes she could be here, but she's out on the road this morning. She did leave this for you."

He handed me a paper sack which contained five large dark chocolate bars.

"I'm going to be very popular with my cellmates."

"We better get back."

He led me back to the cells, even escorting me past Trumboldt.

"She doesn't like me," I whispered. "She looks like a Bolger." Then in a normal voice I said, "Can I pass these out? Rachel even checked to find out how many cellmates I had."

Trumboldt stood by helplessly as I handed the chocolate through the bars to Kim, who passed them out, even handing one to the drunk in the top bunk who barely managed to hang her head over the edge of the bed to see me and take the chocolate. Trumboldt led me to my cell then slammed the door. Merritt followed her to her desk. He leaned over slightly and spoke to her. She nodded and he left. The big, black door clicked shut.

"Oh, my God, this is so good," said Celeste.

"Oh, yeah," said Donna. "But damn, it's gonna give me heartburn. Hey, who was your visitor?"

"My mom," I said.

I sat down to eat the chocolate. Though the breakfast trays had been cleared, my two unopened cereal boxes had been left on my bed. After I finished my chocolate, I started nibbling on the cereal, mostly for something to do. Soon Trumboldt was replaced by a guard in her early thirties with dark, shoulder-length hair and glasses. She glanced at the list as she walked up to inspect us.

"Hello, all," she said. "I hope your night was reasonable. Let me know if you need something…who knows, I might even give it to you." She moved past my cell and looked me over as I sat on the edge of my bed. Her uniform name plate identified her as Kay Steenson.

"Rachel sends her regards," she said.

"Thank you," I said.

I lay back on my bed and quickly fell asleep. I awoke an hour later, thinking of my mom. She said I must endure. Yeah, I needed to endure this unjust condemnation. Those two cops, Baldy and Red, arrested me, but it was that shithead prosecutor and that limp dick judge that sent me here. My anger began to build—I wanted revenge on all of them. I'd spent one night here, and I could spend another. I could do it. I could endure. Anger chased my fear away.

A few minutes later, a cop came to get Kim.

"That effin' husband of mine sure took his time," she said as she put on her coat outside the cell.

"Kim, what are you going to do?" I asked.

"Go stay at my sister's."

"Before you leave Rick, make sure he has dropped the charge against you."

"Yeah, right, I will. See you, jailbirds."

After she left, I started looking through the diary.

"Hey, what was that book you came back with?" asked Celeste.

"It's a diary a woman wrote during the Civil War."

We were interrupted by two cops entering the room. Both Donna and the late-night arrival left.

"Well, go ahead," said Celeste, "tell me what she writes. I used to be good in school…liked history classes the most."

I told her what I knew about the story then found where Mom had left off. I read through a few pages and either summarized it or cited the passages directly. Officer Steenson stopped working to listen. I spent the rest of the morning telling the story of Kate, her father Stuart, and her soldier brother Matthew who had been injured. He and an officer were captured by a couple of Rebel scouts. But the scouts got drunk and Matthew and the officer Tom escaped after killing the scouts as they slept.

My narrative lasted till eleven when Celeste was taken for an interview with Rich Dewey. She returned then I was summoned to talk to my attorney. I met Stan in the hall-way. He said he had nothing to report, except that he'd plead my case to the judge and try to get me out on bail as soon as the judge arrived at one o'clock. I returned to my stale, gray cell.

Soup and crackers on plastic trays arrived at noon. Afterward, I read a bit more from the diary, but quit when I got anxious about my release.

"Hey, Celeste, when do you get to leave?"

"Rich didn't know. He said they're trying to pin more on me than pot."

"Meth? You don't do meth, do you?"

Silence and time for a lecture. I told her about Sheila Ritter and her demise.

"Celeste, don't become that woman. Sheila was on her way to ruining her family and her life. Then she parked her car on the railroad tracks. She left a good man and a good daughter."

I stood at the edge of the cell and whispered, "Celeste, come here."

"Yeah," she whispered back.

I could see her hands on the bars at the edge of her cell. Steenson watched us, but didn't interfere.

"I know someone you could talk to. He's working the meth and cocaine problems in the area. He's not interested in arresting you. He only wants the dealer. He's not local law."

"Who is he?"

"He's undercover. Listen, I know of four deaths related to using it, dealing it, hiding it and another who just got in the way. Just think about it then call me at my office."

"How would it help me?"

"I don't know. I can't promise you anything. Hell, I couldn't even keep myself out of jail."

"I'll think about it."

Chapter 19

ONE o'clock came and went. The minutes ticked by. I sat upright, with my best Victorian posture, ready to deal with whatever came. Still, the wait was excruciating. Celeste's breathing grew heavy and steady. She lacked hope for release, I ached with it. Two o'clock came and went.

God in heaven, please deliver me from this gray hell-hole.

At two-seventeen, the telephone rang and I sprang to my feet. Steenson answered it, spoke briefly, hung up the phone, and then looked at me and nodded.

Finally!

I didn't have anything to pack up except for the diary, so I folded the two blankets. Soon, the big, black door opened and a Sidney officer came to escort me out. I looked back at Celeste, who was standing at the bars.

"See ya," she said.

"I hope I will."

As I left, I said goodbye to Steenson then paused to catch the big, black door. I let it close with a click. Merritt met me at the end of the hall.

"Funny thing, but someone seems to have reached Judge Shelton in the Canadian wilderness. He called Judge Turvey and the bail was quickly set. It's fifty thousand. I was surprised it was that low. Judge Shelton probably had a hand in that. Your mom has already paid what's due, so you are a free woman."

A free woman. What wonderful words.

We passed through a second big, black door. Stan was waiting for me.

"Your hearing has been postponed till next Friday," said my attorney. "Judge Shelton plans to handle your case from here on out. However, with his connection to your family, he'd need to recuse himself from a trial. But for now, you're free to go."

Free to go. What wonderful words.

A few minutes later, I pushed open the front doors, smelled the fresh air and gasped at the throng of admirers. I wondered if anyone remained in Dexter. After I hugged my mom, it took me fifteen minutes to greet and thank them all. Even James sat on a bench in the warm sunshine. Beulah stood with one of several signs that read: "Free Megan!" I managed to dodge the reporters that stood with my fans on the ninety thousand steps. Bud, Jack, and Drew, another Docket cowboy, managed to block their paths to me. In time, Patty hustled me through the crowd to Uncle Bill's pickup, which was parked illegally in front of the station. I waved as we sped away.

Of course, the first thing on my agenda was to take a long shower. I washed again and again, never satisfied I was clean. I finally conceded when the water turned cold. Mom had already returned from the bank after completing a second transaction. Then I made arrangements for Melanie to drive to Sidney and pay Celeste's bail.

A flop onto my bed felt wonderful. Mom laughed when I made a snow angel on my denim comforter. Soon, I was down in the kitchen gobbling up a second, more adequate lunch. I called Vonny, even though Derek or James would have told her the news.

Bill grilled steaks for supper. We invited Beulah, the Wilsons, and the Ritters.

Kayla kept probing me for details, but I didn't really want to talk about it. I described the jail as gray and stale then added that my cellmates were funny and also scared.

Later, James took me aside in the hall. "I'm so sorry, I've been fretting over it…but when the cops asked me…I had to say that I saw you run out there with a gun."

"Oh, James, don't you worry about that. I freely gave up the gun at the scene."

"Still, I hated to testify against you."

"It would do both of us more harm if you lied about what you saw. So come on back to the family room and relax."

As we headed down the hall, his limp appeared more pronounced. Aware that I was watching him, he paused and motioned me forward in a gentlemanly manner so he could walk behind me.

By eight-thirty, exhaustion set in and I excused myself from my guests and went to bed. I couldn't wait to crawl in between those sheets. It was heavenly—clean and comfy and safe—everything jail was not.

The next morning, I went for a run and arrived at the office by eight. My first appointment wasn't until eleven. I resolved not to mention jail unless propriety demanded it. I wasn't even sure why Chuck Hadley wanted to see me. We'd managed to stave off both bankruptcy and divorce, at least while he continued in counseling.

"I hope you're…ah, doing better," Chuck said. "I know Dale Turvey, that judge. He goes by Dale in our gambling anonymous sessions, but someone told me he was a judge. He'd gotten into some bad debt and his wife left him. He likes the casinos on the reservations, but mostly some of those illegal online gambling sites. Anyway, I just thought you might like to know."

"You mean that I might like to spread that news around…get back at him for locking me up? Well, I don't plan to start any scandal-mongering to get my revenge, though it's true I never should have been put in jail."

We discussed his debts for a few minutes then he left. A half hour later, Beulah called, asking me about the gambling rumors.

"I've never met that judge, never got the chance to argue my case." I said. "Chuck seems to know him pretty well. No, I don't plan to stoop to revenge, no matter how wrong and how unjust it was. I have a few things to do then I'll be over for lunch."

Revenge wasn't Christian. But I wasn't going to stop someone else from acting on my behalf, especially if the news sounded true. To prevent the rumor would be protecting that limp dick judge—that was beyond my duty. Well, maybe. Still, half of Dexter would hear about that judge's indiscretions by the time I set foot in Custer's. I suppose people were bored, for all of western Cheyenne County would know the news by suppertime. I bet the news of my incarceration had spread even faster.

When I returned from a mobbing by friends at Custer's, Rachel was waiting for me at my office.

"Thanks for those chocolate bars—it was a big hit with me and my cellmates," I said.

"My pleasure. Sorry I couldn't visit you, only authorized personnel are allowed. But anyway, I thought you'd want an update. Tate did a good job of directing the State Patrol where to investigate. We found disturbed ground, like someone swept away his tracks with a branch...and he or she did a good job. We didn't find more than a heel print in Pooper's Canyon, though we think that's where he fired from."

"I never saw anyone, I just fired into the ground where I thought the shots came from," I said.

"Right, shots. Why does the shooter fire the second time when he's already hit his mark?"

"That second shot felt like it came at me, but I dropped to the ground. Is a Glock accurate from a distance of what...seventy or eighty feet?"

"We calculate it at eighty-four feet. And yes, the shooter was obviously accurate because he hit his mark."

"They can tell from the wound if a shot was fired from close or far, right?"

"Right, that's another reason why the prosecutor was premature in jailing you. A lot of people are pissed about it."

"Little good that does me."

"Oh, I don't know. I know some cops who are ticked off at that prosecutor. And if a man has a good deal of scrutiny on him, well, sometimes he slips up."

"What are you saying?"

"Maybe we can catch that prosecutor at something. I don't know too much about him...but I will."

"An acquaintance of mine told me Judge Turvey has gambling issues. I told my informant that I wasn't interested in seeking revenge. Of course, he immediately went over to Custer's and blabbed it to everyone there."

"Well, we'll see what happens. Oh, and there's an internal investigation on the brutality of the arrest. For now, those two yokels are working tedious desk jobs in North Platte."

"Oh, now isn't that too bad," I said.

"And maybe we can get some dirt on that prick of a prosecutor."

"I sure don't want it to come back on me, especially with a pending charge. I plan to avoid the appearance that I was out for revenge, though I'd love to see them suffer."

"Oh, and we're also tracking sales of Glock handguns."

"Strange, but Raz told me he recently bought a Glock."

"They're quite common. However, we did get a search warrant for his half of the duplex while you were, ah...indisposed. But we didn't find a Glock or any other weapon."

"Well, I'll probably lose that tenant," I said. "Stan told me they released the body this morning, so Nori will take him back to Omaha. I doubt she'd want to stay out here."

I spent a quiet Friday evening, but I was ready for the Cowpoke on Saturday night. It rained lightly most of Saturday, which was good for our dry land, though too late for the crops. Yet it prevented me from riding Strider after I left work. Still, the day went by quickly, as days do when you're not in jail. Tina joined us at the Cowpoke, now that she was finally able to wrap up her job and move in the Wilson house with Derek. Johnny Two Rivers set up a big table to accommodate my gang. Vonny spent the evening talking and dancing with Tony. I danced with several different partners, including Bill, Derek, Bud, Drew, and Jack. Once again, Jay caught me leaving the dance floor when a slow song came on.

"You figured out that I'm not really Faust, do you know who I think you are?"

"Do I dare ask?" I said.

"Lady Chatterley," he said as he pulled me in close.

"How's that?"

"Because you've been disappointed in your man."

"Hmm. I guess so. And she found a replacement."

"But he also disappointed you."

"Actually, it's replacements plural. And I'm not a lady as Raz pointed out. That's why I punched him."

"He was an idiot not to appreciate you."

"Well, thank you for not calling me Madame Bovary. She couldn't see what a good man she had. And she really needed a constructive hobby."

"Her head was full of silly romantic notions. You're not silly."

"Thank you, but I sure make my share of mistakes…with men, in particular."

"I wouldn't disappoint you. I've heard about Brian and Zane. I don't freeze up."

"I need air," I said, yet I let him back me into the dark corner.

"You've said that before. So I come here every Saturday night just waiting to get you in my arms," he said in a soft, deep voice.

I didn't get a chance to reply before his lips were on mine. I did love men, at least those who were hard and strong in all the right ways. And this guy was getting under my skin, which scared the hell out of me. He let me come up for air before he kissed me again. He didn't stop kissing me till the song ended.

"When are you going to call me?" he asked.

"I-I don't know. It's too soon."

Back at the table, Vonny and Tony seemed engrossed in each other. How long had it been since I felt absorbed by someone? When Tony left for the restroom, I sat down next to Vonny.

"There are clean sheets in the guest bedroom," I said in her ear.

She gave me a pinch, but we both knew it was on her mind.

"Ouch. Well, your house is suddenly crowded and Tony lives in those apartments all the other cowboys live in…not your scene. You can stay over if you want. I'll leave the front door unlocked till midnight."

"Well, we'll see. Hey, that salesman is more than a little interested in you."

"Yeah, and I'm hardly ready for him or anyone."

Vonny and Tony were gone by the time I went down for breakfast. After church and lunch, I took Strider out for a run. I stayed clear of the area of the shooting. That day seemed like a nightmare I just kept dreaming. Even though I was out of jail and Raz was dead, the nagging sense of danger persisted; I couldn't get a feel for where or why or from whom the threat came, but it endured. And a question still haunted me—what was I meant to learn from my time in jail?

Chapter 20

THE week was full of appointments. The best one was unscheduled—Stan Spurlock and Sgt. Merritt arrived mid-morning on Wednesday.

"Good news, Megan," said Stan waving a piece of paper. "This is a full release of any and all charges against you."

"Lab tests show that the bullet that killed Raz did not come from your gun," said Merritt. "So you are clear."

"Well, no kidding," I said squelching the more colorful language in my head. "It makes me all the angrier that the prosecutor didn't wait a few more days before he decided I was guilty."

"There's a buzz going around about that judge," said Stan.

"I had nothing to do with that. I've heard the rumor, but it didn't come from me and it wasn't spread by me. I'm not going to dirty my hands with revenge. No way...I'm the model citizen."

"I wonder if there will be a scandal that comes out against Larry Peake?" mused Stan.

"I wouldn't mind that, but it won't come from me," I said.

That news was expected—it was an afternoon visitor that surprised me.

Celeste Percival arrived for her three o'clock appointment a few minutes late. In a strange way, I was pleased to see her. After some small talk, she confirmed she was related to Junior Percival of Dexter, a mechanic at Smokey's sales yard. She looked healthier and cleaner, though she smelled of cigarette smoke. She wore jeans, a simple blue top, and denim jacket; I pegged her at about twenty-two or so.

"I'm grateful that you bailed me out, though I'm not able to pay you back just now...my family was tryin' to come up with the money but..."

"Don't worry about it. I keep a fund from my dad's life insurance policy for certain good causes."

"I don't know if I'm a good cause," she said, twisting her hair through the fingers of her left hand.

"Hey, I was wondering, did you sleep that night in the jail? Everybody in your cell seemed so quiet," I said.

"Oh, hell, what a horrible night. I slept, like, some, not much. What about you?"

"It took me hours to get to sleep then I had nightmares so I regretted it. Yeah, hell is right."

"The chocolate was good."

We laughed.

"I've been eating a lot of it since then," I said. "Did you notice how everything was gray in that place? Gray meant hell, chocolate meant hope."

"Oh, yeah, yeah."

"So you've come to see me. Does that mean you want to talk to that guy I told you about?"

"I don't think I'm ready to talk to any cops. They scare me, especially after that day in jail with 'em."

"There are some cops that scare me, though some are my friends. So, um, you were picked up for possession of what drug?"

She looked at me then looked down at the floor. She wanted to talk or she wouldn't have come.

"Was it meth? There's a lot in the area right now. And some undercover cops."

"No, I got picked up for pot, but they put me in jail, I think, 'cause I had some cocaine in my system."

"Maybe Rich Dewey can get you off on that—claim you ingested it accidentally."

"But that meth—no, I've been warned off that stuff."

"Are you addicted to anything?"

"Nah. Maybe just cigarettes."

"You should get off those."

"I know."

She started twirling her hair again.

"You want to tell me something. We're fellow jailbirds, remember?"

She chuckled then took a single page of a computer printout from her purse, unfolded it and handed it to me. It was a newspaper account of the capture of the Four Bastards, complete with their photos.

"I saw his picture and I know it's him. He said his name was Mark. He sells me pot when I have the money. I've heard he sells meth, too. It says here that his name is Brett Webster."

Holy shit! Was there some connection between the cross burnings and the meth trade?

"Now, I don't wanna get in trouble with those people…so you won't tell anyone I said anything, will you?"

"No, absolutely not. Sometimes the police just need to know who to start watching then they can uncover their own evidence. I'll even strike your name from our appointment calendar. You weren't here." I took out one of my business cards and wrote my cell phone number on the back. "If you think of something or hear anything that might be helpful, call my personal number, okay? But write down your name and address and phone for me. I may have some other questions."

After she left, I walked out into the lobby to Glenda's desk. I walked behind it and turned the laptop toward me. I deleted the entry for Celeste Percival. Glenda looked at me quizzically.

"She wasn't here, right?"

"Right," said Glenda.

I went back to my office to think, so I shut the door. I called my Denver FBI contact, Robert Foxworthy on my office phone.

He didn't even greet me, he just said, "Uh-oh. You're calling on your secure land line. I'm glad you're out of jail. So, what's up?"

"Did the CIA kill Raz?"

"Whoa! You get right to it. I've actually been in contact with my buddy in the CIA. If they did it, I was going to make sure you didn't take the fall for them. But no, they deny killing him. They aren't sure about a hit man for Hezbollah…that was your next question. One could have been hired, they don't know."

"All right then…so tell me about Jason Andrew Young. Is he really State Patrol?"

"Yes, he's actually pulling double duty—he also reports to us, under contract."

"So if I learned something related to the drug dealing in the area, who should I go to?"

"Well, Tony or Jay. Are you questioning the local State Patrol?"

"Let me back up. Do you remember Rachel McNeill?"

"Yes, State Patrol in your area."

"She was involved with that scummy DEA agent RT Martin."

"That you shot and killed."

"Right. Now I don't know how much she knows about the people who were connected to RT. But the Webster brothers, Brett and Nick, were once suspected of working with RT, but no case was brought against them. They could suspect her of knowing too much. And I found someone who bought pot and cocaine from Brett Webster."

"I see."

"And those Webster brothers were part of the Four Bastards, the local name for the four guys captured for the cross burning."

"Great name. So there's a connection between a cross burner and drug dealing."

"Now here's the tricky part—one of the Four Bastards is the son of a local State Patrol officer, Randall Waters."

"And you're wondering if local officers would feel the conflict."

"And then there's this—Officer Waters has been around and investigated several incidents around here. He always seemed very by the book, very professional. Now just being near him scares me and that started before his son was even implicated in the cross burning."

"You are The Woman Who Feels."

"So of the Four Bastards, Waters made bail right away."

"Well, they're all out on bail now. Of course, three of those guys are still recovering from those gunshots."

"I only shot two of them."

"You know, Megan, you've been exonerated. You could back out."

"I could."

"But you won't. I'll let you know if I find out anything new."

After I finished my call to Robert, I fished Jay's card out of my purse then called him.

"Shock of shocks, you called me, but from work," Jay said. "Not very romantic."

"Can you come see me this afternoon?" I asked.

"Just say when."

"My, you're easy. Aren't you supposed to be selling something?"

"I'd sell myself to you."

"Let me see if I have any loose change."

"Funny. But it's nearly five now. I could come over for supper."

"No."

"Someday, Megan Docket, you're going to let me woo you."

"Well, not today, Romeo. I want to talk about murder."

"I'll be there in ten minutes."

He was here in five.

"Nice office," he said as Glenda escorted him in, leaving him with a Danish and cup of coffee. "I've been in some that were the size of broom closets."

"It was my dad's. I took it over after he died."

After I shut the door, I summarized my conversation with Robert Foxworthy.

"So, I need a favor," I said.

"Are you sure you want to owe me?"

"It's your concern, too. I need to know which of the Four Bastards were out of jail when Raz was shot and who was mobile."

"All of them were out. In fact, Mick Spittle never went to jail. He was still in the hospital when his family posted bail. As for mobile, only Jake Waters could run, though the others could drive. What are you thinking?"

"Could one of them have been a hit man for Raz?" Then it struck me. "Could he have been aiming at me? I stepped to the side just as the shot was fired." My stomach cart wheeled. "He shot twice."

"How's that?"

"Why would the gunman shoot a second time if he already hit his mark? Was that second shot or both shots meant for me? I've angered all of the Four Bastards. In the movies, a trained assassin displaces after he's hit his mark."

"I agree that a hit man for Raz would have no reason to kill you, unless you saw him. He'd want you to take the blame for the shot, as you did, even if it was only temporary."

"It seems like an odd coincidence that they used the same model of gun as mine. And why and how does the gunman know where to find either of us right then?"

Why can't I have the kind of enemy that just wants to sue me? Was I the target?

"If you're not carrying a gun, I suggest you start. And the front door here should be kept locked." He studied me for a few moments. "I don't know if you were the objective. But we need to keep track of the Four Bastards."

"And now we have Brett Webster as a part of both the cross burning and dealing drugs."

"I'd like to interview the source of your information about Webster," he said.

"Sorry, I promised confidentiality. But I could ask questions for you."

"Ask about dates and locations for the transactions, the drugs sold, other involved parties...you could probably figure out the questions. But right now I'm concerned about your welfare."

I got up from the big cherry wood desk and walked over to the window. God in heaven, was I the target? At least for the moment, I didn't feel in danger. Yet I felt Jay's approach without seeing or hearing him. He placed his hands on my hips and pulled me back from the window. His lips locked on mine, melting all the cartilage in my spinal column.

"I feel obligated to guard your body," he said into my ear.

Late in the day, I couldn't smell his Zest, but I inhaled him. Damn, there went the cartilage in my knees. Yes, no, I wouldn't give in. I was legally divorced on October eleventh. I planned to be the respectable woman I should have been, despite having already dated two men and getting arrested and spending a day in jail. Meanwhile, we kissed again.

"I need to start packin', but the police still have my gun."

He ran his hand over my abdomen. "Here's a six pack right here." He smiled. "What is this fabric? It's really nice." His hand kept moving.

Oh, help.

"And there's a scar probably right here."

I backed away from him.

"But not as deep as the scar inside. Then there's those disappointing men. They haven't helped. And there's this guy who interests you, but keeps pushing when you're dealing with so many things. How thoughtless."

I grinned at him.

"I can loan you a gun till then."

"But that's not legal," I said.

"Keep it hidden. I won't tell. Give me two minutes, it's in my car."

I sat down at my desk to think while he was gone. He quickly returned with a Smith & Wesson automatic and a box of cartridges. Now that I sat at my desk, he was forced to sit in one of the client chairs.

"Check it out, see how it feels," he said.

"Listen, Jay. I've dated for kicks…but I'm done with that. I'd rather spend my evenings with Charles Dickens. The thing is, you don't live here and I'm not interested in a long-distance relationship. My law firm, my life is here, not Denver, not Omaha."

"I'm going to be around here for a while."

"Then what?"

"I don't know. My condo, my job is in Omaha, for now. Won't you give me a chance?"

"No, it's too risky. I've been discouraged…to put it mildly. But thanks for the gun."

That was his cue to leave. After gazing at me with his intense blue eyes for a few moments, he rose.

"Yes, I'll be at the Cowpoke," I said.

"Now, that's teasing."

"I never said I didn't like your interest in me."

"Still teasing."

"Okay, I'll stay home."

"No, come. May I eat supper with you?"

"I'd like that."

He studied me for a moment then left. I did what I needed to do, but it made me feel lousy. At least, I'd see him at the Cowpoke.

Chapter 21

THAT evening, I read the Civil War diary while Patty watched *Casablanca*. Kate, the daughter, was feeling doubtful about her engagement to the Confederate cavalry leader. Meanwhile, her brother Matthew and an officer had escaped their captors and enlisted the help of two Virginia plantation slaves, a husband and wife, to help them get to the Barton family home in northern Virginia. The two injured men promised the slaves refuge if they helped them. Matthew makes it home, but discovers his father had been stricken with a heart attack. Kate realizes she likes the officer, Lieutenant Tom; although, she thinks it's foolish, for he's likely to go back to war and death once he's healed of his wound. And she was still dealing with the death of her mother, the illness of her father, and the brisk ferry trade. She thinks it's all too much.

Mom and Bill came over about eight. She obviously had something on her mind, so I put away the diary.

"Nori's back," she said.

"Well, she needs to get her things out of the duplex," I replied.

"I saw her this afternoon. She's coming back to work here."

"What the hell?" said Patty, as she paused the movie. "She can't get a job in Omaha, the U.S. capital of employment? Beth, it's demented."

"Mom, she doesn't even work at Wal-Mart, I've checked. And her name's actually Rana and probably not Peters. Why would she want to live here? It doesn't make sense. Mom, console her, but don't trust her. And don't let on that we know she's a liar and a fake."

Mom and Bill stared at me, but it was true. Maybe because she had turned hostile to me, I was inclined to think the worst of her. After Bill and Mom left, I read a little more of the diary. Kate becomes angry when Tom starts to press her. Then one night, he comes to her as she is preparing for bed. Though not old, maybe less than thirty, she'd been a widow for several years. She is offended, but willing to be seduced. She writes, "He did things my husband never thought to do." I flushed warm when I read that. Of course, I read on. After that, Kate pushes him away in anger, though not before visiting him in his bed the next morning.

I went to bed wishing I hadn't pushed Jay away. I wanted him to make me flush warm, no, hot. Yet it was foolish—just as Kate knew Lt. Tom would be forced back into battle, I knew Jay would return home to Omaha.

The rest of the week, I toted Jay's gun, worked every evening, and stayed away from the diary—it wasn't good for me.

On Saturday, I worked during the day, but left in time to take Strider for a ride. This time, for the first time since it happened, I went out to the scene. The yellow tape was gone; the police had completed their investigation. The only arrest they made was wrong. The murderer was free, though his identity and his motive remained mysteries. It incensed me that my childhood playground had been defiled by a murder. This was the land where Derek, Vonny, and I had played games, invented pioneer stories, and wondered at how the wind and water had created the bluffs and buttes.

I led Strider right up to where Raz was shot then looked into the west. Beverly's voice wasn't here, but a mighty blast of wind slapped at me as I steered us westward to where the shooter must have been. We walked up to the edge of the canyon and looked down. For years we laughed at the name Derek gave the ditch after a very young Vonny became in urgent need. Pooper's Canyon was now the besmirched hiding place of a murderer. I yelled into the howling wind. Strider took a few steps back. I stopped yelling, but the wind persisted, lashing at me till I needed to lean forward in the saddle and grip the horn with both hands. Using his good sense, Strider turned us around and trotted back to the Seven Dwarfs. He halted behind one of the Dwarfs, out of the thrust of the wind.

What? What was I supposed to know?

As soon as I came into the house, I went into the study and called Jay.

"Oh, are you calling to tell me you won't be at the Cowpoke?" he asked.

"No. I'll be there and I'll be disappointed if you don't back me into that dark corner. But listen, Nori has come back to live. Doesn't that seem strange to you? I mean, yeah, Lebanon is probably a place to avoid, but why not stay in Omaha? She told my mom she needed the job at Wal-Mart. That's bull. She doesn't work there and probably never has. I had someone follow her once. Check out the third turn north of Highway 28 to Sidney, that's where she went. And has anybody checked on the empty Zimmer house lately? The Krauss Corporation bought that land but who knows if anybody is maintaining that house. We need to find out who Nori Peters or Rana Abboud really is and what she's up to. Once, she mentioned spending time in Nevada."

"Did someone tell you something?"

I couldn't say the wind inspired me, so I just said, "I have a hunch."

"I've heard about those."

"Nori Peters and Officer Waters—what's with them?"

"Randy Waters? Is that another hunch?"

"Yeah, it is. Okay, I'm gonna shower and I'll see you in a bit."

"I won't tell you what I'm thinking."

"That's best. See ya."

At the Cowpoke, Patty, Paul, and Kayla joined me, Mom, and Bill. As Jay sat down next to me, he glanced around the table.

"No James tonight?"

"Derek said he was tired," I replied.

After dinner, Kayla went to the jukebox. This time, no cowhand approached her. Word must have gotten out that she was under the protection of Bill Docket. A dozen or so cowboys sat in the back tables, in their jeans and boots and best shirts, close-shaved and oozing so much testosterone it created a haze that hung in the air, visible only to women. Poor souls—there weren't enough women in the area for them. I could have walked among them, tapped a shoulder and he would have followed me to the dance floor and to my bed whenever I asked. I could have kept a stable of them, one for each night of the week, and given up on ever dating anyone seriously, or of preserving decent reputation.

Jay must have noticed, for he said, "Studying the studs."

"Bill's thinking of promoting one or more of his. I think it's good for morale. It's hard to keep the good ones."

"Why? I thought some men would like that life."

"I think some do. But the pay isn't great, the benefits are zilch, the hours are long, and worst of all, you have all those young, horny men and too few women. Look around, the only females here are kids and married women."

"And you."

"Well, I'm planning to strike up a relationship with Larry McMurtry. I haven't read the prequels to Lonesome Dove yet."

"You are behind. Do you work every evening?" he asked.

"I have been lately."

"Then you're taking on too much work."

"Maybe. So what makes you Mr. Literature?"

"I was an English major in college, but I couldn't figure out many career options, so I got my master's degree in criminal justice."

"I was a lit major, too. But I always knew I'd be going to law school."

"Daddy's girl."

"I guess so. He was a cold-hearted bully in some ways, yet a champion of minorities around here."

"Did he bully you?"

"He tried and failed. But he succeeded in teaching me how to argue."

He grinned at me. He had nice teeth, an indication he wasn't raised poor. I'd seen too many rural families struggling without health and dental care.

The music started and couples began to dance. I took a couple of Advil to quell a headache that was increasing in strength. Vonny and Tony showed up.

"Dad seems better," Vonny said. "He's been dozing off and on most of the evening. We'll stay for an hour or so then switch with Derek and Tina so they can come out here."

Jay and I hit the dance floor. It stayed full when people could do the two-step, but it thinned when a pop or rock song came on. Those were the songs when those without rhythm became exposed. Brian always chose to leave the floor during those songs, though he preferred them to the country songs. To my delight, Jay didn't need to leave the floor—he had a great feel for the beat and looked so damn sexy when he danced. It was a strange fact that among white people, women were more likely to have rhythm than men. On one side of the dance floor, a group of young girls were bouncing to the beat in a circle. Kayla kept looking over at me, which I thought strange until I realized she was picking up my moves. The other girls soon copied her then added their own seasoning.

After another pop song came a slow song and I was in the dark corner, kissing Jay. Before the song was half way done, I pulled away from him, my head pounding.

"It's not you," I quickly said.

"What is it?"

"I don't know."

I turned to go back to the table, but reached back for his hand and he followed. I sat down and gulped water. Paul, Kayla, and Patty were talking together, though I could feel Patty's eyes on me. I began to rub my hands on my legs. Then I stopped. I heard talking, but it became an indiscernible hum. Think, breathe, no, don't think, clear my mind. I sat still and shut my eyes, as the hammering continued in my head. The music disappeared. Everyone disappeared then one appeared and I saw him through the darkness. The pounding started in my chest and my head snapped up. I don't know how long I'd been that way, but Mom and Bill were at the table. They were all staring at me. I stood then scanned the dance floor for her. Vonny returned my look then hurried to the table.

"What, Megan?" someone said.

"Call an ambulance," I said to Mom. "Tell them to go to the Wilson house."

"Oh, Lord," said Bill as he jumped to his feet along with the rest of the table.

Jay wanted to keep staring at me, but I sent him to tell Johnny we'd settle the bill tomorrow. In a flash, we were in our trucks and cars and speeding north to Harney Street. Bill had barely come to a stop in the street in front of the Wilson house when I flung open the door, jumped out of the pickup, and then dashed up the front steps. The front door was open—Derek or Tina must have called the ambulance, too, and were waiting.

James lay on his back in the front room next to his brown recliner. I had been right, but it was a shame I couldn't do anything except kneel down next to Derek.

"We called for an ambulance," I said.

"They said someone had already called when we did," said Tina, who knelt on the other side of the motionless, unconscious James.

"He kind of convulsed for a few seconds then fell to the floor," said Derek. "But first, he reached up to his head. He said a while ago his headache was better, so I don't know what happened."

"Vonny's on the way."

"Derek, when did you call her?" asked Tina.

He shook his head.

As I reached down to feel his pulse on his neck, Mom then Bill came into the room. Vonny soon followed. She dropped hard to her knees.

"He has a pulse, but it's not strong," I said.

I leaned toward him to listen to his breathing; it was irregular, a sign of a gravely serious stroke. His skin had that green tint I saw when he had his mini-stroke. As a means of avoiding the looks of Vonny and Derek, I kept my eyes on James.

"What? What do you know?" asked Vonny.

"Just that we have to wait."

A few minutes later, the paramedics hauled James out the front door past Tony, Jay, Patty, Kayla, and Paul, who shivered in the chilly evening wind. Derek and Vonny rode in the ambulance with James, and the rest of us, with the exception of Kayla and Paul, piled in various vehicles and met at the all-too-familiar Sidney hospital waiting room. I called Beulah, even though it was close to her bedtime. She thanked me for thinking of her. I promised to call her if anything extraordinary developed. The message was a calculated attempt to get her to call a number of people, who in turn, would hopefully start praying for James.

We gathered in the waiting room and did as we do in such places—we waited. Even Derek and Vonny were banished from the ER. I went to look out the windows into the darkness. A small town like Sidney didn't put out much light, which made for great star-gazing, except from a well-lit room. Jay came to stand beside me.

"I've heard about you, but that was bloody amazing," he said.

"'Bloody'? Do you watch Harry Potter movies?" I asked.

"Yeah, they're brilliant."

I smiled.

"Really though, what do you know? Will he live?"

"Oh, he'll die some day. I don't know when. I just knew something bad was happening to him."

"When do you know?" he asked.

"Well, it has to be someone close."

"Did you know Raz was going to get killed?"

I studied him for a moment.

"I did feel alarm…danger, but I think I was feeling it for myself. Oh, I should call Rachel. She's fond of James."

"I should leave then."

"Why? Afraid I'll blow your cover? She still doesn't know, does she?"

"I don't think local State Patrol knows about me. But I should go. I need to get working on the information you gave me. See ya."

He left, which increased my sadness. I called Rachel then rejoined the group. Around midnight, the doctor came out and confirmed that James did have a stroke, but had stabilized. He suggested we go home. Derek and Vonny remained rigid in their chairs. Tony yanked Vonny up then he and Bill pulled Derek to his feet.

Rachel walked with me down the hall.

"I heard you're dating that new guy, Rob Faust," she said.

"I don't know that I'm dating anyone. It seems like a bad idea right now." I wondered if she suspected something about him.

"What do you know about him?"

I didn't answer.

"Megan?"

"Huh? Oh, you said something." Then I leaned toward her and said quietly, "James was unconscious and his breathing was out of whack. From what I've read, those are bad things. Oh, and he had a headache earlier in the evening."

"Yeah, it's bad."

Fortunately, she let the Faust issue drop. We all trudged out to our cars and drove home.

The next morning before church, I drove out to Sidney with Mom and Bill. Derek, Vonny, and Tina were already in the waiting room, looking sad and tired. Dr. Dearborn, who had attended James when he suffered his TIA, spoke briefly to them then headed to the doorway. Mom and Bill went in to get the doctor's report, but I waited in the hall for the doctor.

"Dr. Dearborn, Mr. Wilson has a Living Will."

"Good."

"Here is a copy that I had because I drafted it last year. If you need the original, you'll need to get that from Derek or Vonny." I took a deep breath. "It's quite serious, isn't it?"

"Yes. He may improve in some areas, but most of the brain damage is permanent. It will take some time to determine how much if any physical or cognitive function will be regained."

"You'll be asking them about a DNR, won't you?" I asked.

"I'm afraid we will."

"Well, let me mention it to them first, so it won't be such a shock."

I remembered the jolt it gave me when the doctor asked Bill and me that question about my dad.

The doctor nodded as I went into the room. It was best to get it over with.

I stood before Derek, Tina, and Vonny with Mom and Bill at my side.

"Okay, it's time to put on my lawyer hat," I began. Then I took a deep breath. "I gave the doctor a copy of your dad's Living Will. He may or may not ask you for the original, which should be in the house. It simply says they won't go to extreme measures, to, ah, prolong life." Derek and Vonny looked to have stopped breathing. I tried to keep my voice steady. "They will be asking you about a DNR, a directive that says they won't resuscitate, if you wish. I mention these things now, when they are not an issue." They looked positively devastated and I wanted to cry. "You may not use that Living Will or the DNR anytime this decade, but it's best to know now, so they won't be such a shock if they should come up." I really wanted to run away, especially when the tears began to run down Vonny's face. "The DNR question was a shock to me...with my dad. I wanted to spare you that."

I sat down at the end of the row, trying to avoid their eyes. Mom sat down next to me, wrapped her arm around my shoulders then handed me a tissue to wipe away my tears. My guts churned—maybe I shouldn't have eaten breakfast or maybe I should've eaten more, I couldn't tell, but I needed to keep it down. After a few minutes of silence, Bill, Mom, and I left for church. Vonny gave my hand a squeeze as I walked past her. Still, I couldn't look either of them in the eyes.

Chapter 22

AFTER church, we ate a quick lunch, packed food for Derek, Tina, and Vonny then headed back to the hospital. Once there, we learned that James had slipped into a coma, but it didn't surprise the physicians. What was there to say? It tore at me, but I wanted to stay strong for Derek and Vonny. Tina probably wondered if married life could start any worse.

An hour of near silence followed as Derek, Tina, and Vonny ate their lunches then stared at the floor. Then Mom brought out the diary. Derek and Tina knew about the story, but Vonny didn't, so Mom gave a summary of the lives of the Pittsburgh family and their ferry business during the Civil War. It even interested the silver-haired volunteer, for she sat down in the row behind Mom to listen.

Despite being smitten by Lt. Tom, Kate lets him leave with Matthew to rejoin the army without any assurance of her affection for him. While he is marching across Maryland toward the bloody battle at Antietam, a drunken Kyle, the confederate officer, arrives at the Barton home, alerted to the news of a rival. In his malevolent jealousy, Kyle carelessly kills a bystander, a runaway slave who had survived decades in bondage only to be killed when he was just a river away from freedom. Kate becomes distraught over the death of the innocent man. When Kate breaks off her engagement to Kyle, he threatens to shoot Kate. Kyle is then killed by a Rebel deserter, who had been hiding in the area with the help of Kate.

"Dang, they could make a movie out of this diary," said Vonny, who seemed to enjoy the distraction of the story.

"We think it's the second of two diaries," I said. "I wrote to Lynne Zimmer to see if we could locate the first diary, but Lynne never knew of any other diary. She's not even sure why Max had it in his possession. But this diary helped me get through jail time, so I wrote to Lynne and waived her bankruptcy and probate fees."

Rachel joined our group then said, "I know of another story. It's about a judge who wrongly sends a woman, a really short one, to jail. Well, Shorty had some friends who knew this judge and that he had a really bad gambling habit. Well, it turns out some of his gambling was illegal. The scandal breaks and the judge decides to take an early retirement, starting November first. Now isn't that a nice story?"

Even Vonny and Derek chuckled.

My cell vibrated. I took the call from Jay and walked out into the hallway.

"Hey, your bit of information on Brett Webster convinced Judge Shelton to give us, the FBI actually, a search warrant," said Jay. "That idiot started dealing as soon as he was out of jail. Brother Nick joined in, so we were able to nab them both. The judge didn't even make us find the source of your information—he said your word was good enough."

"I'm at the hospital, so I can't say much. James is in a coma."

"Oh, man. I'm really sorry," said Jay.

"Okay, so go on."

"Right. Oh, it was Tony who made the arrests, so his cover is blown, but mine is safe. Nick is a blabbermouth—he implicated Mick Spittle right away. So, all three are in jail and Judge Shelton is not setting bail for any of them."

"Who is the attorney for those idiots?"

"Ah, Rich Dewey for the Websters, I'm not sure on Spittle."

"Have Tony contact Judge Shelton and tell him Dewey has a conflict of interest and needs to terminate representation. Rich will thank me. So nothing on Jake Waters?"

"Not according to Tony."

"Anything on Rana?"

"We're still working on it, but Abboud was probably not her last name either."

"Makes her look more suspicious of something," I said. "Hey, here comes Tony down the hall. He's ditched the cowboy look. Oh, and the doctor is back."

"Okay, keep me updated on James."

"I do feel safer with those lunkheads in jail, but…"

Tony stopped in front of me.

"But what?" asked Jay.

"It's not over. There's stuff still out there."

"You got that gun?"

"Absolutely. Better go. Bye."

Tony smiled at me. He was clean shaven and wearing khakis. It was the first time I'd seen him without cowboy boots and a big brown hat.

"Nice work, cowboy. But no evidence against Jake Waters."

"Not so far. But thanks for the tip on the others."

"Well, please keep that to yourself. I'd like to stay out of trouble."

Tony and I stood behind the doctor as he announced that James had come out of his coma. He told Derek and Vonny they could go see him. Derek took Tina's hand and they followed the doctor. Vonny greeted Tony then she grabbed my hand and pulled me along.

In James' ICU room, he was hooked up to several machines. His eyes were open and they looked from Derek to Vonny then to me. A plastic oxygen mask covered his mouth and nose.

"He's not speaking," said the doctor, whose nametag read Neil Robertson, M.D. "He does have some movement in the fingers of his right hand."

"But he'll get better, right? He did before," said Derek.

"We can't predict his recovery right now. That could take some time."

"Is it normal for him to be on a respirator?" I asked.

"Ah, let's go out in the hall."

We followed the physician into the hall. When I glanced back at James, his eyes focused on me. He looked aware, but trapped in his condition. I shuddered.

"He's suffered a complete stroke, which began suddenly and developed rapidly. It's an ischemic stroke, which means he had significant blockage in the arterial pathways...we think probably the carotid artery, possibly another smaller artery as well."

Shit. I wondered if Vonny and Derek understood just how bad this sounded.

"And yes, with a stroke of this extent, ventilation is common. Trach tubes are rough on the throat, so we'll remove that when and if we can."

"So can surgery help?" asked Vonny.

"No, the affected brain tissue is dead and surgery to the artery won't restore brain function."

Vonny looked woozy, so Tony wrapped his arm around her shoulder. It was sinking in.

"Rehabilitation is possible with stroke victims, right?" I asked.

"Yes. But first we must do what we can to stabilize his blood pressure, pulse, and breathing."

"How long does that take?" asked Derek.

"Well, um, let me be frank, it's going to be difficult given the extent of the brain damage, and the other complications, ah, his breathing problems, his existing high blood pressure. But we must wait and see how much improvement he makes this week."

"What are you doing for him?" I asked.

"Of course, we're treating the high blood pressure and giving him mannitol to help reduce the swelling and the pressure on the brain. The heart is closely monitored. We used MRI and CT scans to check for blood clots. We believe we can keep him from worsening for now."

"Should he be moved to another facility? Maybe one that specializes in stroke victim care?" I asked.

Clearly, I needed to ask these questions, for Vonny looked unstable and Derek seemed frozen with shock.

"It would be catastrophic to move him now. No other hospital could do more than what we're doing. Now if rehabilitation is possible, yes, there are better facilities for him. We can aid you in selecting a facility when…ah, and if that time comes."

It couldn't be good that the doctor was stumbling through his explanation. It was also strange that they were allowing five people in an ICU room.

"Perhaps it would be best if Derek and Vonny sat down by their father," I said.

Tina led the stiffened Derek and Tony hung on tight to the wobbly Vonny as they reentered the room. Too bad no Saint Bernard wandered up with a flask of brandy.

I turned to the doctor and said, "I warned them about the DNR question."

He nodded and looked down at his file. "He has a Living Will. Good, good. That helps. Did you draft it, Ms. Docket?"

I nodded. He didn't say anything else. Grateful he didn't launch into a story of how he knew me or when he treated me, I shook his hand then went into the room.

"Hey, Dad, you just hang in there, okay?" said Derek.

Vonny's lips were quivering so badly, she couldn't speak. I put my hand on her shoulder. When I looked at James, his eyes moved from Vonny to me. Vonny held his right hand in both of hers. I could see his fingers moving in spasms. With Derek and Vonny struggling so badly and James watching me, I couldn't indulge myself in a fit of tears as I wanted. James looked at each person in the room one more time. When his eyes closed, Derek jumped from his seat. The green line kept squiggling. All the other numbers on the machines remained constant.

"I think he's just gone to sleep," I said. "If something was wrong, those ER nurses would be rushing in here. He's had a tough couple of days, he should be tired."

Derek sat down. "Well, you're the ICU veteran. You should know."

A few minutes later, I told the gang in the waiting room, which had quadrupled in size, that James had suffered "major stroke" and he was now sleeping. For most, "major" shocked them to silence. Mom and Bill stared at me. When I didn't elaborate, they just nodded, certain they'd hear the details later in private.

Bill approached Tony and said, "You on vacation today?"

"No, I'm undercover FBI. I made some recent arrests involving drug dealing."

"I'll tell you about it," I said to Bill.

"Well, I'm down a cowboy. You were pretty convincing."

"Eric is finishing the fence I was working on."

Beulah shuffled over.

"Heh! What's this? You're not a cowboy? Heh, figured. You talk too good and tip too good for a cowboy."

Tony smiled; meanwhile, Beulah looked at each of us in turn, waiting for some news.

I looked to Tony, "Should I?"

"That's fine, I just came to get some coffee," he said.

He headed over to the volunteer, while Mom, Bill, and Beulah crowded in close to me. I told them of the arrests. Beulah nodded then walked away to do what she loved most—deliver news. After I coaxed Bill and Mom away from the others, I told them that Jay was undercover and was trying to stay that way.

"Why do I suspect you had a hand in this somehow?" asked Mom.

"I gave information I learned from a confidential source," I said. "It led to search warrants and arrests. But my role and Jay's status is top secret."

"I thought he had to be more than a salesman to interest you," said Mom.

Bill stepped away to talk to Tom Sedlacek, James' main supervisor for his landscaping business.

As soon as Bill left, Mom leaned in close to me. "So jail did have a purpose, didn't it?"

I nodded.

"James is going to die, isn't he?"

I cleared the lump from my throat. "Soon."

"Vonny and Derek need to get out of here…get some air," she said. "We should get them to come for supper."

"They might need to be kidnapped. Hey, Patty just bought a big ham. Derek loves ham. Is there time to cook it?"

"Patty and I can go start it. Are you going to stay?"

"Yeah. The doctor is letting me go into James room, so I'll go back there. We should keep the group small."

"Okay, I'll let you know the time."

I nodded.

After she left, I spoke to a few people then went to James' room, all the while thinking how to get Derek and Vonny to leave their father.

The room was silent with shock. James locked his eyes on me as soon as I appeared in the doorway. I walked around Vonny and stood next to James.

"James, my friend, do you know who I am? Blink twice for yes, once for no."

Derek and Vonny rose from their chairs.

After a few moments, he closed his eyes then opened them then closed them again.

"Ah!" said Vonny. "Megan, how did you know?"

"By watching his eyes and how he looks at us." I looked back at James. "Do you understand what we say?"

Again, the hesitation indicated his slow-working mind, but he blinked twice. A nurse entered the room.

"Okay, I have a question for you. Do you think Derek, Vonny, Tina, and Tony should come to my house for a ham dinner?"

He blinked twice then made an attempt to move his mouth, but only succeeded in pursing his lips inside the ventilation cup.

"Okay, you two," I said. "Now are you going to disobey your father?"

"But—" started Vonny.

"Oh, you both disobeyed him enough as kids, now it's time to behave," I said.

Derek smirked and shook his head. Tony and Tina were on my side—they were probably ready to run screaming from the room, as I was.

"Plus, it will give your dad a chance to rest without everybody staring at him and fretting over these damn machines. We'll make sure the ICU staff has every possible phone number that they can call at a moment's notice. My mom will let us know when they expect dinner to be ready. Then you can come back. ICU doesn't have specific visiting hours."

"You're like Great-aunt Megan, laying down the law," said Tony with a smile.

"Or General Megan," said Tina, who winked at me.

James worked his mouth.

"I think that's a smile," said Tina.

Both Derek and Vonny seemed to perk up. Tony talked about the arrests, but left me and Jay out of it. James watched him the entire time, while I watched James—the tragedy of him ripping at my insides. When I was a kid, he taught me how to dribble, trim rose bushes, and play backgammon. Life in Dexter had been lonely for me until his family moved next door. Beverly was gone and Vonny would go back to Denver in time. Now James—I could hardly recall life without him.

FIRE IN THE WIND

My phone hummed. I left ICU to answer a call from Mom.

"Hi, how is James?"

"Alert, but he doesn't speak or move, except for a few fingers. Derek and Vonny are taking it hard."

"We'll eat at six-thirty. And there's something else. Nori called a few minutes ago. She wanted to spend time with me tonight. I was in a pickle, so I invited her over to your house. I explained it would be a quick meal then people would be going back to the hospital. She said that was okay."

"Hmm. She better behave."

"She's suffered a great loss…I hated to put her off."

Maybe I could understand more about her. Surely, she would respect Derek and Vonny's plight. With her own loss, I assumed she'd be quiet and not combative.

"It'll be okay," I said, but I wasn't really certain. Something was eating at me—was it something other than James?

Chapter 23

BACK in the room, I mentioned to the group that Nori would be joining us for dinner. Then I said I didn't think we should mention the arrests, though she might already know.

"Why not?" asked Derek.

"I don't know, but it seems best."

Vonny stood and said to Derek, "We need to talk."

He nodded and rose. I backed away, but Vonny grabbed my hand and pulled me out into the hall with her. Oh, no, she wanted my advice or at least my interference.

Out in the hall, Derek stretched his arms and back. "It's good to move."

"And you guys need to get out of that room now and then," I said. "You can't hold a twenty-four hour vigil. Your dad needs the chance for some peace and rest."

"I think we should talk about the DNR," said Vonny.

"Then I should go," I said.

"Nah, stay, Miggy," said Derek. "This is some heavy stuff to deal with."

I nodded and waited in the silence. Vonny rubbed her temples.

"Oh, God, this is horrible," she said. "But I don't know about giving up on him…I mean, he could still improve."

"Sis, you know he's in bad shape. What if his only improvement is more finger wiggling? He's got a lot of brain damage. We can't expect a miracle."

"No, but he's obviously got something going on. He hears and sees us. Megan proved that. I'm just not ready to give up…as we'd be doing if we told them okay on the DNR."

"Have they asked you about that?" I asked.

They both shook their heads.

"Then maybe the doctors think it's too soon," I said. "I'm not going to tell you what to do. Maybe you just need to wait. Your dad is thinking about this stuff, too. He knows how bad he is. Last summer, I knew how close to death I came. I think there was even a time when I could've made a choice…"

"What do you mean?" asked Vonny.

"It's hard to describe…um…I wonder if your dad might decide something…I don't know."

"Miggy, I don't understand," said Derek.

"Neither could your dad till now or in a few days. He may wish to stay as he is and fight to live, or he might choose to go to God and your mom."

"But he's on all those machines," Derek said.

"The doctor said rehabilitation is possible," said Vonny.

"No, he said we have to see if Dad improves enough to start rehabilitation. So, is he only alive because of those machines? Wouldn't that violate the Living Will?"

"It would, but it may be too early to know if he needs machines to live." I took a deep breath. "The Living Will was his idea. He told me he didn't want science keeping him alive."

"When did you write it?" Vonny asked.

"In August. I think my brush with death got him thinking. Lots of people have Living Wills—I've drafted them for Mom and Bill and Beulah and others. I have one, so does Brian. I would have approached your dad about it in time."

"What does it say?" asked Derek.

"Simply that extraordinary measures won't be used to keep him alive, but that every attempt would be made to keep him comfortable. So they could keep him on pain meds to make sure he's not suffering."

The both stood stiffly, staring down at the brown speckled carpet.

"I don't think you need to make any decisions right now." They both looked up at me. "The Living Will solves some problems for you. And you're thinking about the DNR, which is the right thing to do."

They clearly needed a boost, and I wanted so badly to help them.

"So, your dad is closely monitored. The ICU staff would know if he sneezed. The doctors are doing everything they can right now. We'll just need to watch and wait to see how he does over the next few days or so. I guess I don't know what kind of time period we're looking at. But nothing is going to happen today."

It wasn't much, but it was enough for both of them to lift their heads. They walked back into the room. A text from Brian stopped me from following them. He was in the waiting room. People probably wanted an update, even if there wasn't much to say. So I excused myself from Derek and Vonny and found Brian in the waiting room. He walked over to the windows to get away from the others and I followed him.

"You could have called me about James," he said. "I had to find out at Custer's."

"I'm sorry…there's just so much going on," I said.

In truth, with James and Jay and the arrests, I hadn't even thought of him. And the one shall become two—he was disappearing from my mind and life even faster than I expected.

"It's really bad, isn't it?" Brian asked.

"Yeah."

He wrapped his arm around my shoulder.

"We're down to days now. You could still stop it."

"Huh? Oh, the divorce. No, I think it's best."

"So jail didn't soften you."

No, it didn't, you jerk. I moved away from him. "It just scared me. Listen, this is the right thing to do. I'm always going to care about you. But we aren't right together."

"I'm never going to hit you. I think you know that, but you're using that as an excuse."

"No, I don't know that and no, I'm not using it as an excuse…I'm using it to make sure you cooperate, which you have. And I thank you for that."

"I can change."

"No, you don't need to change. And I wouldn't try to force anything on you. It's foolish to try and change anyone…well, except for kids. You're fine. It's us, our…um…dynamic is wrong. Like I told you before, go find someone normal. I'm not and that isn't your fault. What's wrong with Jessica Fenton? I know you were dating her before I even filed for divorce."

He opened his mouth then shut it. I left him toying with the curtain cord. Beulah had been watching us, so I walked over to her and sat down next to her.

"I see you've got your Christmas lights up," I said.

"Well, it is October," she said.

"I like that single string of blue lights framing your house. Very classy."

"You think so? Heh. I was gonna have Tom do more, but he's been here."

I looked over a couple of rows and spotted Tom Sedlacek, James' main worker and now supervisor. James added Christmas house decorating to his business a few years back. We had a substantial graying population in town who appreciated help with the lights. Next to Tom sat Zane, whom I hadn't noticed when I entered the room. He'd probably accuse me of ignoring him, the hypocrite.

"James is really bad," Beulah remarked.

"Yes, he is," I said.

"Tough on those two kids."

"Yeah, they're hurting and scared."

"What was that fancy word?"

"Ischemic. It means there was some kind of blockage, like a clot. The other kind of stroke is when a blood vessel bursts in the brain and blood hemorrhages into it, causing damage. Either kind is very bad."

"Oh, pshaw, I can't say those words."

"Just say a blockage stops blood and oxygen from getting into the brain. Use the words 'major' or 'severe' and that will be enough for most people. And folks will want to know when they come into Custer's tomorrow morning."

"Yep, they'll be askin' me."

"We'll be relying on you."

She nodded, now deep in thought.

At six o'clock, Derek, Vonny, Tina, and Tony filed out of the room. James looked at me, his mouth moving. I squeezed his hand, swallowed hard then followed my friends. When we arrived at my house, Bill, Mom, Patty, and Nori were waiting. Nori displayed kindness toward Derek and Vonny. To their credit, Derek and Vonny remembered to offer their sympathies over the death of her brother. When Nori spoke to me she was polite, yet I sensed her loathing. Why does she hate me so much? Even people in court don't give off hate vibes as strong as this. Derek and Vonny relaxed a bit with the meal and the fresh air and break from the hospital. I wanted to try and read them, but it made me angry that Nori's abhorrence for me was a distraction. My mind was in swirl—danger and sadness were tangled in my mind. I worked hard to eat a normal meal. I didn't want to draw any attention to myself, for Derek and Vonny needed our support. I was just Megan feeling weird again.

After the dinner, Nori went to the family room with Vonny, Tina, and Tony, so I went to the kitchen to help with the cleanup. Bill and Derek went home to tend to the dogs. By the time they returned, the kitchen was clean and Vonny was anxious to go. So, everyone loaded into vehicles for the drive back to the Sidney hospital, except I stayed behind because I wanted to drive the Barracuda so I'd be free to come and go. Bill and Tony's pickups pulled out of my driveway followed by Derek's sedan as Nori climbed in the silver XTerra. She had decided to keep the SUV Raz formerly drove. That made sense with winter coming. As the autos left, the house phone rang. I left the front door to answer it in the kitchen. No one was on the line. I checked the caller ID, but the name was blocked.

Something suddenly changed. My stomach cart wheeled.

Triple shit.

As I walked toward the front door, I heard it pushed shut. I froze. My heart pounded so hard it nearly burst through my chest. Who was here? My guts told me it wasn't a friend. Where was my gun? Shit. It was by the front door with my car keys. It was too light to dash outside, as I'd be seen. The floor creaked in the other hallway. I tip-toed to the basement door, opened it, and then closed it quietly behind me. I flicked on the light then scampered down the steps. I took a quick look around before I opened the fuse box on the wall next to the stairs. I cut the power. The room went dark.

Chapter 24

I stood in the black for a moment, listening as fear rose up into my chest, constricting my lungs. I gasped for air. Whoever was upstairs was after me. Why? The floor above me creaked. That was the sound of someone trying to be quiet, someone who didn't make the noise of a larger person. It was Nori or Rana, whatever the hell her name was. I crept behind the hot water heater, aware that I didn't have much time before she'd know to come down here. Why did she hate me so much? A sister wouldn't blame me for the death of Raz. She'd be grieving back in Omaha with friends and family. Wait, oh, shit. Jealousy. Like Kate's fiancé in the diary—angry with jealousy, he'd sought to kill his rival.

Rana was the wife of Raz.

She tried to kill me out in my backyard, but missed when I stepped to the left. Instead, she killed her own husband—now she was enraged with vengeance, ready to finish the job. Oh, sweet Jesus, please help me!

The door opened. But she didn't come down. While I was plotting my defense, she was probably looking for a flashlight. Upstairs she'd have the evening light from outside to see. Down here, the windows were small and covered with insulated Roman Shades; it was blacker than the night sky.

I pictured the basement, what could I use to help me? I needed a weapon. I needed more than one diversion to defeat the green-eyed monster. Rana would know I didn't have a gun, she'd seen me and she'd seen my purse on the foyer bench. Maybe she swiped my gun, well, Jay's gun. She would shine the beam first down the stairs then around the room, which was a full-sized basement with lots of old furniture. She'd spot potential hiding places. I needed to stay mobile and absolutely silent. I removed my shoes—in socks I'd have no traction, but I'd be quiet. I dashed over to set my shoes just to the right of the staircase that ran down against the wall. Under the stairwell was a steel-reinforced cave-like space meant to be protection from tornados. She'd look for me hiding in there. We had a rack of clothes covered in plastic—she might fire at that because something upright might startle her.

I dashed over to a shelf with an old golf bag. After unzipping a pocket, I stuffed three balls in my jean pockets then ran my hands over the clubs till I found a thick-headed wood. I needed something to smash in her skull—she'd show me no mercy—I didn't intend to show her any. I yanked off the cover and pulled it out.

A step sounded at the top of the stairs. It caught my breath; I exhaled quietly as my heart started beating again. A beam of light shone down the stairs. She took another step forward and swept the light quickly around the room, probably hoping to catch me in my flight. But I was now crouched low behind an old sofa from Bill's first marriage. I didn't need to see her, the flashlight would tell me her location; yet, to be caught in the beam meant death.

She shone the light around the room, which should dishearten her given the size of it and the labyrinth of old furniture, boxes, and shelves. Suddenly, I was glad I never forced Bill to take away his old furniture, though I'd made suggestions. God bless him for ignoring me.

Rana eased her way down the steps, the light moving from the stairs ahead of her to various spots in the room and back to the wood steps. When she reached the bottom, she flashed the beam around then stepped forward, tripping over my shoes. Bones hit the concrete floor and a string of profanities spewed forth. Back on her feet, I could hear her frantic, angry bursts of breath. The flashlight caught the rack of bagged clothes in its beam to her right then she fired several shots into it. She proceeded to fire into each corner, probably hoping to flush me out. She went over to check near the bag of clothes.

"I'm going to kill you, bitch!"

Maybe she would, but first I crept back to the golf bag, which was in the open—all she had to do was shine it on me. I grabbed three more balls from the pocket. I rolled one ball across the room at her feet; then I bounced another into the corner near the base of the stairs; the third ball I lobbed into a group of dining room chairs and a table where it pinballed against chairs legs. Rana fired wildly at the sounds, the bullets chipping at the poured concrete walls. More profanity.

Meanwhile, I moved to cover, always staying low, deeper toward the far wall where I knew we kept a stack of old bricks left over from one of our landscaping projects. With the stack of bricks between the source of the beam and me, I knelt behind it, feeling for the top brick. I started to move a brick, but another one was on top of it so that it made a brief scraping sound. The light flashed toward me. I froze for a moment then hurled a golf ball from my pocket toward the Cave. The light shone on it as I grabbed the topmost brick and crawled behind a bookshelf, the gold club tucked tightly under my left arm.

Rana walked toward the Cave, sweeping that corner of the room with the light. She found the treadmill and the TV, but kept walking toward the dark space under the stairs. A blast of gunfire erupted as she ran forward, shining the light inside. More profanities punctuated her disappointment. She was getting creative—now I wasn't just a whore, I was a bitchy hick whore among other things. I took exception to that—I was not a hick. More accurately, I was someone who longed to smash this brick over her head.

I waited to see which way she'd move. She spotted the water heater just a few feet from me then fired on both sides of it. Thank you, bitch, for not destroying it. She turned back from where she'd come and began to work her way through the furniture. Even with the flashlight, she bumped into end tables and stubbed her feet on chair legs. The noise she created allowed me to move forward away from her. She knew where I'd been.

Suddenly, she sprinted to a row of furniture and fired low. She then located the stack of bricks. She fired at them. She was moving faster than I was and now following me. I needed to move faster and get behind her. The light darted quickly to an area near my location. The moment it moved away, I heaved a golf ball toward the corner opposite of me, hoping it would ricochet off both walls—it did. Staying low, I scurried forward, but stopped just in time to avoid knocking over a wooden stool. My breath came out in quick, quiet blasts. Shit, if only I could see how to get behind her.

The night goggles! I needed to stop and think where I'd seen them. Then I remembered I'd seen them when I tumbled off the treadmill. As she moved through the chairs only a couple dozen feet behind me, I slithered on the floor toward my destination. I felt the edge of the shelf then dropped my hand to the lowest shelf. I felt a pair of the goggles, but checked to make sure nothing was on top of it. I grabbed them, ran my hand around them to make sure they weren't upside down, and then slipped them over my head as the flashlight shone just over me.

Now I could see a dresser drawer was the last sizable piece of furniture until I reached the open space near the treadmill. I crept behind the bureau then peeked out the side. There she was, sweeping the flashlight beam over the furniture then stopping to check around each piece. She came to the dresser. She stood on the other side of it as I watched her. I only needed to be silent and out of the beam of light. When she turned to check along the wall, I swung the golf club, just as she stepped back. The shaft hit her on the side of the head, the golf club clamoring to the ground. She went down, the gun fell, and the flashlight rolled away from her. She screamed in anger. I picked up the brick then moved back towards the furniture.

Her hands were moving along the ground and hitting against chair legs as she searched for the gun. Suddenly, she rose to her feet and ran to the flashlight. She now had a gun in her hand. Did she find the gun or was this another? I crouched back down then moved to where she'd searched for the handgun—if she didn't find it, maybe I could. She grabbed the flashlight from the ground—I ducked just in time to avoid getting caught in the light. She dashed back toward where she dropped the gun. She knew I was close by—she couldn't let me find the gun. I only had a few seconds to search, it was too late. As soon as she ran by the musty recliner I hid behind, I rose then took a few steps behind her. Then I smashed the brick down on the back of her head.

She fell hard and the flashlight rolled against the wall. She groaned then rolled to her back. I stepped behind the hot water heater as she fired behind her into the black. Why don't you die? When she turned over onto her hands and knees to rise, I jumped knees first onto her back.

She grunted then growled.

I reached for the gun she dropped, but her hand found it first. I pinned that arm down with my knee, but then she got a leg underneath her body and tried to buck me off. I stayed on top, but I slid to one side. I grabbed her by the forehead then with my hand behind her head, I smashed her face into the concrete.

Without good balance, I didn't deliver a strong blow, probably breaking her nose at best. But then she recovered. As she fumbled with the gun, I lunged forward to seize it. Just then, I felt a searing pain in my left hip. I plucked the knife from my side. It would end now.

As she tried to maneuver her gun to point it at me, I lifted her forehead with my left hand then with my right, I pressed hard and slashed across her throat. I let her head drop with a thud to the concrete as a pool of dark liquid spread out from her head and upper body. I retrieved the flashlight to shine on her. She was still with her eyes open, her face resting in the blood. I sat down in a nearby armchair.

Lord Almighty, thank you—I'm alive. But why was I lousy with a golf club yet good with a knife? Never mind.

My mind spun with exhilaration and disgust. I shone the light on the gun in her hand. It was Jay's gun. I found her gun under the wooden stool I almost knocked over. I pried Jay's gun from her hand. It was illegal for me to have that gun and illegal for him to loan it. Why complicate things? I wiped it off with the clean side of my shirt then shoved it under the seat cushion of the recliner. With my foot, I slid her gun next to her right hand. It was a Glock.

"Bitch, you needed to die," I said to a dead body.

I limped back down to the chair and stared into the darkness, my entire body trembling, inside and out. My left hip burned. I pressed my hand onto it; my jeans and blouse were sticky with blood I wanted to keep. I needed help. Why didn't I have a phone down here? If I didn't bleed to death, I'd get one installed. Sucking deep breaths, I hobbled to the stairwell. Clearly, I needed to make it up those stairs. Blood oozed out of me and my wits felt strained. Hospital. Drugs. Sleep. I hobbled toward the staircase.

Suddenly, heavy footfalls were above me. If it was Bill, he'd be running and yelling. No, this was a big man, searching, trying to be quiet. I limped back to the chair, put on the night goggles and plucked Jay's gun out from under the seat cushion then shuffled back to the Cave. My heart pounded inside my ears. My God, who was this? He started to make me mad, for the longer I had to wait, the more blood I lost. Yet, when the big man stepped onto the landing of the basement steps, it was too soon. He walked down a few steps, shone his flashlight around the room then it darted to the row with the bloody body, the gun and the flashlight on the floor pointing away from Rana, but still on. He had his gun drawn as he took the steps by two. He stepped on one of my tennies—I'd need to remember those. The man, who I could now see wore a State Patrol uniform, stopped abruptly when he came to the body.

As I came out from under the Cave, I barked: "Officer, don't move! Don't turn around."

The cop froze.

"She's dead. Now listen, I know your son Jake is in trouble and maybe you blame me for that. Maybe he's gotten you in trouble, I don't know."

Trooper Waters straightened, but didn't turn.

"Now, I don't know why you're here. Did you come to kill me? Know this—you're a dead man the moment you start to turn around. I've heard you're a good shot, but you've seen what I've done. I'm also wearing night goggles and I have a bead on your skull. So please don't turn around. Just wait."

"I didn't come to kill you," said Waters.

"Okay, good. My guess is you were mixed up with Nori...Rana...somehow. Maybe she had evidence against Jake. But I need you to stay still. You call this in to the station, say you saw the lights were off and you thought that was strange...which it is because I always have the lights on in the evening. Tell them you came in the unlocked front door and heard gunfire, so you came down here. That is all true and I'll back you on that. I don't want you as an enemy. I don't have any evidence against you. So, get on your phone and call for backup or whatever and for an ambulance."

"But I'm in so deep," he said in a weakened voice.

He started to turn his shoulders.

"No! Stop! What are you doing? You know I'll kill you to save myself. Why would—"

Duh. I gasped.

"No, you don't want to die, Randy. Just stop, that's right. Now let's be calm. I'm not going to oblige you and put a bullet through your head, but I will shoot off your balls. I only got one of Mick Spittle's, but that's because I was on a moving horse."

He didn't turn around. But I could see he was taking big breaths.

"Did Rana kill Raz?" I asked.

"I think she was aiming at you."

"I swear I didn't know they were married. I only figured that out because she hated me so much that she wanted to kill me. She's not big, but she was tough and hard to kill."

Feeling weak, I had to lean back against the stairwell.

"Randy, make the call. I promise I'll back you. But first, put your gun back in the holster, so it doesn't look like you were after me."

He called the State Patrol, reported the attack then asked for an ambulance; but he still held his gun.

Big boots clomped in the hallway above us. Waters put his gun in his holster.

"That's my uncle."

Boots stopped on the landing.

"Uncle Bill, down here!"

"Megan, where are you?"

"I flipped off the power. Will you come down and turn it on? Officer Waters is down here, too."

Bill shone his light down into the basement, spotted Waters then he came the rest of the way down the stairs. He opened the fuse box. Click, lights, I shielded my eyes.

"Megan, what happened?"

I pointed toward Rana.

"We played a bloody game of hide-and-seek. I won."

Mom scurried down the steps.

"Mom, you don't want to see this."

"Oh! Megan! Look at you!"

"I do think I'll sit down."

More footsteps above and on the steps as I walked over to the nearest chair with my hand at my side. I shoved the gun down the back of the seat cushion just before Mom got to me.

"She stuck a knife in me," I said as I leaned on my right side across the seat cushion and armrest.

Jay descended the stairs, looked at me then at Rana, and then turned to Waters. Other officers followed Jay, who pulled his badge out of his back pocket and held it in front of Waters.

"Put your gun on the ground. Now!" barked Jay.

Waters complied.

"You are under arrest. Down on the ground."

"No! I killed her."

Jay gave me a strange stare then turned back to the other State Patrol officers. "Cuff him, read him his rights, and book him."

Was I missing something?

"Randy, you'll be all right. He didn't kill her, Officer. He told me he came here when he saw my lights off. Then he heard gunfire. Rana shot the hell out of this place long before he got here. Randy, do you want me to call an attorney for you? Luke Spencer in Denver practices in Nebraska, too."

Jay gave me an angry look. "You're not his attorney so stay out of this. He knows why he's being arrested."

Uncle Bill walked over to me and said, "Enough of this. You need to get to the hospital, you're bleeding like crazy."

Bill scooped me up and carried me up the stairs with Mom close behind, toting my shoes. The gurney was coming down the hall. Bill set me down on it then they wheeled me out the front door. It surprised me that Jay was the one in the ambulance with me. After one of the paramedics started me on a drip and staunched my bleeding, Jay asked them to wait for a minute or two up front. They started to protest then he whipped out his badge.

"Yes, Sergeant," said one of the medics as the ambulance lurched forward.

Once the door closed behind them, I said, "Sergeant? Your card didn't say that."

"What was going on down there?" he snapped.

"Well, there was this undercover cop acting so damn anal. That's what was happening. This guy charges down the stairs and thinks he knows, thinks he understands, but he doesn't have a damn clue. Rana came to kill me. Then Waters came. He claims he didn't come to kill me and I believe that now, because I took the time to listen. I tried to convince him that I didn't know anything about Jake. I needed him to think I was on his side so he wouldn't ever come after me. Actually, I don't know what he's done. I don't care...I'm just happy to be alive. But he needs to be put on a suicide watch."

Jay stared at me.

"That's the trouble with thinking you know a person or a situation—you can end up looking like a stupid brute. You don't know me and you didn't understand the situation with Waters."

"All right, I get the message. So tell me what happened down there."

"She came to kill me because I think she was the wife of Raz. I cut the power, I hid, I ambushed her, she died, I lived."

"So did she kill Raz?"

I heard the question, but my brain was slowing down.

"Ah...yeah, now let me be."

I closed my eyes. That was better. Pounding, the paramedics came back, pushing Jay out of the way. I closed my eyes again. Did someone ask me a question? I fought the darkness because it scared me. It came anyway.

Chapter 25

I awoke in a hospital room wearing a gown. I didn't open my eyes because I could hear whispering. I wanted to think. I could feel the bandage on my hip. I felt weak, but stronger than in the ambulance. Then it came back to me—the smell of her, death—like bloody meat.

When my head cleared, the truth smacked me hard—I'd committed adultery with Raz. That thin-souled viper deceived me. And his wife tried to kill me twice. She was dangerous—I'd bashed her head two, no, three times, and she still put a knife in me. I certainly didn't know hand-to-hand combat—perhaps I needed to remedy that. It was probably more valuable than learning golf.

Wait, did Raz set me up for Rana to kill me? Why would he risk that danger to himself? Raz didn't love me, but it didn't seem like he intended me to be murdered. Maybe Rana was trailing me and acted on her opportunity. I would never know the answer, though other questions began to bother me.

Did Waters follow Rana to my house? Did he want to kill her? Did he really want to die? He said he was in deep—with Rana? Rachel said the drugs were passing through or in the area like it was invisible. Was Waters the one with the blind eye? Was he getting kickbacks? Was he being blackmailed because of Jake's troubles, which might have included dealing meth? Either would put Waters in a ton of trouble. How was Rana connected? Wait, oh! She was dealing the drugs. How stupid was I to miss that? Was Raz involved in the drug trade? He must have known about it. Maybe he was with me those nights when Rana was sending or receiving drug shipments or however that worked. With Rana dead, and Waters and the Four Bastards arrested, maybe that pernicious pipeline finally burst.

I opened my eyes. Nurses, Mom and Bill were in the room, a regular room, not ICU. Good. Why? Oh, wait, I was in recovery after the stitches, and then the ceiling started moving. I wanted to stay still. The bed stopped in a new room. Mom's face appeared before mine.

"Hi," I said with great profundity.

She kissed my forehead. "Hi, hon. How do you feel?"

"Like I need a bourbon float...with double bourbon."

Uncle Bill came to the other side of the bed. I gave him a smile.

"You know all that furniture in the basement you never removed? Well, thanks for ignoring my requests—all that stuff saved my life."

"It's a story I'd like to hear," he said.

"You will, though maybe not tonight. I just want to go home."

"Oh, you can't," said Mom. "You need to stay here tonight."

My body flushed hot with anger and panic.

"What the hell? I'm fine. I've got my stitches, right? So I want to go. I have a legal right to leave. I'm not in jail."

My mom's expression indicated she understood my fear.

"I want to go home."

"Shortstuff, you lost too much blood," said Bill. "They need to monitor you. And you need to lay flat so your head has enough blood in it."

Trapped. Trapped in the dark. Trapped in a blasted hospital bed. I wiped my sweaty palms on my sheets.

"Will you stay if I promise to bring Derek and Vonny to see you?" asked Mom.

Damn, that was cagey.

"I'll stay if I get to see them and I get to visit James."

"I don't know if they'll permit that," said Bill.

"Ha! They won't be able to stop me, though I wish I had something other than this gown."

"Patty brought you some clean clothes and your purse…but you won't feel like putting on jeans."

In truth, I didn't really feel like socializing.

"And I want some bourbon. Bill, surely you could find a way to smuggle some in."

"I don't know…you're on meds."

"I'm ah…afraid I won't sleep here. I did kill a woman tonight."

"Okay, we will work on that," said my mom. "I'll text Vonny, though she might not have her phone on if she's in ICU. They're not allowing other visitors to see James."

"Well, I'm going."

"What if you bust your stitches?" said Bill.

"Then they can sew me up again. I'll need you to commandeer a wheelchair for me."

Mom was smirking as she finished her text.

"Oh, she's already replying. They are on their way."

In short order, Vonny, Derek, Tina, and Tony were standing around my bed.

I gave them a nutshell version of the attack.

"Dad was crying when we arrived from your house," said Vonny. "He seemed very upset. It sent his blood pressure through the roof. The staff couldn't figure out what was happening. Then he suddenly stopped crying and he was all right."

"He knew," I said.

"Knew what?" she asked.

"Tony, you have a badge. Get me a wheelchair, will you? I need to see him."

He saluted me. "Right away, General."

"Miggy, are you sure?" asked Derek.

"Oh, yeah."

"We were on our way to the hospital, but I knew something was wrong. So I demanded that we turn around and come back," said Mom.

"Is this some sort of Lebanese thing?" asked Derek.

Mom shook her head and turned toward Tony as he parked the wheelchair inside the door. Mom and Vonny made sure my robe strings were tied tightly in the back. Then Bill lowered the side railing on the bed then scooped me up in his arms and set me in the chair with Mom's guidance. Sitting upright made my head spin. I hung on to the sides of the chair and said nothing. As we turned toward the door, we saw Jay standing in the threshold.

"I'm not talking to the police tonight. I invoke my right to silence."

"You haven't been arrested," said Jay.

"Let's go."

Derek pushed me past him into the hallway. In the ICU ward, two nurses sat at the monitors as another came out of a room.

One of the female nurses at the desk stood up and said, "Mr. Wilson has had enough visitors for today."

Right on cue, Derek slowed the chair for my retort.

"Don't bother me. I've already killed one woman tonight."

I didn't even look back.

James saw me as soon as I entered. He'd probably had his eyes on the door ever since his visitors left. Derek parked me right next to James' bed. He worked his mouth hard, as I briefly described my ordeal. When I finished, he stopped moving his mouth and his face relaxed; the skin seemed to stretch down from his prominent cheekbones. After a few minutes, he started to shut his eyes for seconds at a time. Sleep was feeling more and more welcome. I said goodnight to James and his visitors. He was asleep by the time Bill wheeled me out of the room.

The combination of blood loss and sleeping pills produced a hard sleep free of the nightmares I feared. The next morning, I called Melanie at the office to discuss my day. Gus was handling the hearing on a bankruptcy case in the afternoon for me. Otherwise, she would ask Glenda to reschedule my other appointments. Spending the night in a hospital wasn't like a night in jail, but in either case, I still had the tremendous burden of my job. How would I catch up on the work I would miss? I wasn't sure I was ready for work—I still felt light-headed, even though I convinced the nurse to bring a second banana, a third orange juice, and a cinnamon roll after I finished my breakfast. It seemed natural to treat blood loss with extra food and drink.

The doctor told me my blood count was progressing well enough that I could leave at noon. I was ready to go home and be at peace in my haven, my castle.

After the breakfast rush at Custer's, Beulah arrived. "What a stupid girl…attackin' you on your own turf. She learned like Salt Eldritch did when he attacked you and James out in them hills. Stupid, stupid, dead." She cackled. "Heh! I bet you gave Beth and Bill the heebie-jeebies. Girl, you're gonna make your mom old before she's meant to be. You look a mite puny…I'm leavin' so you can rest." Shuffling away, she gave me one of her Queen Elizabeth waves that always made me laugh.

Later Zane walked in from the hallway and knelt beside my bed. "Lordy, Megan."

"Yeah, I know. I can't wait to go home."

"How bad is the cut?"

"Not that bad. It's the loss of blood that wiped me out." I looked him in the face. I had missed him. "I haven't seen you in weeks, except in the waiting room. So how are you?"

"Still at Cabela's."

I waited, but that's all he said. I ate a chunk of chocolate, but he declined my offer. Why would anyone turn down chocolate? He really was screwed up.

"The thing is, Zane, if you can't get the help you need here then you need to find it."

"But you wouldn't be waiting for me," he said.

"No. We've failed twice. You've never given me enough of yourself to grab onto. I just get pushed away. Come here."

He rose and leaned over to me. I hugged him and gave him a kiss on the cheek, as permanent a farewell as I could give him. He reddened a bit then straightened.

Bill wheeled me by James' room on our way out of the hospital. This time, the ICU staff allowed Mom and Bill to enter. One of the nurses even gave me a thumbs up when she spotted me as she came out of a room down the hall. James tore at my heart as I studied his face. He gazed at me and worked his mouth.

"Remember how your basement used to scare us?" said Vonny. "Derek would hide down there and scare the crap out of you and me."

Derek chuckled.

"And that was just last year," I said.

They laughed and James worked his mouth even harder, fogging his ventilation cup.

"We never could've guessed that six golf balls and a brick would one day save my life."

Derek and Vonny smiled as I departed. I was glad they didn't need to worry about me along with their father.

At home, Patty started making sandwiches for us to go with the potato soup she'd made yesterday in last night's nervous fit of cooking. I found Jay at the top of the basement stairs, waiting for me.

"Look, I don't really think you're a stupid brute, though maybe all cops have their moments," I said.

"I had mine last night. I made the arrest of Waters more important than your health. I'm sorry."

I nodded. "I need to sit down."

He followed me to the kitchen where Mom and Patty were waiting. Patty placed a sandwich and a bowl of soup in front of me then offered Jay lunch, which he accepted.

He had apologized to me. Maybe he would have done so at the hospital, but I didn't give him the chance. When I finished eating, I dropped my head on my hand.

"Oh, I need a nap and not in a hospital bed."

Jay stood then pulled out my chair. I headed out of the kitchen.

In the hall, Jay asked, "Why did you tell me to put Waters on a suicide watch?"

"He was probably following Rana, probably hoping for a gunfight. But she was dead. I told him not to move or I'd kill him. Then he started to turn around. He wanted suicide by Megan, but I talked him out of it…told him I'd back him…and I did. But I didn't think we were out of danger even when you came. I thought he might provoke someone to shoot him."

"I see. And you were right, I didn't understand the situation."

"He may have been blackmailed because of Jake, but you know more about his situation than I do."

At the base of the front stairs, Jay scooped me up in his arms.

"Say where."

"Up the stairs and down the hall to the right."

"You know, this is the most beautiful house in the panhandle," he said.

"I guess that's a compliment, even though hardly anybody lives out here."

He didn't put me down at the top of the stairs, but carried me to my room. Despite my fatigue and pain, my love parts started to stir. He placed me on the edge of my bed then he backed away from me.

"Please tell me you're not going to undress for your nap." He bent over and ran his hand over his face. "I need to go back to work." He looked down at his groin. "Damn."

"Think about your mother."

He laughed. "That should work. See ya."

The door closed. I pulled off my pants and crawled under the covers. Heaven.

The next morning, I went in to work with a bottle of Advil. I must have looked puny because Glenda the Good Witch kept bringing me cinnamon scones. She even brought me a brownie she saved from yesterday. One of my early appointments was the single mother of a young autistic man.

Later in the afternoon, I texted Vonny. She called me back a few minutes later.

"Vonny, I'm feeling like a big wimp, but I think I'm going to skip a visit today. I'd like a day outside of that place," I said.

She said she understood, though I still felt like a wuss as she spent all her waking hours there. Mom and Patty already visited, so I knew James could lift his right hand off the bed. Still, I acted pleased and impressed when she told me. In truth, it seemed like limited progress. He was still getting his air, food, and water from tubes connected to machines. The DNR question was looming, so I made a couple of calls to the hospital. At least I could be of use to them tomorrow.

A half hour later, Jay called to check on me. Being near him muddled my brain, but away from him, I could think.

"So, the meth assignment is finished," I said. "When will you be going back to Omaha?"

"Oh, there's a lot of things up in the air still," he said.

"Things not to be discussed over the phone."

"I might have something on Thursday. Can I come see you tonight?"

"No, I don't think so. It's a bad idea to get close to you when you could leave anytime. I'm just not looking for that."

All of that was true, as was the fact that he drew me in. I was in danger with him—I didn't plan to risk my heart on anything fleeting.

Chapter 26

AFTER work the next day, I went to see James. He still followed people with his eyes, but he seemed a bit slower than on Monday when I last saw him. He was also getting slower with his blinking responses. The only progress was with his right hand and arm, which he could raise off the bed as high as the top of his hip. While I was there, Derek gave him a pen and a notepad to see if he could write. The hand could grasp the pen, but the markings were like the scratch marks of a two-year-old. Derek worked hard to conceal his disappointment. He started a discussion with Tina and Vonny on their supper plans, which quickly ended when they all confessed to a lack of appetite. I left the room to call home then returned.

"Come home with me," I said. "Patty says she was planning to grill steaks. We have plenty. Is Tony working?"

"Yeah, till six," said Vonny. Then in a whisper, she said, "We need to talk."

I gave her a nod. "So call Tony and tell him to meet us. Men will go anywhere for a steak and a beer. And hallelujah, we're getting some rain at last. It's a good soaker."

A half hour later, as Bill, Mom, and Patty finished supper preparations, I sat at the dining room table with Derek, Tina, and Vonny.

"They asked us about the DNR today," said Derek.

"I still think it's too soon," said Vonny. "It's not like they say he's terminal."

"He is," I said. "Something related to the stroke, which includes the brain, the heart, the lungs, one of those things will eventually kill him. Or he could simply die from another stroke. We just don't know if something bad will hit him next week or in five years."

"Oh, my God!" said Derek. "He can't go on like this for five years. Then he'd be suffering through all of this for a long time then he'd still haveta die on top of it. It kills me to see him like this."

"And it doesn't bother me?" snapped Vonny.

"It's just what Dad never wanted—to be kept alive by machines as he is now."

"But he's still on the ventilator because he could still improve," she said.

"And he could. But dang, Dad doesn't even have control of his bowels. It all has to be so humiliating. The brain damage is permanent...we gotta accept that. I'm sure he does."

Vonny sat heaving big breaths of emotion as Derek stared at the wall.

"The problem is that you are both right," I said. "You know and see the same things, but none of us can predict the future. Wouldn't you both agree that your dad needs to be given the chance to improve?"

They both nodded.

"And wouldn't you both agree that if God wants to take him, you wouldn't want science to prevent or even delay that?"

They both nodded.

"So here's something to think about. I called the hospital and they talked to me because they think I'm the family attorney and because I give them lots of business. So, your dad won't be permitted to stay in ICU indefinitely. He'll be moved to another room, hopefully a private one. But even then, he can't stay for months while we wait for enough improvement to go to a rehab facility."

"The doctor says he hasn't really made progress at all, except with the right hand. So he's nowhere close to going to rehab," said Derek.

"Then what do we do?" asked Vonny.

"I stopped by room 122 before I came to see your dad," I said. "The hospital has two rooms which they reserve for hospice care. These private rooms are meant to be a comfortable place for the family to visit. The room includes two armchairs, a coffee table, a sofa, and a TV."

"Dang, that sounds nice. Will my dad's insurance pay for that?" asked Derek.

"I asked staff here to check for sure, but they thought so. I talked to a woman named Dorothy Withers. She's going to come see you tomorrow. But here's the deal—they would allow the respirator and the catheter, but you wouldn't have the constant monitoring you get in ICU. But like I said, he's going to be pushed out of ICU anyway. He'll still get nursing care, but less, and a DNR is required."

Vonny stared at the table while Derek stared at her.

"So, that's something to think about, okay? Nothing is going to happen or change tonight, so let's have supper."

The next morning, Jay called.

"I need to tell you a few things about Rana and Raz or Rariq," he said. "You have a right to know some other things, too."

"Okay, um, where?"

"You could come to the station. I have an office here now."

"Oh, I'd love to spend more time in that gray hole. No, you can come to my house. I'd say come here, but I'm booked up till after five."

"You work a lot of hours."

"I'm working on that, too. In fact, I plan to hire another attorney for the firm. Anyway, I'll even feed you, though I don't know what we're having. So come at six-thirty."

A few minutes later, I got a call from Derek.

"Vonny and I went to look at the hospice room. She thought it was great and she consented to the DNR. We're moving Dad in about fifteen minutes…they need to line up a couple of orderlies. You should come see it."

As soon as I could, I grabbed my umbrella then dashed off to Custer's to get a quick bite before heading to the hospital. The move must have knocked out James, for he slept the whole time I was there. Tina and Derek reclined on the sofa, while Vonny sat in an armchair. As much as anything, they would be more comfortable. Also, the new room featured softer lighting, as opposed to the stark illumination of the life and death ICU rooms.

"Vonny, how are you able to miss so much work?" I asked.

"I'm taking family leave time. Hopefully, I'll still have a job when I go back. Hey, how's your hip? You're starting to walk normally again."

"Oh, it's still sore, but it's getting better. I won't get the stitches out for another week."

It pleased me that Derek and Vonny looked more relaxed. Tina, to her credit, worked to keep their spirits up, but stayed out of the decision-making processes. Tina and Derek started dating three years ago; she even attended my dad's funeral. And she must approve of my interference, for every time I looked at her she smiled at me.

Back at the office, I didn't seem to get much work done, for I'd packed in so many appointments, half of which were new clients. I needed to bring work home, but I didn't because I assumed Jay's revelations would take most of the evening. As Mom, Bill, and Patty would be there, I hoped they would be allowed to hear some of the news. So I'd listen to what Jay planned to say, then he'd need to leave. I resolved not to screw up my life with a couple of erotic weeks only to get abandoned.

However, the butthead arrived wearing cologne and a ribbed sweater that showed off his physique. If he thought the lack of a belt would make for an easy exit for his thang, he was so wrong. At dinner, he was gentlemanly, even pulling out the dining room chair for Patty; I gave him credit for showing kindness to the cook, always a good plan. He avoided any heavy topics during the meal, but shared some humorous tales of the misadventures of him and his older sisters. I concluded that they were the mischief makers and he was the malleable brawn, who never snitched on them. They must have loved a younger brother who wasn't a brat and could keep secrets.

After a quick kitchen cleanup and the customary pouring of the Jim Beam Black, we sat down in the family room. Patty sat in an armchair, Bill in the recliner, and then I sat down next to Mom on the sofa. Jay came into the room, grinned at the bourbon on the coffee table in front of him. He sat down next to me, inappropriately close, took a sip, opened a notebook, and then put on a pair of reading glasses. I loved the effect; I loved his deep voice.

"Tracking the backgrounds of Raz and Nori was tricky. Raz was actually a childhood nickname for Paul Johnson," said Jay.

"Johnson? Hmm." I remarked.

"Yes. He was born in Minnesota then his mother divorced and married a man named Johnson. Rana had so many aliases that we're still tracking them. And yes, they were married and they did lie about it. They met and married in Lebanon using yet another surname. Rana was dealing opium from Afghanistan then. Things got hot, so they moved to the U.S. She kept them moving…sweeping into an area and taking control. She heard about the death of RT who was the major dealer here—they met in Nevada and had an affair a few years ago. Anyway, she moved here then recruited the Websters and Mick Spittle."

"What about Jake Waters?" I asked.

"We may not know that for a while. He's clammed up, though the Websters and Spittle all point to Rana. It may be that Rana found a way to get Jake tied up in things, which then opened up Officer Waters to blackmail to protect his son, or maybe he was taking kickbacks for letting the drugs pass through on his shift. He may have been more involved, we aren't sure yet. Oh, and he did hire that attorney you suggested, Megan."

I nodded.

"Not only did Megan catch the Four Bastards, excuse me ladies, but she also exposed the Websters in drug dealing, guessed at the marriage, though too late, figured out Rana's meth dealing, and may be right about Randy Waters being blackmailed. Oh, and she prevented his suicide."

Mom stared at me. "Megan?"

"The last time I got people close to me involved, you almost got killed, Zane got his head bashed in, and Brian nearly got into a crash with Bert Bolger. No, I learned my lesson."

"But you don't hesitate to use my best cowhands on dangerous missions," said Bill.

"They love it," I said with a smirk.

"Actually, they do. Do you know what my cowboys call you?" Bill asked.

"Oh, I don't know if I want to hear this," I said.

"The Goddess of Kick-Ass."

"Oh, brother. Well, maybe that's better than the Shelf Elf or the Pocket Docket," I said.

"Wait, I don't get those," said Jay.

"When my house got hit by the tornado, she was in the basement when the floor started to collapse. So she jumped into a shelf to dodge the crash."

Jay chuckled.

"So is anybody else in the State Patrol involved?" I asked.

"We haven't found any evidence to that effect. They had suspicions, but nobody could pin anything on Waters. Of course, the lieutenant supervising him looks bad. I demoted him. Oh, by the way, the Sidney police nailed the Sidney prosecutor with a DUI. As it turns out, State Patrol off-duty officers have been watching him. Somebody reported Larry Peake and they caught him just today."

"Ha! Now that's justice," said Bill.

"Okay, what do you know about the cross burnings?" I asked. "Were they meant to intimidate James or were they a diversion?"

"It depends on who you ask. The Websters say a diversion to shift the State Patrol's focus from the drug trade. Mick Spittle is a racist so-and-so. He was probably the ideal accomplice."

"Did Rana set up the cross burnings?"

"We think she did, though she made sure she wasn't around when it happened."

"God forgive me, but that witch needed to die," I said. "Think about it, she dates RT when both of them are married then tries to kill me when I date Raz. And she was part of the sibling deception, which was meant to conceal her and help her drug dealing. What a bleepin' hypocrite."

"She got her justice," said Patty.

"So was Raz a dealer?"

Jay shrugged. "We've found nothing to indicate that."

"But he must have known. Then he gets shot dead by Rana when she's trying to kill me."

"More justice," said Bill.

I took a big swig of bourbon. "So how is it that you're doing the demoting and promoting around here? You were undercover from Omaha."

"Well, I'm now a lieutenant and the head of the area State Patrol office. It was just finalized this morning."

"So you got promoted...and Merritt, too...mostly based on the work I did. Hmmm."

"Yes, thank you very much."

"I think we need to celebrate with root beer floats," I said.

While my gang was up and moving about, I went into the kitchen. At the desk was a box wrapped in brown postal paper.

"I bet I know what this is," I said as I unwrapped it. When I pulled out my trusty Glock and three night goggles,

I turned to Patty, who was handing a root beer float to Jay. "Who delivered this?"

"Officer Merritt brought it by at about noon," Patty said then wandered off with her float.

"I killed another person…a woman. And a man last summer. It's a strange thing to know you've wiped out a person's existence on earth." I sighed. "Have you ever killed anybody?" I asked Jay.

"Yes, ah, once, when I was out on patrol. We stopped a car and the guy got out and pointed a sawed-off shotgun at my partner. I shot him twice in the head."

"Sounds like you were calm and efficient."

"Like when you took down RT. That was pretty damn effective."

"So were my nightmares at unhinging me."

"Have you had nightmares from killing Rana?"

"No, but it seems like I should. I worry that I've gotten hardened to it. To be honest, that night in jail was worse."

"It's a terrible thing to imprison the innocent. It's—"

"Kafkaesque."

"Exactly."

We were talking about killing people, yet his eyes were soft when he looked at me.

"You know, I'm not always a stupid brute."

He leaned forward and down to kiss me.

"Sometimes, I'm just a brute."

"Exactly."

Soon, I was backed up against the fridge. He backed away from me when we heard footsteps in the hall. I'd soon be losing my chaperons. We walked them to the front door. Then they were gone. Jay locked the door behind them then turned to me.

"You know, I really do have so much to thank you for. I'd love the opportunity to show my gratitude. First, I'd like to put my iPod in your port."

"Oh, my."

"Do you have one?"

"Um, yeah. A big one."

He took my root beer float out of my hand and went into the kitchen. My resolve was melting into a puddle on the floor. Nanoseconds later, he was carrying me up the stairs. Sometimes it's good to be compact. He didn't start kissing me again until he stepped onto the hallway. Very wise— smooching on a staircase could prove disastrous.

In my room, I turned on a lamp then pointed to the player port. Then the sexy R&B voice of Anita Baker started and he was in my arms.

"Tall boy, we don't match up very well for dancing."

"Think of it as foreplay."

I didn't think he could, but he drew me in tighter. We couldn't have been closer if we were sharing the same clothes. Our sway became imperceptible as we kissed.

"Nice sweater but it looks too warm for you."

I took the lower edge of it in both hands and pulled upward. When I reached as high as I could, he pulled it over his arms. I drank in the sight of his hairy pecs with a man trail that led down to the top of his khakis where his stallion was ready to bust out of his stable. He ran his hands down from my ribs to the top of my hips then kneeled. One hand continued onto my right hip as the other slid to my lower back. He slowly moved his face toward me then lightly kissed my wounded left hip. He steadied me when my legs began to tremble with excitement.

I took his hands and tugged him toward my bed. Once there, I whipped back the comforter and top sheet with the efficiency and accuracy the moment demanded. He put his hands on my cheeks and kissed me softly on the lips then on my neck. Oh, how those soft kisses kill me. Soon I'd want his hard, but his tenderness made me moan. In a flash, we were both naked and scorching the sheets with our excited bodies.

He put his lips close to my ear and said in a low bedroom voice, "Please let me stay over. I don't want to be banished by you."

So much heat and excitement was welling up inside me that it took a couple of moments to summon my vocal cords into unexpected action.

"Okay."

Chapter 27

JUST before dawn, our hips rolled together. He kissed my neck igniting us and revving our pistons. He fell back asleep with his arm across my waist and tucked under my right hip. I waited till he was soundly sleeping then I rose, put on my robe, and then walked down the hall to the guest room to peer out the window at sleet. Uncle Bill drove slowly down the street in his Ford pickup with two cowhands shoveling gravel out the back onto Harney Street.

I called Bill's cell phone. "Is my generator gassed up?" I asked.

"Yeah, I did it on Tuesday when I heard we might get ice," he said. "They're getting snow north of here. I've got my hands out moving the herds."

"Do you have the calves in the barns yet?"

"That's next. I hope we can get it done before the snow hits here."

I asked Patty and Melanie to stock the house and the firm. The area homeowners and businesses possessed a few generators, but not nearly enough to house everybody if we lost power. Many would be forced into the middle school if temperatures dropped low enough.

I went back to my room to wake Jay. I looked down on him. What a fine specimen. His eyes opened and he smiled at me then pulled me into bed with him.

"I gotta say, babe, I didn't know if I'd ever get between your sheets."

"You transplanted yourself out into the sticks just to get here. So, what do you think—they're 1000 thread count sateen...new last spring."

He kissed me hard then said, "No fair, you brushed."

"You might want to take a look outside," I said.

He strode over to the window. "Oh, great, sleet. They had storms yesterday south of Lincoln."

I flipped on the TV to the local news. After a summer of drought, wildfires, and flooding, we now had a blizzard and tornados. Because we showered together, and opted for scrambled eggs and toast, neither of us made it to work as early as we planned.

By mid-morning the sleet turned to snow. When Gus turned on the TV in the conference room, we learned the power outages were moving south. Meanwhile, I sent Melanie to Shavers for more groceries and supplies then directed Joy, Glenda, and Gus to check on friends and family who might be in trouble if the town lost power. Then I started on my own calls. Patty and Mom went for more supplies. I contacted Paul Ritter and Lew. Beulah assured me that Custer's generator was ready to go. Derek said he, Vonny, and Tina were all at the hospital, which had backup power. At eleven-thirty, Dexter lost power. Jay reported that Sidney lost power at eleven, but the police station and courthouse had backup generators.

"Well, there might be an empty bed for you in the jail," I said.

A few minutes later, I met with the staff in the dimly-lit lobby. We'd conducted various emergency drills, so everyone knew what to do. Gus left to start the generator. Then everyone left to go get bedding, clothes, and family. Glenda was the first back. She immediately started making sandwiches from the office stock. Brian arrived then he and Gus started shoveling the sidewalks and putting down salt. Later in the afternoon, Marva Gush arrived with a troop of girls from her Interpretive Dance class.

"Quick, someone get a lute," I whispered to Melanie, who failed to squelch her laughter.

Brian went out to help the neighbors negotiate the slick paths. Our firm was filling with the snow-covered desperate. Gus assured me that all was in order, so I left for home.

By the time I got there, Mom, Patty, Paul and Kayla, Lew, Hank, and Linda were already there. Hank and Lew went out back with me to fire up the generator. What a wonderful invention. We turned on the TV to learn that northwest Nebraska had been hit by a blizzard that dumped two feet of snow, in addition to their power outages. During supper, we learned that Wayne, Nebraska, northwest of Omaha, had been hit by a powerful tornado.

"So weird," Hank said. "On one end of the state we've got a January blizzard and on the other end we have an April tornado, all on October twelfth."

By suppertime, Jay brought over Beulah and the house filled with cowboys. Patty fed our group from a vat of sloppy joes. By ten o'clock, the house was nearly quiet. Jack thanked me for letting the guys stay the night in the basement, on hallowed ground he dubbed the "field of victory."

"Well, don't defile it by plugging that toilet down there," said Bill.

After Mom and Bill retired for the night, I led Jay up to my room and started the gas fireplace. Then we plunged into hot sexual waters. When we came up for air, we cuddled together, sipped our bourbon, and stared at the fire.

Oh, how I loved big, strong men, especially if they don't mind me being strong or strong-headed. I slit a woman's throat; he knows I'm the boss at the firm; and that I've killed more people than he has—yet, he was still pursing me. Those were good signs. What else did he know about me?

We slept in till nearly eight. Jay was scheduled for a day off work, but there would be a ton of auto accidents. While he called in to work, I heated water for tea in an electric pot. I wasn't eager to join the crowd in the house, especially with Jay in tow. I decided to hide a bit longer so we could breakfast in peace.

"I'll keep checking, but I may need to go into work," he said as he sipped his Earl Grey.

I took a sip then decided to ask an incredibly important question.

"Do you believe in God?"

He gulped his mouthful of tea then said, "That's random. But yes, I do."

"Jesus, the Resurrection, and all that?"

"All of it...I can't necessarily explain or understand everything, but yeah, I believe. I'm Lutheran, but you don't have a Lutheran church in Dexter."

"Nope. We only have three flavors—Methodist, Presbyterian, and Evangelical."

"You're Presbyterian. I've done my research," he said as we dressed.

"What does that mean? I suppose you read the stuff that can be written down, quantified, explained. I'm sure the FBI has a file on me."

"Yes, all of that. I also spoke with Robert Foxworthy. He says there's more...things that he couldn't explain, but said he believed."

"He's right...it's hard to explain." I hoped he didn't require an explanation right now.

"Looks like a foot of snow, maybe not quite. It's hard to tell with the drifting from the wind."

"Thousands of cattle will be in trouble. I think the snow was much worse up north in Pine Ridge. Bill and his cowhands will check on Docket herds then they'll drive around the county looking to help other ranches. When they can, they'll work their way north."

"This is weird," Jay said as we descended the creaking stairs that let out near the rear of the house. "I mean it's cool that you have two sets of stairs, but it's...ah—"

"Like going down stairs in a closet? They used to scare me when I was little...the strange echo and these squeaky wood steps."

We proceeded to the kitchen where I showed Jay our cereal offerings. He selected Wheaties then got a call. I led him to the study for privacy. Meanwhile, I started on a bowl of Life, but after a few mouthfuls, I started to gag. Mom wandered into the kitchen just as Jay came back. I greeted her then went to stare out the back door. Something was stirring in me or was it someplace else? I opened the door to a cold north wind. In a flash, I knew what I needed to do. I walked by my guests in the kitchen down to the hall closet. I put on my winter coat and a stocking cap to cover my wet hair. Patty, Kayla, and Mom stood outside the mud-room where I was zipping up my winter boots.

"Are you going to play in the snow?" asked Patty who had just joined the group.

"Are you going to do something scary?" asked Kayla.

"I just need to—" How could I explain to them what I didn't understand myself?

When Jay returned he asked, "Should we do something?"

Mom answered, "No, she's doing what she needs to do."

"What is that?" he asked.

"We always find out later."

Chapter 28

I yanked on my gloves and pushed open the back door. At first, I started walking straight out toward Rufus, but then I cut west and headed toward Raccoon Creek in a snow-sloshed sprint. James liked to walk out to the cottonwoods along the creek in good weather, so maybe that's why I needed to go there. I didn't hear Beverly's soothing voice, so I kept running.

Then it all hit me—the blast of wind, the blast of Beverly, and then the blast of James. I'd never heard him before; his wail sliced me deeply. Her voice summoned me to listen. Double-barreled blows hit me—desperation, the heart-retching kind, urgency, the forceful kind—from my beloved surrogate parents, my friends.

"What do I do?" I yelled as the wind hurled icy particles of snow in my face.

Close eyes, breathe, don't think, listen, focus on James, feel him, know his pain, know his longing, let Beverly's voice guide me, let it be right with God.

I opened my eyes to find I'd fallen into the snow. I jumped up and ran back to the house. Time became urgently important. The people were milling around the back door and mud room. I pulled off my boots then strode past them. I took the closet stairs by twos then came back again in dry jeans and with my purse.

"Should we come with you?" asked Mom.

"Huh? No, I'll call when—" I didn't finish; I went out the garage door to the Barracuda.

I headed north to Highway 30 and Sidney. I ran from my SUV to the hospital doors, then slowed once I entered the building to avoid calling attention to myself. When I arrived at the hospice room, a nurse was just leaving.

"Oh, they just left to get lunch," the short, chubby-cheeked nurse said.

"Okay, I'll wait. Thank you."

Was it lunch time? They were gone. Timing, right. It was eleven-thirty. I shut the door. James' eyes were already on me. His face was slackened from the lack of movement, the loss of vigor. In the silence, he called for me to come close. As I stood next to him, it nearly overcame me; yesterday, the smell was faint, but today it was strong, forceful, grave. He reeked of decay—he was dying inside, despite looking clean and well-groomed on the outside. I touched his gray-black hair. His face and hands displayed an ashen tint.

What was I supposed to do? I walked to his right side. Why did I do that? My purse landed on an armchair. His fingers started twitching then cupping into a fist. Then his elbow bent and he grasped the top sheet, which he pulled into a bunch under his hand and arm. He pulled it until it was taut then his hand clutched and moved up his hip and onto the bottom edge of his gray and navy striped pajama shirt. What was he doing?

He pinched the edge of the shirt then worked his hand upward, sometimes pinching the flesh he probably couldn't feel. He grasped and pinched, moving his hand upward. The pinching grew frantic when the upward movement ceased, but he persisted. He reached his pocket then hooked his index finger over the top edge of it. His hand stopped moving, as if he was resting. Riveted, he pinned me motionless with his eyes, a witness to the greatest and most difficult task of his life.

Soon the hand started pinching, grasping, moving up his shirt where he clutched the bottom of his shirt collar. He worked his hand along the collar to the side of his jaw. He rested his hand for a few moments then with a spastic flutter, his hand jerked to his face, but it fell back onto his shirt. He worked his hand back up to and along the collar. This time when he thrust his hand upward, his index finger touched the elastic band that held the respiration cup over his nose and mouth, but his hand fell back down to his shirt. His mouth started moving as if he was talking. But he didn't need to—I heard his soul just fine.

I stepped closer to him, my heart rending, my guts churning. He tried once more to lift his hand to the ventilation cup. This time I caught it.

Though I knew the answer, I felt it morally or legally or somehow necessary to ask, "James, are you trying to pull off the cup?"

Ten or fifteen seconds passed. Then he blinked twice.

"James, do want to die?"

Another painfully long pause. Two eye blinks. The tears rolled down my face as I kissed his forehead. Then I hooked his index finger over the band at the edge of the cup. I took a step back.

"I love you, my dear friend."

His fingers gathered together and he yanked the cord and the cup off his face. The cup lodged under his chin and his hand fell away. I put his cool, smooth hand back up to the cup, hooking two fingers over the band and a third over the edge of the cup.

This would be another secret I'd keep.

For the first time in two weeks, I saw his face—it was relaxed for a moment or two then he gasped and squeezed the cup. For an eternity, he panted and wheezed and even tried to force his lips closed. He then sputtered as if his lungs were convulsing. I wept.

Oh, God! Won't you end this?

His upper body shook as he struggled to close his mouth, but his body still fought to breathe. In the movies, people drown and choke to death in seconds, but this seemed like days. God, take him now! The panting and coughing and snorting continued in sounds that cut me to the core.

He wheezed and rasped then his face turned—what color was that? The color of death maybe, as his final breaths left him. His eyes, still fixed on me, emptied until all that remained was brown glass.

I stepped toward the armchair and collapsed into it. I dropped my head into my hands and gushed tears that rolled down my arms. I don't know how long I cried before Derek, Tina, and Vonny walked into the room. Time stopped for James; I sensed my stretch of tribulation had just begun.

"Dad! Oh! Dad!" Derek blurted.

"Dad, no!" said Vonny. "He pulled the cup off!"

In that instant, all of their eyes were on me.

"He died right in front of you," said Vonny.

Derek and Tina stared at me. I couldn't take both his death and their condemnation, so I grabbed my coat and purse then rushed past them out the door. In the hall, I was the one gasping for air. James had been miserable and living the life he most dreaded—off machines. He told me he didn't want science to keep him alive. He was like a father to me when I was young; later he was my friend. I did the right thing for him. He knew I would. Was it the right thing in the eyes of God?

I hurried down the hall, not wanting to talk to any of them. Back home, I set my purse on the kitchen desk then turned to the crowd that still populated my house. Damn storm, I would find no peace.

"James died," I said.

"When?" somebody said as I sat down at the kitchen table.

"Just before I left."

The room exhaled. A few minutes later, the doorbell rang. Soon, Beulah shuffled into the kitchen to stare at me as I hunched over the table.

"Give her some chocolate," Beulah said. "Got any? Her face is—what is that? Green? I never seen it like that."

I shook my head. I was waiting. People spoke in low tones. Jay was still here, as was Mom, Patty, Kayla, and Linda. Hank and Lew had been outside shoveling, but they came in the back door. They'd be able to stare now, too. Patty set a banana in front of me. Kayla said nothing, but stood next to my chair, probably wanting to hug me. I probably looked like I needed it. But I would wait.

It didn't take long. The doorbell rang. I heard her footsteps in the hall, walking fast. This would be brutal.

"Why didn't you call one of us? Huh?" Vonny asked.

I looked up at her then back down at the table. Go ahead, my friend. I'll love you no matter what you say or do to me. Go ahead.

"You sat there and watched him pull the ventilator cup off his mouth. He suffocated to death."

I looked up once more to see Derek and Tina enter the room. Then I dropped my head again.

"You let him die. You had no right." She was breathing hard.

I lifted my head slightly. "That's all true. But he wanted to die."

"What? How do you know?"

"He was miserable, trapped in medical limbo, kept alive by science, just what he said he'd never want."

"But how do you know that he wanted it then, when we were gone? We never got to say goodbye."

"He knew you never would and you and Derek would fight and…he didn't want that. He trusted me. He wanted to go to God."

"How did you know? Huh? Did the wind tell you? You know you're crazy, don't you?"

"I asked him if he wanted to die. He blinked twice then reached for the cup."

"H-how could you sit there and watch him die like that?"

"Should I have let him die alone?"

"But how could you not help him?"

I shook my head. I had no words for what I endured.

"That was my father, Megan. He loved you. You could have saved him."

"I did."

Dead silence.

After a few moments, Vonny turned and walked down the hall toward the front door. Derek stood by the sink—I never looked at him, I was too chicken. After a few moments, he left without a word of kindness. That stung as hard as anything Vonny said.

Quick footsteps crossed the floor then Tina's hand squeezed my forearm. "It'll be all right." She hastened after Derek.

Drama and tragedy froze everyone to their spot in the room, except me. I left for the bathroom where I vomited my heart. The little food I had eaten was long gone, but the. dry heaves persisted until I thought I might upchuck a few small organs. Then I sat back against the wall and cried into a hand towel.

After a few minutes, my mom tapped at the door. I lived in a big house all by myself—I wasn't in the habit of locking doors. She sat down next to me on the floor, took my head in her warm hands, and then pulled me to her. I proceeded to sob onto her plum turtleneck.

When we came out, Patty shooed people out of the room; however, Beulah, the obstinate, refused to move from her spot against the wall. Everyone else milled about the hallway outside the kitchen. I sat back down at the kitchen table and slowly worked at eating the banana. Kayla sneaked back into the room and stood next to Beulah as Jay hovered in the doorway to the dining room. Patty set a container of yogurt and a spoon in front of me. I stared at it for a few moments then dropped my head. My roiling stomach wasn't ready.

"Have any of you had lunch?" I asked.

"No," said Patty. "I have this potato soup simmering and I have plenty for sandwiches."

"Okay, let's get that going." I departed for the family room.

As soon as I sat down, Kayla and Beulah sat right next to me. Mom walked into the room and stood on the other side of the coffee table.

"You're not going to bolt, are you?" Mom asked.

"I couldn't if I wanted to…these two are practically sitting on me."

Jay sat down in the recliner. He studied me for a few minutes as I stared out the window at my backyard.

"Can we eat in here?" he asked.

"Sure," I said then went back to gazing out at Rufus.

I did want to bolt, but I wanted to do it for more time than the cold would allow. In an instant, I concocted a plan. I rose when Kayla left to get her lunch.

"Where you goin'?" asked Beulah.

"Some things I insist on doing without a crowd."

Chapter 29

WITHIN a few moments, I was searching the Internet. I then called to verify the reservation. I'd found a cabin in Colorado near the Big Thompson River, refurbished after the Colorado floods from last month. I grabbed a big suitcase and started packing a few items. I needed to return to the crowd or they would get suspicious. I'd send Jay home tonight and finish packing, though it would all prove tougher if the area didn't get power.

Back in the family room, I sat down beside Kayla, who had a tray on her lap. Without asking, she handed me half of her turkey sandwich and a napkin. I summoned calmness and ate it. A few minutes later, Jay handed me half of his sandwich. I smirked then took it.

"When we were kids, we discovered that food tastes better when you steal it from someone else," he said. "My sisters found that out the hard way. One time, they tried to swipe my Pringles. So I took out most of the container and licked down one whole side then gave it to them. They gave up bothering me after that."

"Ew, that's so gross," said Kayla.

Beulah cackled. I laughed then bit into his sandwich.

"Once, I drank an entire gallon of milk," he said.

"No way, that's, like, impossible," Kayla said.

"It did take the whole evening and the Oreos helped. My sisters said it was 'groady.'"

Kayla got up and came back with a bowl of soup that she passed to me.

"I always thought it would be good to have a big brother, like, if someone was bullying me," she said.

I stopped eating my soup. "Does anyone bother you?"

"Not anymore. Louanne Spittle and her friends used to. But I just give it back to them."

"Heh! Wonder where you learned that," said Beulah.

"Sometimes I think what you would say, Megan. Now my friends come get me when they want to tell someone off."

"I used to stick up for Vonny and Derek. In school, some kids called them the N-word."

Mentioning them made my stomach cartwheel. I set down my spoon. Kayla didn't seem to notice.

"What did you say?" she asked.

"Well, in elementary school, I just punched them. In middle school, let's see, oh, I'd call them hicks and tell them to go deep fat fry something."

Jay smiled at me and Beulah cackled.

"Then what?"

"Well, by high school, Derek was so tall nobody wanted to mess with him. Vonny scared the guys because she looked beautiful and exotic. And I never got the growth spurt I was waiting for, so I just kept telling them off."

"Heh! You are a shrimpy girl...always was," said Beulah. "I knew her when she and her Pa was out here and the Wilsons moved in. Kayla, her Pa waited to sell the house till someone moved in who had kids Megan's age. Been close friends all these years." Beulah turned to look at me. "Megan, hon, they'll come around. They've had a powerful shock. You know you did right. I hope you'd do the same for me."

Later we watched the Huskers play. I gave it my detached attention. At about four, the power came on, or at least that's when Patty noticed the Ritter's outside lights were on. Paul came by to coax Kayla home. The news of James' death has already spread through town. Hank, Linda, and Lew drove Beulah to Custer's then went home. Soon I was left with Jay, Mom, and Patty.

"Well, I guess I better be working on the stew," said Patty. "We'll have a whole herd of cowboys looking for food."

"No. No more crowds. Send them to Custer's. We can pick up the tab. But I don't want to see anybody else today."

"But, Megan, your uncle will be coming."

"He's fine, but he needs to come alone." I looked over to Jay. "And I'll be kicking you out after supper. James was like a father to me when I was young. I think I deserve the right to grieve alone."

"You would send me home without any bourbon?" he said with a twinge of a grin.

"Well, okay, then you go."

Mom left to help Patty.

"You didn't like it when Zane pushed you away." Jay said.

"These are extraordinary and temporary circumstances. And we've only been dating since yesterday. And why would you want to be around me? Do you like to watch people mope?"

"You're a mystery I'm trying to figure out."

"I think there's a club to join on that score."

"I mean, you go out into the cold wind then you know to drive to the hospital just when a man decides to die."

"Don't assume I know all the answers."

"You're hurting and you're vulnerable. Maybe you shouldn't be alone."

"Oh, now I'm catnip for a wolf?"

"I want to find your tender underbelly."

"It's been done...with a switchblade and I thought you needed to work."

"I have been. But back to you. You have an insight. And yes, I've heard about The Woman Who Feels. You knew when your father was having a heart attack from two blocks away. You knew where to find the young man Davey who died. You figured out the crime then found the corpses from a murder committed forty-five years ago. You knew when and where the Four Bastards would strike. Then I saw you in action today."

"What do you expect me to say?"

"I'll say it for you. What you did today…watching and letting him die…that took a ton of courage."

"Are you angling for a second bourbon? One is the house rule. Though I may break it myself. I'm going for one now. Do you want one?"

"Sure."

But I didn't move; I looked down at my lap and prayed to God to forgive me if I'd sinned. Then I looked at Jay.

"If it was wrong, why did it feel right?"

Jay shook his head. It wasn't a question he could answer. I sighed. Just as I rose, the doorbell rang. I walked to the kitchen.

"I don't want to see anybody. But I do think we should all drink brandy—that was James' favorite."

Mom came back. "It's Tony."

"Nobody, especially from that house."

"I'll take care of it," said Patty.

By the time Bill arrived at eight that evening, Patty had shooed away Zane, Brian, Rachel, Merritt, and Tina.

Bill sat at the kitchen table eating his stew. I sat with him, eating a large chunk of dark chocolate. Every now and then Bill would stop eating and stare then he'd go back to eating.

During one stoppage, he said, "I can't picture this world without James in it."

"Dad and James. It's a different world."

I felt a cry coming on, but I was able to wait until everyone left before I let loose a big wail on my bed.

In the morning, just after dawn, I rolled my suitcase and toiletries bag out to the Barracuda. This would be my first road trip in my new SUV. I loaded the back with emergency travel gear, a cooler, a box of food, and firewood. I stopped at my office to return the work I hadn't done and to leave instructions to reschedule my appointments through Thursday. Before I left, I sent two texts, one to Mom and one to Jay, saying that I needed a vacation, but I would return for the funeral. Mom tried to call but I didn't answer, so she sent a text telling me the funeral was Wednesday at noon.

As I headed west, I drove by the snow that caused so many people so many problems. But I couldn't take care of everyone. I took care of the people who needed my help when we lost power. Now I needed some mental and spiritual health time to take care of me.

Why was I running away? It wasn't my nature to flee, except for the occasional dashes to Big Leo or another destination close to home. Was I feeling guilty? Maybe, I needed to ponder that. I definitely wanted to avoid Vonny and to a lesser extent Derek. Even if they admitted I'd done the right thing, I didn't want their drama. This was the time for them to deal with their own tragedy. In the past, I had always been ready to console them, but their condemnation still stung. Then again, by leaving town, I didn't make reconciliation possible, though I doubted Vonny was ready.

So I drove onward, away from trouble toward the taste of tranquility I hoped the mountains would provide. The Wilsons had been the great friends of my life—now they'd become a burden. Why did James put this on me? Had he tried and failed before? Did he know I'd help when his own blood couldn't or wouldn't?

I'd done more than I'd admitted—I didn't just watch him—I helped him die. Was it suicide? Assisted suicide? Murder? He wanted to get rid of the science, the machines that kept him from finding peace. Had I simply fulfilled the terms of the Living Will by removing the medical obstacles the document prohibited? It made my brain spin, forcing me to clear my head and focus on driving.

I turned south to drive parallel to the mountains, to my destination. I pictured Sweetie a year from now, ten months old, with brown eyes, brown hair, and dimples every-where—on her cheeks, and knuckles, and elbows, and knees. She'd be crawling, maybe even standing, maybe even pondering how to put one foot in front of the other. My dad told me I walked before I hit eleven months. What would it be like if she was in the back seat now? It would have meant that Brian summoned the courage to save us. He'd be with us now, in a doomed marriage, but probably intact for now.

I could tell my daughter the story of a little girl born with a twin brother disabled from cerebral palsy. I wouldn't tell her that I probably stole all the best of the womb for myself and left him with a body that wouldn't live past age twenty-six. I wouldn't tell her that my father took me away from him and our mother, and then I forgot them. No, I'd tell her about growing up with my dad, and my uncle, and my neighbors, the Wilsons, and the strange lady named Bear Lake Beulah. I'd tell her about me as a little girl who wandered alone out into the wild rough land of scary even-ing shadows, gusts that could knock me down, big moun-tains of dirt and rocks that I tried to climb and failed but tried until I could, and the wind that brought voices to me sometimes from one direction, sometimes from another, and of a young child like me who had no words, and the voice of a sad woman who had no words just pain, but sometimes happy sounds that came to me when I went out to the curly, gray-green buffalo grass.

Something happened to me then and it never went away. Maybe somewhere deep I did remember them, for I never stopped yearning.

Then suddenly, two dark kids appeared like gifts and we told each other stories and played in the rough land, in their house, on the basketball court, and in the attic and basement of my house. And I loved their mother like she was mine; I loved their father like he was mine.

Over the years, powerful forces existed in my life—three men. Frank, Bill, and James—and I loved them all.

Bill and James were kind and fun and taught me cool things. And then there was Frank Docket, Esquire. He raised me and talked to me and argued with me—he was my anchor. He was strong, but not always in a good way; domineering and demanding, he molded me and I tried hard not to disappoint him. But he was gone. I wanted so badly to find the good kind of strong character, someone I could love and respect. But he eluded me. Could Jay be that man? But I couldn't picture Jay's face—all I could see was James, reaching for that cup, reaching for death and God, and then gasping and sputtering. Would his death be like my brother's or my daughter's—something from which I'd never recover?

Now the tears were coming so hard it impaired my vision, so I pulled off the road. Forty miles, I needed to make it that far. Breathe, deeper, more tissues, glad I brought a box.

When I arrived at the resort, I found out that only three of their twelve cabins were rentable. The rest still bore the effects of the devastating floods. From the office window, the Big Thompson River looked to be in its normal churning, roiling mountain river state. My cabin smelled of new stain and new carpet.

After I unloaded my SUV and put everything away, I drank a glass of bourbon with my soup and sandwich. Then I donned my coat and went to sit on the deck. The cabin overlooked the river with a mountain, well, it was probably a tall foothill. To the west of my cabin were two others, the one next to me looked refurbished though the one beyond it hosted construction workers repairing a deck. Beyond it was a couple who stood on the deck gazing at the hill. The hell with looking, tomorrow I'd climb it.

But for now, I opted for a less strenuous alternative. I took a pillow and blanket from one of the beds and settled on the main room sofa for a snooze. I awoke in time for a walk around the resort then I cooked a frozen pizza—I'd known I wouldn't want to be fussing with preparing supper.

I spent an evening with Charles Dickens and Jim Beam. My mind was wonderfully clear of anything serious, except for David Copperfield's time as a child laborer. Before I went to bed, I watched the moon climb through the gap between the foothill and the mountain behind it. After a few more swallows of bourbon, I climbed into bed with triple blankets. This was going so well. I planned to sleep late then hike in the morning and afternoon.

In the middle of the night, it all came crashing down—the burning cross, James stricken, Zane and Raz, so disappointing, so tragic, gunshots, Raz down, jail, Rana's attack, another person I killed, Jay pressing hard, searching for weakness, Brian, I'm here, you're not, here's my dust, James grasping for the cup then gasping for air while trying not to, then empty eyes, Vonny's reproach, Derek's silence. I awoke in a sweat; I flung off two blankets then fought to regain sleep.

In the morning, I crossed a makeshift metal bridge to get to the foothill. The area hadn't received the panhandle's snow, so the climb was easy. Atop the hill, I lingered to enjoy the view. But my mind began to drift as I descended the hill—it stunk that I needed to abandon my home so people would leave me alone. Back at the cabin, I checked my voice mail and texts. Just chatter and annoying questions—I'm fine, I just needed to get away from pests like you, I thought after I played each message. The only interesting message was from Zane, who was leaving on Thursday to go to Omaha for treatment where he'd been accepted as an outpatient at the veterans' hospital. I sent him a cryptic good luck text. Derek also called to say he wished I hadn't left. Yeah, right. Maybe I wouldn't have left if you had found your nerve in time to either settle down Vonny or say something nice to me. But you didn't, buddy, so don't expect me to return your call.

Jay's messages were actually kind and supportive, encouraging me to clear my head and grieve in peace. I returned the calls from Mom, Bill, Beulah, Jay, Gus, and

FIRE IN THE WIND

Kayla with a text that read: "I'm okay. See you Wednesday."

I spent the afternoon driving into the Rocky Mountain National Park, gazing at the high peaks and taking short hikes on various trails where I didn't think I'd encounter anyone. By four o'clock, I was tired and ready for my book and bourbon. After a couple hours of reading, I started a charcoal fire in the outdoor grill for my brats then warmed and ate a half can of corn and a half can of baked beans. After a cleanup, I went out on the deck to read the Civil War diary. The mystery of the mother's death was finally revealed. She had become incapacitated by a terminal illness, cancer I assumed, and stricken by excruciating pain. After months of pleading, Stuart gave in to his wife's wishes and smothered her. He took to the bottle after that. Matthew is angered by the mercy killing of his mother. He is still livid when he and the officer Tom rejoin their regiment. Both he and Tom are wounded at the battle of Antietam. I recalled that James said that battle was the single bloodiest day in American military history—22,000 men killed—more fathers, brothers, and sons than my puny brain could comprehend. I got cold and went inside for an evening of Charles and Jim.

By ten-thirty, the words were blurry and running into each other. I knew I was sloshed because Mr. Micawber's speeches began to make sense. So I went to bed piling the pillows from the other beds around me as if they would protect me from reality. I wished I could read more, no, I wished I could escape and plunge into David's Victorian world. Then again, I'd need to wear corsets and hoop skirts. Never mind.

I awoke hung-over and angry. Shit. Why did James and Beverly die? Why were Vonny and Derek so blind and dense and, well, selfish? They wanted to keep their father alive when it was against their father's wishes. Why could I see that and they couldn't? Damn them.

I downed a couple of Advil and swilled several glasses of water. As I ate a bowl of cereal, I listened to a voice mail message from Zane he'd left late last night:

"I remember when Zach and I were kids. My mom didn't like us playing with black kids. I think she thought blacks were either obsessed with sports or headed for prison. Then one day, I told her that you loved Mrs. Wilson like a mother. That shut her up. Later, when she realized Derek and Vonny were good students, she became their supporters. And here's a secret that I hope you will keep to yourself—she voted for Obama both times."

I laughed into my Wheaties. I'd never warmed to Mrs. Whitfield, but that was a hoot. I sent him a text back thanking him and telling him I'd see him at the funeral.

The funeral. Tomorrow. I dreaded going home. I would work. I would lock myself in my house. Patty, the Wilsons, Mom, and Bill all had keys to my house and knew my security code. But nobody could get past the floor bolts.

I stripped the bed and trudged over to the office. I gave them my sheets and paid for an extra half day. That way, I could stay until late afternoon before I had to leave. I flipped on the TV to catch the news. Nebraska was the big story, just as the devastation in Colorado consumed our attention the month before. The news shocked and saddened me. The cattle losses for Nebraska, South Dakota, and Wyoming could reach into the tens of thousands, including breeding stock and calves that would wipe out the next generation of cattle. The livestock, which also included horses and sheep, were still in their summer pastures rather than their more protected winter lands when the storm hit. The news showed dead Black Angus and heifers piled in heaps in ravines and along fences.

I hoped Uncle Bill and our cowhands hadn't gotten stuck in the muck. The soil in the hardest hit areas to the north was known as "gumbo" because it turns into a quicksand-like gunk when soaked. Ranchers and their cowhands would be working in treacherous conditions, trying to pull

1,200 pound cows out of the goo as they tried to avoid getting sucked in as well. I sent a text to Mom asking about Bill and our hands. She must have been walking around with her phone in her hand because she responded immediately. Bill and our cowboys were fine. Bill was back home supervising our stock, though a few of our hands were still north. My text stated I didn't plan to be home till nightfall and that I'd see her at the funeral.

Then I texted Patty to inquire about Jackson and our friends on the Pine Ridge Reservation in southern South Dakota. She also replied immediately. They were fine and since they planned to come to James' funeral, they had already traveled south to get to where power was restored. She hosted four Lakotas at her apartment last night. It made me feel guilty that my big house was empty.

I spent most of the day hiking or reading. At four, I packed up and left, stopping in Cheyenne, Wyoming for supper. I came home to an empty house. Patty had left a lamp on in the family room; other than it, I didn't turn on any lights. I still wanted to be alone. I ignored the phone, but spent the evening listening to phone messages and sorting through the mail. I texted Mom that I was home, and then I took a bowl of roasted peanuts and a glass of root beer up to my bedroom and sat in front of the fireplace, dreading the next day.

Chapter 30

WHEN I awoke, I recalled how badly I wanted to enliven myself after Sweetie's death. No doubt, surviving Rana's attack had stirred me up. Yet it was ironic that instead of coming back to life, whatever that meant, I helped a loved one end his.

After I showered, I called to ask if Mom and Bill wanted to have breakfast with me. They must have driven or run down the block, for they were at my door in two minutes flat.

"Where'd you go?" asked Bill as I poured him a cup of coffee.

"Estes Park. It's still pretty soggy and there's a ton of construction, but a few of the cabins have been restored."

"What did you do out there?"

"Oh, hiked and read and drank."

"David Copperfield?" asked Mom.

"Of course."

"Are you back to stay?" asked Bill.

"Oh, yeah. I'll be working evenings and through the weekend."

"We have a few things to report," said Bill.

"Jack broke his arm helping to get a calf out of the mud," said Bill. "And yes, I've made arrangements for the hospital to bill us. And I do plan to promote him to my well, overseer position."

"I hope you don't call him that," I said. "It sounds so antebellum slavery."

"Yeah, 'supervisor' sounds better. And Bud is quitting in January to start classes in Kearney. He'll finish his classes in Sidney by then."

"Derek and Tina have decided to stay," said Mom. "Derek will continue his job long distance. They'll run Wilson Landscaping together. Tina has a degree in business. Tom Sedlacek will be manager and take care of the nitty-gritty. Oh, and Tony got reassigned back to Denver on Monday. But he'll be here for the funeral."

She was ready to say something else, so I waited.

"Vonny and Derek have been calling me for information on you. They've been concerned."

"They called me, too."

"Did you ever answer them?"

"I texted Derek that I was fine. What do you want to eat?"

"Oh, we ate."

"Oh, I have something for you."

I went to the study, extracted two forms from a folder and returned. I handed the multi-page documents to them.

"Wills?" said Bill.

"Well, it's appropriate because your marital status changed," I said.

They read through the first page then looked up at me.

"All the land and stock goes to you and none for Kyle," said Bill.

"Right. All your other assets go to him. Every penny. Kyle never cared about ranching or this land. He'd sell his portion to some corporation or a warehouse. You'll have plenty of opportunity to provide for him financially."

He nodded.

"You know I'll protect this land."

Bill grinned at me. "Yeah, I do."

"Megan, is there something behind this? Something on your mind?" asked Mom.

I could ask, I could find out if she thought Bill was my father. Maybe she wasn't absolutely sure. No matter what she said, it would stir up so much emotion and at a terrible time. It always felt like Frank Docket was my father and it still felt that way. Bill and James always seemed like the genial alter fathers. If something was different than it appeared, perhaps it was a secret no one knew but God—I'd let Him keep it.

"No, well, James' condition got me thinking about it. Last week, I drafted wills for Paul Ritter and Junior Percival. Junior paid me with an old rifle his father owned, a special edition Winchester."

"Well, if anyone knows about guns, it's the Percivals...they've got a small arsenal," said Bill. "Oh, and I need to get something out of my truck."

After he left, I said to Mom, "I'm adding another attorney to the firm as you know. I'd like to hire more support staff. The job is yours if you want it."

"I do get stir crazy...at least when nothing's happening with you...but that's been awhile. It does feel strange because I've always worked."

Bill came down the hallway.

"You think about it. It's hard to make decisions right now," I said to her.

I immediately recognized the long box Bill placed on the table. He drew the rifle from the felt bag. It was the Sharps carbine James so prized; it belonged to his great-grandfather in the Civil War when his group of runaway slaves joined a Pennsylvania infantry troop in battle.

"Derek and Vonny brought it up to the house yesterday," said Mom. "They're leery of you right now. They hate the way things were left between you."

They'd need to prove it.

"They were in a panic when they learned you ran away. They said you'd never done that—well, not farther than the bluffs, that is."

"It's a strange peace offering," I said.

In truth, it thrilled me given its history, but it failed to warm my heart. Instead, it made me sad because James cherished it.

"I'll get a special case for it to commemorate the Wilson family and add it to the firm's Civil War collection."

At the funeral, I lagged back when Mom and Bill sat near the front behind the Wilson relatives. I sat down with Gus and his family. In a flash, Jay was in the pew next to me. I nodded to him, but wished I was back at the cabin, miles from here. It did please me that the turnout was huge, with people standing along the aisles and seated in folding chairs in the narthex. As with most funerals, it passed by with me in a trance. Though I did hear Pastor Ryder say, "James was trapped in his affliction, but God has set him free." Free. That made me gulp hard several times. Jay must have known I was struggling, for he grabbed my hand. The warmth and feel of it smacked me in the chest. No one had touched me in several days. Neither Mom nor Bill hugged me this morning—they were leery of me, too.

At the internment, I hung back from the Wilson family, standing instead by Sweetie's grave, which made me feel even worse. At the luncheon, I went to an open table, followed by Jay, ate sparingly, and rose to leave before Mom and Bill could join us. I heard voices directed at me, I saw people I knew, people dear to me, but I didn't respond. I needed to get away—it was all closing in. As I turned to go, I discovered Derek standing behind me.

"Why don't you come and sit with us?" he asked.

"So you can add to my pain? No thanks." That was mean, but it came out anyway.

As I walked up the stairs and out of the church, Jay got caught in the throng and couldn't follow me. I drove to the office, which Gus had closed for the day. I worked till eight then finally returned Jay's call. I remembered the touch of his warm hand in mine, so I let him come over. In my bedroom, we moved the loveseat from the wall and placed it in front of the fire. I didn't talk much, so he let me sit in the silence with my head on his shoulder. In time, I climbed onto his lap and dropped my head onto his chest and cried. He held me tight and waited. He earned high marks for his patience; he didn't know me well enough to anticipate that

I would eventually want to crawl into bed and burrow underneath his hot body for comfort.

I worked late the next day then went out to Big Leo, a bluff I'd mostly avoided since Bert Bolger displayed the corpses of Mary and Julie Quinn on its northern incline. I climbed the snow-crusted eastern slope then sat on the far western edge on a rock, with my back to the Wilson house. So Derek planned to stay. A big part of me wished he'd move away and leave me be. Up on the bluff, the wind lashed at me, whipping around me, mocking me and my frailty.

Where do I go from here, God? Can I ever forgive James for the burden he crushed me with? He had trusted me with his death. What am I to do with my anger? How do I get out from under this dark cloud that hangs over me? So much loss, so much death haunted me. Where's my brother? Where's my daughter?

A hand grasped my shoulder. I wished it was Jesus, but he had more important people to worry about than pathetic me. Yet only God could help me. The hand stayed. It was somebody who would cause emotion. I overflowed with it, let me be. Would they go away if I didn't move? I stared at the hawk overhead, to be free of it all. Just live, just survive, no attachments, no emotions, just hunt and live.

Then a blast of wind swept in from the west. I stood. Despite the strength of the wind, Beverly's voice came to me softly. I stood and the hand stayed on my shoulder. What would it be like to be only a voice in the wind? Just sounds, never words? I looked down the steepest pitch of the bluff, swaying in the powerful wind.

The grip tightened and another hand grabbed my shoulder. Bound now, bound to this earth by strong hands. Closed eyes helped me to hear her soothing voice. I waited, dropping to my knees. How would James torture me? Other voices came from behind me, but they weren't of the wind. I needed to know, I needed to hear him.

Then I did—low and smooth. He tried to calm me, but I wept instead. Was God speaking through him? Is this how God spoke to people like me, strange souls tortured by the wind?

The hands still held me. Why was I bound to so much pain? They all hurt me—Dad, Mom, Bill, Brian, Zane, Beverly, James, Derek, Vonny, even Scottie. The people I cared about the most hurt me the most. If I gave Jay the chance, he would probably hurt me, too.

Then I was picked up, turned around, and hugged by a tall woman. She had been crying. Derek hugged me, too. He had been crying. How long had they been with me? Words were said, but I was only feeling their embraces and hearing the soothing voices in the wind.

They climbed down the easier side of the bluff with me. At first, they tried to assist me, but I could climb up and down a bluff like a spider on the wall. They gave up speaking, for I was still listening to others as we walked toward home. Mom, Bill, and Jay stood in my yard, shivering in the chilly wind. They'd been watching and wondering about me. What would that crazy girl do? They were quiet when we approached them.

"We need root beer floats and *Young Frankenstein*," I said.

Why did I say that? Why didn't I send them away? Why, when they would someday hurt me? Why?

Smiles.

Love.

That's why.

About the Author

JUDY Bruce is a resident of Omaha, Nebraska, USA, where she lives with her husband and two children. She has a law degree from Creighton University. Judy is the author of the Wind Series: *Voices in the Wind, Alone in the Wind, Cries in the Wind* and future stories in the series, as well as *Death Steppe: A World War II Novel.* She maintains a website at judybruce.com and a blog at heyjoood.com.